THE MISSING YEARS

CLAUDETTE BECKFORD-BRADY

Copyright © 2012 Claudette Beckford-Brady

All rights reserved.

ISBN: 148259126X
ISBN-13: 1482591262

DEDICATION

To all the people who have told me that I have written *their* story; all the fostered and adopted children who do not know their biological families.

CONTENTS

	Acknowledgments	i
1	A Letter from Delisia	1
2	Accident!	26
3	My Own Line, and a Happy Grandma	47
4	Robbery Under Arms	64
5	Where is Richard?	78
6	Marital Disquiet	96
7	Jungle Telegraph	114
8	I Make the News, and Revenge on Devlin	132
9	Reconciliation…at last	152
10	Malicious Gossip	169
11	A Pleasant Interlude with Delisia	185
12	A History Lesson, and a Californian Vacation	206
13	Delisia's Story – The Finale	229

ACKNOWLEDGMENTS

There are a number of people who have constantly been behind me spurring me on with their support and encouragement:

My two sisters, Silvia Edmondson and Navlette Guy
My good friends Miriam Clayton and Dave Rodney
My "daughter" Keisha Banton, who is usually my 'Artist-in-Residence and last, but certainly not least, my lifetime partner and the love of my life Ronney Brady.

CHAPTER ONE

A Letter from Delisia

The sun crept up over Morant Point, and, kissing the tops of the Blue and John Crow Mountains of Portland and St. Thomas, he made his way westwards across the parishes of Kingston & St. Andrew, through St. Catherine and Clarendon and the parishes beyond, until he reached Negril, the most westerly point of the island, where he generally left spectacular sunsets.

Before he got to Negril, though, he passed over the hills of south-western St. Catherine, where he found two people standing on a hilltop, eagerly awaiting his arrival.

His much anticipated entry heralded a melodious dawn chorus of magical proportions; it seemed every single bird in the island had been waiting for his arrival, along with we two humans on the hilltop, and the feathered friends sang is if their very hearts would burst from sheer joy.

The morning sparkled; the sunlight glistened and danced

Claudette Beckford-Brady

and created dewdrop diamonds; the sky was a cloudless sky-blue which promised another scorching day, as was to be expected in late August.

Grandma Miriam and I stood on the hilltop and gloried in the beauty of the morning, as we welcomed the sun, and the song of the birds.

Here, where we were standing, we could look out over an expansive vista of blue hills, and green valleys, rising and dipping off to the north and east, while to the south, a glimpse of the blue waters of the Caribbean could be caught, way off in the distance at Old Harbour Bay, a couple of thousand feet below.

I loved it up here in my country district of Gravel Hill, where I had been born nearly thirty-two years ago, and where I had spent the first year of my life, before moving down to the town of Old Harbour, and subsequently to England, when I was just three years old.

In 1974, a few weeks short of my fourteenth birthday, I had discovered a controversy surrounding my birth. It had come as a great shock to me when I found out that Mavis, my father's wife, whom I had always assumed to be my mother, was in fact *not* my mother at all. My father had temporarily strayed from his conjugal base, and I was the tangible result.

My birth mother had been just seventeen years old, and had the promise of a golden future. She was extremely bright, and had ambitions of becoming a lawyer. Her father, my maternal grandfather, Carlton Campbell, now deceased, had been extremely proud of his only daughter amongst eight sons, and had been looking forward to sending her to study at the University of the West Indies, known at that time as the University College of the West Indies.

The Missing Years

My mother would have been the first person from the district to attain that distinction – several of her brothers had university degrees, but they had been obtained abroad – and the fact that she was female had made Grandpa Carlton even more proud. Needless to say, he had been *extremely* angry and disappointed when her pregnancy was discovered.

At four weeks old, I had been forcibly taken away from her, despite her pleas and protests, and given to my father, George Freeman, who took me home to his 'baby-mother' Mavis, to be raised by them. Mavis had accepted me as her own; she already had one child with my father; my brother Delroy, who was three years old when I was born.

It seems that there had been no plans to acquaint me with the circumstances or the facts of my birth, but a major difference of opinion with Mavis when I was thirteen had caused her to unintentionally blurt out the fact that she was not my biological mother.

The discovery had started me on the quest to find out the whereabouts of my real mother, Delisia Campbell, and in the search I had discovered that I had a large extended maternal family I had not known about. I had also discovered my island home, fallen in love with it, and found within myself my 'Jamaican-ness'. I had subsequently made up my mind to leave England and come home to the land of my birth.

So here I was, on a glorious August morning in 1992, standing on my very own hilltop with my maternal grandmother, Miriam Campbell, enjoying the sunrise.

Grandma Miriam was nearly eighty-seven years old, but could pass for younger. She was still mobile, although she now used a stout stick to help her walk, mainly as a result of

Claudette Beckford-Brady

having hurt her ankle some time back. She was in great health; no hypertension or heart disease or diabetes, and all her faculties were still intact; her mind was clear as sparkling spring water.

She was a diminutive woman; I stood a head and shoulders taller than her, and her hair was now completely white, as opposed to when I had first met her back in 1978 on my first visit to the island. She hailed from Bartons District, a community in the hills across the valley from Gravel Hill, and had married Grandpa Carlton and borne him nine children, of whom Delisia, my mother, was the youngest, and the only girl.

Grandma Miriam had spent time in Canada during her growing up years, and had been a schoolteacher by profession. Although she lived in a rural country district where most people were poor and under-educated and spoke the local patois dialect, her English was nearly always impeccable, except when she was under emotion, when she would lapse into patois.

I loved Grandma Miriam to death. She, in turn, had latched on to me as the living embodiment of her missing daughter, Delisia, whom I resembled remarkably, and who had left the district in 1965 and disappeared into thin air, cutting her entire family out of her life.

For years no-one had known whether she was dead or alive, and the family and I had spent years and large sums of money in trying to locate her. When we had all but given up hope, I happened to be at the airport in Kingston one evening, awaiting the arrival of Daddy and Mavis from England, when a friend pointed Delisia out to me, mistakenly believing that she was the mother I was waiting for, because of our remarkable resemblance to each other.

I had accosted Delisia, and because her response to me, her long lost daughter, was not the happy and tear-jerking reunion I had envisaged and fantasised about over the years, I had attacked her verbally and we had developed an animosity toward each other.

However, my husband Richard, along with my cousin Daniel, had worked tirelessly to bring about forgiveness and reconciliation, and eventually Delisia and I had been able to communicate, and had developed a tentative, fledgling friendship.

But the best part of all was that Grandma Miriam was totally and completely happy again. She had missed her only daughter terribly, and had expressed the wish of seeing her, or at least finding out what had become of her, before she, Grandma, died.

Her wish had been granted, and Delisia was now in communication with her family once again, and was expected in December for the five-yearly Campbell Family Reunion.

I took my eyes away from the beautiful panoramic view I was enjoying, and gave Grandma my attention as she spoke.

"A got a letter from Delisia this week. She's looking forward to the family reunion." She touched my cheek. "Am really glad you two found each other."

I had taken great pains not to let Grandma know how much antipathy I had initially felt toward Delisia, as I had not wanted to dampen her joy at finding her long-lost daughter. I had had many angry and negative thoughts about Delisia, but had voiced them only to Richard, my husband, and Mavis, my stepmother, who I considered to be my "real" mother.

I had thought that I was successful in keeping my

animosity secret from other members of the family, but my cousin Daniel had picked up on it, and so, as I now discovered, had Grandma. Her next words took me by surprise.

"A was really afraid for a time that yu and Delisia were going to hate each other. It would have been so easy, because *both* of you are stubborn and opinionated, and the antipathy I sensed between oonu seemed too large to get over, but Am glad to know that both of oonu were big enough to leave the past behind and concentrate on a promising future."

I stared at Grandma. "You *knew* there were bad feelings between us? After I tried so hard not to let you see it? Did Delisia say anything to you about it?"

Grandma grinned, her pearly white dentures flashing in the early morning sunlight. It never failed to amaze me how she could get her dentures to stay so white. "Yu can't hide anything from me, Chile; A read yu like one of yu books."

I had been an aspiring writer for years, and had achieved some financial success – if no great recognition or acclaim – with my short stories. I had recently had my first novel published; it had been given moderate reviews by the critics, but it was too early to know what sort of impact it was having on the market. It had only been a few months since its launch and I would not know for some time if it was enjoying good sales.

Grandma took my hand and we turned to retrace our steps down the hillside back to the yard. We called out our goodbyes to my cousin Maisie, who lived in my house on the hilltop with her two children. Grandma had given me the hilltop, saying that it really belonged to Delisia, and was mine by right of succession. She and my uncles had collaborated and had the house built for me.

There had been rumblings of discontent among some of my local cousins, who felt that I, who least needed it, was being given preferential treatment, and I had been guilt-tripped into offering the use of the house to one of them, since I lived at my own *Sweet Home* some three miles outside of Old Harbour.

Maisie Campbell, the cousin who lived in the house, had not been one of the disgruntled ones; on the contrary, she was a bright, friendly, and down to earth soul, who never failed to thank me every time she saw me. I had not known her as well as I did the cousins who lived in or near the yard; prior to her living in the house, she had been staying at Bullet Tree with one of her brothers and his family, and had not visited the yard at Gravel Hill often.

She had had more need of the house then anyone else, and so Grandma had suggested that I allow her the use of the place. I had agreed, and never regretted it, because she kept it as I would myself, and she had made good use of the available land space on the west side of the house – steep though it was – by planting a food grung (ground) where she cultivated a few plantains and bananas, some yam, coco, sweet potato and dasheen on the slope which led nowhere but down into a deep gully.

She also had some corn and gungu, and a few tomatoes, okra, and cucumbers nearer the house. I was impressed with her industry, and the way she kept the place neat and clean.

She was a single mother, and worked hard to feed and send her children to school, sometimes doing "day's work" if she could get any, and selling her surplus food to put a little extra cash in her hand.

She came now from around the side of the house, wearing a wide cheerful grin on her chubby face. Her children were nowhere in sight and I assumed they were still in bed; it was just past sunrise. She said, "Oonu gone? Is a shame oonu have to waak suh far fi si di sun-rise; mi si it every day fah free, t'anks to yu, Cousin Shellie."

"You're more than welcome, Cousin Maisie," I smiled at her. "It couldn't happen to a nicer person."

Grandma and I set off down the hill, me shortening my stride to accommodate her age and slower movement, although I myself was a little ungainly due to my six-month pregnant belly.

On the way to the yard, near the base of the hill, was a stand of pimento trees. As we approached, I caught the aromatic scent of the trees, and saw the twinkle of sunlight between the glossy, dark green leaves.

This was a sacred spot for Grandma, and we always paused here on our way down from the hilltop. In accordance with an old Jamaican country tradition where each child born on the land had their umbilical cord planted together with a young tree, mine and Delisia's umbilical cords, or navel strings, to use the vernacular, had been planted here, seventeen years apart, with two pimento saplings, now full grown trees.

My cousin Daniel, who was a master carpenter, had built a bench under the trees for Grandma, who often came here to commune with herself and think of her formerly missing daughter. It had been a sweetly sad place, but now that Delisia had been found it had once again become a happy place. We sat down on the bench.

The Missing Years

I felt a particular affinity for the pimento and considered it a perfect choice for my navel string tree. I loved to pick a leaf and crush it, to intensify the pungent aromatic scent which it gave off.

Pimento, also called allspice, is Jamaica's only indigenous spice, and is the most sought after in the world, having a virtual monopoly on world markets. It is called allspice because it is purported to have the combined flavours of cloves, cinnamon, nutmeg, and pepper.

All parts of the tree is aromatic – the bark and leaves, as well as the berries. Locally it is used to flavour cooking, and also for medicinal purposes. Grandma kept a bottle of rum in which pimento berries soaked, along with camphor and wintergreen. This was used as a pain rub, and also as smelling salts. A wine could also be distilled from the pimento berries.

I broke the companionable silence that Grandma and I were enjoying, sitting there on the bench in the pimento walk. "Grandma, now that Delisia has been found, will I have to relinquish the hilltop to her? I mean, you did tell me that it was hers, and I only got it by default. And what about the house? The hill might be hers, but the house was built for *me*."

Grandma squeezed my hand. "Don't worry yuself. Ownership is irrelevant; we can all share and enjoy the hilltop."

"But what if she lays claim to it and *my house*? You did say it was her favourite place, and when she comes she might want to stay up there."

"Well, if she does, Maisie and the children can 'small up themselves,' and let her stay. She has her life in California; I hardly think she would be interested in a small piece of rural hillside."

I hoped Grandma was right. Although I had my house at Island Farm, where I lived with my husband and two children, I felt a particular thrill of ownership for this place. It was quiet and secluded; could only be approached from one direction – through the yard – and it was where I had done some of my best writing.

The infant in my stomach stirred, and I realised that I was starving. Breakfast was being prepared back at the yard and I licked my lips in anticipation. My earlier bouts of morning sickness were a thing of the distant past, and I was eating more than enough for two, however, I was lucky enough not to be gaining too much weight.

I told Grandma that I was starving, and we got up and walked the short distance back to the yard, where we broke our fast with ackee and saltfish, which is Jamaica's national dish, and roast yellow-heart breadfruit. We washed it down with our own home-grown coffee.

I was spending the weekend up in the country with Grandma Miriam and my paternal grandparents, Mamma and Pappa Freeman, and had also taken time out to visit Mavis' family over at Ginger Ridge.

My two children had been at our farm in Walker's Wood, St. Ann, for the last three weeks, spending some of the summer holidays with their paternal relatives and their two half-brothers from Richard's former marriage. The boys lived in Miami with their mother, and had already returned to the States; their school resumed earlier than the ones out here. Richard, too, had been at the farm for the past week.

I was missing them terribly. Richard had suggested that I join them for part of the holiday but I did not fancy the drive

The Missing Years

to St. Ann at the best of times – I hated both Flat Bridge and Mount Rosser – both of which had to be crossed to reach St. Ann, so I had declined. But feeling a little lonely, although Daddy and Mavis lived right next door, I had decided to take the opportunity to visit my Country and spend some quality time with my three grandparents.

I had been alternating my stay between the grandparents, and I was planning on staying overnight with Mamma and Pappa Freeman up at Joe Ground, or Joe *Grung* as it was pronounced.

While we were eating breakfast Grandma Miriam returned to the subject of Delisia. "When yu finish yu breakfast A will show yu Delisia's letter. She send some pictures too."

It had been a matter of a mere month since Delisia had reappeared in our lives, and two weeks since she had returned to California. I was surprised that she had written so soon.

After I had been taken away from her and given to my father and Mavis, she had withdrawn into herself, ostracizing her entire family, although only Grandpa Carlton, who could be described as a tyrant, had been responsible for my being taken away.

She had eventually left Country in 1965, had apparently taught school in Kingston for a while before obtaining a United States visa and migrating. For nearly thirty years there had been neither sight nor sound of her, despite the best efforts of her family to find her.

We had all but given up hope of ever knowing what had happened to her, but Grandma Miriam's most fervent wish had been to see her daughter, or at least to know what had become of her, before she died. I too had been anxious to find Delisia, more for Grandma's sake than for my own, or so I had tried to fool myself.

But I had not been able to fool my husband Richard, who knew how much I really wanted to find and be accepted by my biological mother. I had a great Mum in Mavis, whom I loved dearly; we had become very close after some initial stormy times when I was in my teens – but I had still wanted – needed – to find my birth mother.

During the intervening years I had woven all kinds of scenarios about the happy tear-filled reunion we would have when we finally met. So when I had seen her at the airport in Kingston, after my initial shock and surprise, I had approached her with eager anticipation. However, she had responded with a cold, impersonal indifference, and when I realised that my fantasies would not be realised I had reacted with scathing anger.

I had surprised even myself with the amount of resentment I felt toward her. I had not realised until that moment that deep down I blamed her for not having made any efforts to communicate with me over the years. I had not known where *she* was, but she could easily have found me if she had wanted to, by simply writing to my father's parents. She could have monitored my progress, or even written to me – but she had not.

So I had attacked her verbally, all my pent up resentment spilling out, and we had developed an animosity toward each other. For Grandma's sake, I had tried to get her to give me some means of contact – a phone number or an address – but she had declined, saying it was best to leave things as they were because it was "the easiest thing to do."

The Missing Years

She had also said that she had put me out of her mind and gotten on with her life because that too had been the easiest thing to do.

My hurt and resentment had known no bounds, and I had decided that as far as I was concerned Delisia could return from whence she had come, or even to hell. As far as I was concerned, she was dead and buried, and I thanked God for Mavis.

Richard, though, had been determined to bring about reconciliation between Delisia and me, and by extension, Grandma and the wider family. He had stoutly defended her to me, stating that she was obviously as distressed as I was, and I should put myself in her shoes and try to see where she was coming from. He said she was in conflict with herself, and that I had further alienated her by my verbal attack on her. He said he was sure that given time and the right encouragement she would be glad to embrace her family once again.

So he had instigated a search for her, starting with the Kingston hotels. It had not taken long to track her down; she was staying at a hotel in New Kingston, and he and my cousin Daniel, who was also Delisia's nephew, although they were the same age, had gone there to see her. She had been persuaded to return to Old Harbour with them, and the process of reconciling with her family had begun.

She and I had gotten off on the wrong foot, but I had been persuaded to go and visit with her at Daniel's house, and we had had a fairly civil conversation, after I had apologised for my earlier aggressive mode. She had accepted my apology, but the air had not really been cleared, nor had my resentment fully abated.

Claudette Beckford-Brady

I had resented too, her relationship with Grandma. It was an open secret that I was Grandma's favourite, and now that Delisia was back, she was taking my place in Grandma's heart. Of course I knew this to be flawed reasoning, but I had been too consumed with anger, resentment and jealousy to be entirely rational.

But I had given serious thought to the things that Richard had said, and my innate sense of fairness had brought me to a place where I was able to accept Delisia with an open mind. I had made up my mind to offer her the Olive Branch of Peace, and by some weird coincidence, she had also come to the same decision. Before I could enact my plan, *she* came to *me*.

We had spent a couple of hours talking, and this time the air had truly been cleared, and a tentative friendship established.

She had returned to her law practice in California, promising to return in December for the third quinquennial Campbell Family Reunion which had been inaugurated in 1982 and which was held in the yard at Gravel Hill, and to which large numbers of the extended family from England, North America, and the wider world, came. This year would be a special event, in honour of Delisia, and again I felt an unreasonable little stab of jealousy as the thought entered my mind.

We had finished breakfast; I washed up the utensils we had used while Grandma went to fetch Delisia's letter. She came back, all beaming smiles, and we went to sit outside on the babbeque, or barbeque, which is a flat area of hard-packed earth where certain crops such as coffee and cocoa beans are spread out to dry. We sat under the large guinep tree which was my grandfather's navel string tree.

She handed me the envelope and I drew out the contents; a handwritten letter and several photographs. I examined the pictures before turning my attention to the letter.

One showed a swimming pool and patio decorated with ferns and potted palms; another showed a large and obviously expensively furnished living room, and another, a full frontal view of a beautiful single-storey ranch style house. The last two were of Delisia herself, one in a cap and gown, obviously a graduation photo, and in the other she was standing in front of a building looking at a name-plate which read *CAMPBELL, CHAMBERS & ASSOCIATES*.

"Impressive. She seems to be living very well," I remarked to Grandma. "Her business is obviously successful."

"Yes," Grandma replied, "I'm glad she fulfilled her ambitions of becoming a lawyer. Her father would be so proud... Anyway, read the letter." I did as she said.

Dear Mamma,

I hope you are in good health and spirits.

I can't begin to tell you how happy I am that we have finally reconciled. I acknowledge the fact that had it not been for my stubborn pride, not to mention my guilt, this event could have taken place a long time ago. Thank you all for the way you have accepted me back into the bosom of the family with no recriminations.

I want you to know, Mamma, that I have never stopped loving you, and I know you did your best to persuade Pappa to let you keep and raise Michelle for me. I had no right to cut off the entire family for Pappa's unilateral decision.

Claudette Beckford-Brady

None of you were to blame for what happened, and now, being older and a lot wiser, I can look at things from Pappa's perspective, and although I don't agree with what he did, I have made my peace with it. I still feel partly responsible for Pappa's death, but realise that that is something I will have to work out on my own and in my own time. I only hope and pray that wherever Pappa is now, he is aware of my penitence.

However, I have no time for "if onlies". The past cannot be undone, and since all is well that ends well, let's give thanks, leave the past where it belongs – in the past – and make a new beginning.

I expect Michelle told you that I stopped by to see her on my way to the airport. We had a good talk and I think we made some progress toward a future friendship. Although I have no right to be, I am extremely proud of Michelle and her achievements. George and Mavis did an incredible job in raising her and should be very proud, and of course Michelle herself deserves much credit too.

I am so looking forward, although with a little trepidation, to the family reunion in December. I am just now realising how much I have missed having my family, and I can't wait to renew acquaintance with everyone.

Give my love to the extended family, and tell them that I look forward to seeing them all in December. And you, Mamma, have an open invitation to come and visit me whenever you please. I know you don't like to travel, but honestly, age is no barrier these days; just say the word and I will make the arrangements.

I love you, Mamma. God bless and keep you, until I hear from you.

The Missing Years

Your beloved daughter,
Delisia.

PS Here are a few photos of my home. You would be very comfortable here.

I replaced the letter and the photos into the envelope and handed it back to Grandma. She looked at me expectantly, waiting for my comments. "Well," I said, "the reunion should be interesting this year. It's a nice letter, Grandma, and I appreciate the tribute she's paid to my parents. It's generous of her."

"It's no more than the truth. Yu probably benefited from being raised by George and Mavis; if you had been raised here you might have turned out differently." She got up, adding, "A going to get ready fah church."

I was not a church-going person, so after breakfast I set out to walk the half mile up to Joe Grung to my father's parents.

Part of Joe Grung was actually in the adjoining parish of Clarendon. The road from Old Harbour to Gravel Hill and beyond marked the border between the two parishes. Several of my Campbell cousins lived in Clarendon, although only across the road from the yard.

It was a beautiful Sunday morning and I felt exuberant to be out in the fresh clean country air; no traffic fumes, no great thundering trucks or buses; just pure, peaceful, countryside. I sang loudly as I walked slowly up the road, which was uphill. *"Sunday morning, up with the lark; A think I'll take a walk in the park; Hey, hey, hey, it's a beautiful day..."*

Claudette Beckford-Brady

As I passed the various board residences on my way up, the locals who lived close enough to the road to hear me singing, came out to greet me. For years I had been known locally as "Delisia's girl" or "Miss Miriam gran'dahta," or just plain "Shellie." I was treated with a friendly familiarity tinged with a certain amount of respect due to the fact that the Campbell family were the largest landowners and the most affluent in the district.

Lately, however, there had been a subtle change in the way I was greeted. The friendliness was still there, but the familiarity had gone, and been replaced by an almost subservient formality. I had now become "Miss Armstrong," a Very Important Person. Their body language spoke volumes.

This new type of respect probably came from several sources. Part of it, I suspect, was due to the fact that I was now a published writer with my book in the stores for everyone to see. The locals were awed by the fact that they actually *knew* someone 'famous' because they had seen me being interviewed on TV and heard me on the radio.

Then there was the fact that I part-owned and ran a successful business, but I believe the greater part of the increased respect was a spin-off from Richard, my husband. He commanded great respect, with his air of confident self-assurance, his obviously expensive mode of dress, his gold jewellery, and his brand new Range Rover proclaiming his affluence. He looked like a man who was used to giving orders and having them obeyed.

He was "Marse Richard" to nearly everyone except Grandma and my parents, who treated him as an equal, but even Mamma Freeman was in awe of him, and we could not get her to stop curtseying and calling him Marse Richard, despite his protests, and the fact that he was her "grandson-in-law" (?) and called her "Mamma" as I did.

The walk up to Joe Grung, which should have taken no more than twenty minutes, took over an hour. I had to keep refusing offers of 'tea' which could mean anything from coffee or cocoa to Milo, Ovaltine, or 'bush tea'.

Bush tea could be a great variety of things, including mint, fever (lemon) grass, citrus leaves or peels, ginger, and a number of other plants and bushes.

One 'tea' I would have nothing to do with was Cerassee; "sirsy" to the locals, which tastes bitter, and is actually a toxin, being a member of the Deadly Nightshade family. However, the country folk swore by its cleansing and medicinal properties and, particularly the older ones, drank it regularly with no obvious ill effects.

I finally accepted a jelly coconut from Miss Vinette, and two yards up the hill, I borrowed Miss Tiny's pit latrine to empty my bladder. We talked for a few minutes and then I went on. I finally reached Joe Grung and the Freeman yard.

I walked down into the yard from the road. Uncle Linval, Daddy's older brother, was sitting on an old tree stump sharpening a cutlass with a file. He looked up as I entered the yard and said, "Waapen, Shellie; what a gwaan?"

"Mi deh yah, Uncle. Everything cool?"

In general, I rarely spoke patois, but I was beginning to use it more and more as I assimilated myself into the culture of the island.

Uncle Linval said that Pappa had gone "a-bush" and Mamma was "roun' a kitchen-side."

"Gone a bush pon Sunday? Him should be resting. How di sugar?" I asked.

Claudette Beckford-Brady

Both Mamma and Pappa had diabetes, known locally as "sugar" and Pappa was also a hypertensive. He really had no need to work the land or "guh a bush" at all; there were only a couple of acres of land which was mainly in tree crops, and Uncle Linval looked after the food grung and the few animals. In addition Daddy and Aunt Violet supplemented their income, as did I myself.

But Pappa did not like sitting around doing nothing, and went to bush nearly every day, pottering around, doing nothing substantial but keeping happy and active. He and Mamma were both some years younger than Grandma Miriam, but were not as fit and strong as she was.

"Di sugar aanda control. Him tek him medicine dem an him seh him feel fine, so wi juss leave him."

I left Uncle Linval and walked over to Mamma's house and round behind it where the outside kitchen was, stepping over two sleeping dogs on the way. Several fowls scratched away at the hard-packed earth, vainly searching for delicacies, but there had been no rain for weeks, and the pickings were slim.

The yard was quiet. Uncle Linval's wife and daughter-in-law had gone to church, taking the children with them. My cousin, Bertram, or Bulla as he was nicknamed, was the other resident of Top Yard. He was nowhere in sight; he did not go to church, and I assumed he was still in bed, as he operated a sound system disco and was often out till the small hours.

The yard was actually two yards; Top Yard and Bottom Yard. The original house was situated at Top Yard or "up a top" and Uncle Linval and Bulla had built their own houses there, near to Mamma and Pappa. Uncle Linval's other son, Everald, had also built a house at Top Yard, but it was now empty, as he had recently migrated to the States. But it would not stay empty for long as cousins were growing up and starting families all the time.

Several other houses had been built on a lower level of the land, and this became known as Bottom Yard, or "dung a bottom." Various cousins resided at Bottom Yard, including Aunt Violet's children and grandchildren.

One of the houses "dung a bottom" was where I had lived with Daddy and Mavis for the first year of my life, after I had been taken away from Delisia. The houses were small board structures with zinc (corrugated iron) roofs, and contained two rooms, three at the most. In recent times more rooms and verandas had been added to some.

The kitchens were situated outside in small huts, and the pit latrine toilets were away behind the houses.

Most people up here had electricity now, unless they were way off the main road, and many had piped water, but most of them still had pit latrines. A few, and gradually more and more, were adding bathrooms to their houses and installing plumbing and flush toilets. Mamma and Pappa had a flush toilet and a shower, courtesy of Daddy and Mavis.

I found Mamma at the fireside cooking rice and peas and chicken, traditional Jamaican Sunday dinner. I pecked her cheek and said, "Hmm, Mamma; that smells divine. I just had breakfast less than two hours ago, and I'm starving again!"

Mamma laughed and said, "Mi nuh know which part yu put all dat food, y'know Michelle. Yu eat like a horse and yu still kyaan' get fat. Here." She handed me a chicken leg and I bit into it enthusiastically. "I swear, Mamma," I said, around a mouthful of chicken, "No one in the world cooks like you, except maybe Uncle Bertie. Yu should open a cook-shop; yu would make nuff money."

In fact Mamma was famous in the district for her cooking, and often on Friday and Saturday evenings she would fry up a batch of bammy and fried fish, garnished with vinegared onions and hot scotch bonnet peppers, to sell to the locals. At other times she would bake sweet potato or cornmeal pudding. Everything always sold like hot cakes.

Mamma used to sell in Old Harbour market on Fridays and Saturdays, but we had retired her a few years ago. Apart from the diabetes, she also suffered from arthritis and often complained of being in pain.

I belatedly realised that I had not even asked Mamma how she was doing. I guiltily rectified my mistake. "How yu feeling, Mamma?"

"A not too bad, Chile. Di pain dem ease off likkle, and di sugar aanda control."

"That's good Mamma. I hate it when you hurt."

I stayed overnight at Joe Ground and left early on Monday morning to return to Gravel Hill to say goodbye to Grandma Miriam and the others, before catching a taxi down to Old Harbour, where I went straight to the office.

SmallRock Publications, which I ran with two partners, was situated almost in the centre of the town of Old Harbour, on South Street. We put out a weekly parish newspaper, *The St. Catherine District Bell,* and a monthly glossy magazine, *Jamaican Woman* which was an island-wide publication.

My two partners and I had started the business with a skeleton staff, a lot of borrowed money, and a great deal of faith and hope. To our relief and delight, we had become almost an overnight success. We enjoyed good support from our subscribers, both local and abroad, and almost from the beginning sales and advertising revenues had been good.

Before going into my office I stopped to say "hi" to my cousin Daniel, whose furniture workshop and showroom was next door. I gave him half dozen Alligator pears (long-necked avocados) which Grandma had sent for him, along with greetings from the country cousins.

I left him and went next door to my office, looking in on Miss Lyn, who ran our bookshop and variety store, on my way. As I approached the door to enter the newspaper offices, George, our general handyman, saw me and opened the door for me. "Maaning Miss Shellie," he smiled.

"Good morning, George. How was your weekend?" I smiled back at him.

George was a treasure. He was around sixty years old; a short man with greying hair cropped close to his head. He did all the cleaning for the offices, and took great pride in having everything spick and span. In rainy times he could be seen with a mop perpetually in his hands; he could not bear to see the wet marks that were left by people coming and going, and lurked in the reception area, mop at the ready.

"Mi 'ave a nice weeken' Miss Shellie. Mi son carry mi an di missis guh dung a Salt River mineral guh bade (bathe) Sunday maaning. It was nice."

"Good; I'm glad you enjoyed it."

I took a few minutes to greet Denise, the Receptionist, and then went on into my own office. My personal assistant, Debbie, was just placing a sheaf of papers on my desk, and looked up at my entry. "Ah; morning Mrs Armstrong. Yu just missed Mr Armstrong's call. He wants you to call him as soon as you come in."

"Thanks Debbie; I'll call him in a few minutes. Did you

have a good weekend? How are your children and your mother?"

We spent a few minutes on pleasantries, and another few minutes on matters pertaining to the business, and then Debbie returned to her own office, adjoining mine, and I picked up the phone to call Richard.

He answered the phone himself, on the first ring, as if he had been waiting beside it. "Honey?" he asked. I deepened my voice, trying to disguise it. "Who?" I growled.

"Oh...!" He was momentarily taken aback. "Sorry... A thought yu were my wife... Can I help yu?"

"I want your body," I growled, trying hard not to laugh.

"Excuse me?!" And then light suddenly dawned on him. "Michelle Armstrong! Yu wait till A catch yu, yu wretch yu!" In between fits of laughter I said, "And I love you too, Honey."

He said that everyone was fine and all missing me, and that they would be coming home on Wednesday. I was glad; I missed them too, and *Sweet Home* seemed much too big without them. Wednesday seemed too far away.

We chatted awhile, and then I spoke to the children, after which I phoned Mavis (phones had finally reached the Island Farm/Nightingale Grove communities) to tell her that I was back from Country and would see her and Daddy this evening.

The day passed uneventfully; I made some headway into the paperwork on my desk, looked over our latest sales figures, signed some cheques, and looked at several articles for the next edition of the *Districk Bell,* as the paper was known locally. At six o'clock I left the office and walked around to the taxi stand at the front of the market to get a taxi home.

The Missing Years

I now owned a fleet of four taxis; two on the Spanish Town route and two on my local Spring Village route. They were commuter taxis, and were always overloaded, carrying two passengers in the front and four or five squeezed into the backs. Small children were not allowed to occupy a seat but were squeezed in a standing position in front of the adults.

The type of vehicle generally used in the taxi business was the Russian made *Lada* with one or two old BMCs, along with a couple of other makes and models. I did not see either of my drivers so I got into the first available car.

I was home in ten minutes and went straight over to the Big House to have dinner with Daddy and Mavis. I had given my household helper, Lurline, some time off, and she would not be returning until tomorrow.

I did not linger at my parents' house. After dinner I went straight over to *Sweet Home*, showered, put on my nightdress, and switched on my computer. I was working on my second novel, and decided to put in a couple of hours before going to bed.

The computer was now in an alcove of the living room; my study upstairs had been turned into a bedroom for the children, and now that the family was growing, we had been considering our options. I loved my home and did not want to move, so Richard had suggested we build-on to the house. It would mean cutting down a few fruit trees, regrettably, but we had plenty more.

I wrote till ten-thirty, and then went up to bed, after checking that everywhere was locked up. I had let the dogs out and felt quite safe, although I was all alone. I couldn't wait for Wednesday when Richard and the children would be home.

CHAPTER TWO

Accident!

I surfaced slowly, reluctantly, and grumpily from a deep sleep. Something had penetrated my consciousness, and I lay in the darkness, listening and trying to identify what that something was.

Oh, just some inconsiderate and no doubt drunken louts on their way home from some shindig or the other. I reflected sleepily that it was unusual for this to occur in the early hours of a Tuesday morning; most dances took place at the weekend, although of course, not always.

But why the heck did they have to be blaring the car horn like that? And the damned dogs weren't helping, with their everlasting barking at everything that passed the gate. I looked at the illuminated display on the radio beside my bed, and saw that the clock said a quarter past three.

I kissed my teeth and prepared to snuggle back down and start counting sheep – or since I was in Jamaica, goats – when I realised something. The ruckus was not moving past, but seemed to be stationary outside my house. And then I realised something else; the intercom buzzer was ringing, and my name was being called.

"MISS ARMSTRONG? MISS ARMSTRONG...?!"

I was alone. Richard and the children were not due back until Wednesday. I most certainly was not going to answer whoever the devil was calling at this ungodly hour. Various scenarios flashed through my mind. Did they want to rob the house and was trying to lure me into letting them in? Did someone want to kill or harm me? Did they *know* I was alone?

And then I began to think logically. There was too much noise. If they were up to no good, they were certainly broadcasting it to the entire neighbourhood. As the thought crossed my mind, the phone started to ring. I grabbed it up and said, "Hello?"

It was Daddy calling from the Big House. "Shellie, yu ahright?"

"Yes Daddy, but there's a heck of a hullabaloo going on outside, and someone is calling me by name. I don't know what to do..."

"Doan't do anyting. A coming right ovah. Tek time an pull di back grille." He hung up before I could respond.

I turned on a light so that whoever was outside would know that they had been heard. I put on my dressing gown and went downstairs, going through the kitchen to the back veranda where I unlocked the grille and waited for Daddy. In a few minutes he arrived, followed by Mavis, who was saying we should call the police before responding to whoever was at the gate.

"I don't think that's necessary, Mum, they're making too much noise to be up to no good. Let's find out what the problem is."

It went without saying that there was a problem. I had already ruled out something happening to Richard and the kids; I had spoken to Richard at 10 pm, the kids were in bed, and he had been about to turn in himself. If a catastrophe had struck in St. Ann I would probably be notified by phone or a visit from a police officer, not a group of very vociferous persons outside my gate at three in the morning.

I went back into the living room, followed by my parents, and Daddy pressed the intercom button and said, "Hello. Who is dere, an what oonu want at dis time a di night?"

The noise abated somewhat, and then a voice which I recognised as belonging to Wilbert, one of my drivers, came over the intercom. "Missa Free, is bad news, sah. Is Lizard; him dead."

The words hit me like a blow to the solar plexus, and I placed my hands protectively against my pregnant belly. I do not know what I was expecting to hear, but it was not this. I had had no real feeling of apprehension; no premonition of disaster, which I should have had, given that I had been awoken from my sleep in the pre-dawn morning. That did not happen for less than a disaster.

The next few minutes passed in a kind of daze. Mavis guided me to a chair on the veranda, and I was dimly aware that Daddy was opening the grille and going outside. I heard him sending the dogs around back, and in a few minutes he returned with Wilbert, Kenute, and Shortman, three of my drivers, in tow. I owned four commuter taxis which were operated by these three and Lenny, who was nicknamed "Lizard." But now they were telling me that Lizard was dead.

The Missing Years

Mavis and I were waiting on the veranda. I was still trying to assimilate the words I had heard. *"Is Lizard; him dead."* Baldly spoken, with no attempt to soften or cushion the blow.

Since coming to Jamaica I had discovered that death was a part of everyday life. In my entire life before coming here when I was twenty-five, I had only known one person who had died. That had been my first love, Clive, who had been killed by a skidding car one wicked winter's day back in 1978. But since arriving on the island in 1986 several people I knew had died or had been killed.

But people I had known only in passing, for the most part, away from my Uncle Kingsley, who had died of lung cancer earlier this year. But Lizard I knew well, and his death was too close to home. He had been driving for me for over four years, and was on his way to earning assistance from me to buy his own car. I would have been sorry to lose him as a driver, but he was, or rather had been, a good honest worker, who took good care of my vehicle, and he had deserved a step up in life.

He could not be dead. He had a wife and young family; what would they do now? *He could not be dead.*

Wilbert was telling us the details of Lizard's death, and when I realised, I controlled my wandering mind to listen. He had taken a charter fare to Montego Bay, waiting while the fare conducted his business, and had made the return trip to Old Harbour. He dropped off the fare at Bowers District, and was making his way home at about 1.30 am, when a speeding drunk driver failed to give way at the junction where Colbeck Road, Lennon's Ville and Darlington Drive met.

He smashed straight into the driver side of my car,

killing Lizard instantly. I dimly heard Shortman consoling that the car, though badly damaged, was not a total write-off, and suddenly I was engulfed by a searing anger.

I rounded on him angrily. "Oh for Christ sakes SHUT UP! Who cares about a stupid old piece of machinery when a man has *lost his life*?! What about Lizard? Can he be repaired? A man – fi oonu friend – is dead, and all you can think about is a twisted old piece of metal. Shame on yu, Shortman!"

He had the decency to look shamed. My outburst had roused me from my stupor, and I now took back control from Daddy. Lizard was gone; there was nothing I could do for him, but his wife and children would need support. I asked Wilbert where Lizard's wife was, and he said he had left her at the hospital. "Who is with her?" I asked.

I was relieved when I learned that her mother and brother were with her at the hospital. I did not want to go to the hospital. I did not want to even view Lizard's body. Jamaicans were remarkably ghoulish and loved to look at dead bodies. Every car accident or other kind of death in public drew a crowd of sightseers, and some scavengers who picked the body clean given the opportunity, sometimes even if the victim was not yet quite dead.

I asked about the condition of the other driver and learned that he was in serious condition in the hospital; his female companion, having been in the front passenger seat and nearer the point of impact, was critical, and not expected to live.

I decided I would wait till daylight to go and see Verna, Lizard's wife. I ascertained that the police had been notified, asked for the name of the investigating officer, and thanked the drivers for letting me know. Daddy let them out, and

The Missing Years

locked up again. Mavis went to make coffee, while I sat thinking about the events of the night. There would be no going back to bed.

It was now after 4 am; I debated phoning Richard, but decided to wait half an hour; he was usually up by five. Mavis returned with the coffee and the three of us sat in the living room, still trying to come to terms with Lizard's death.

Daddy and Mavis only knew him in passing, but over the years he had worked for me, I had gotten to know him and his family very well, as I had with all my drivers. Lizard was thirty-three, and had four children all under the age of twelve.

My heart broke when I thought how they would react to the loss of their father, who was a good father to them, unlike many others who did not support or cherish their children. I remembered how devastated I had been at the death of Clive, my first love, when I was seventeen, and I knew the pain of their loss would be agonising, especially with them being so young.

I told Daddy and Mavis that they should go back to bed, but they both said it was already morning. Daddy was always up before daybreak anyway, and Mavis also loved the early morning. They said the beauty of it was that they got up early because they *wanted* to and not because they *had* to.

Still, I wanted to be alone, so I told them I was going upstairs to shower and get dressed, and that they might as well go and do the same. Mavis was doubtful about leaving me alone, but I convinced her I was quite fine. I told her I was going to phone Richard, and she and Daddy left through the back grille.

It was already light outside. I had a leisurely bath,

knowing there was nothing I could do immediately. I dressed, made my bed, had another cup of coffee, and then I phoned Richard.

I had left it too late; Richard loved inspecting his farm in the early morning. His aunt, who ran his father's household, and whom everyone called "Auntie", answered the phone.

"Morning Michelle; yu up early, but as early as yu be, Richard gone down on the farm already."

"Oh dear," I said, "I should have followed my mind and called earlier. Can you give him a message as soon as he comes back up – his pager doesn't pick up when he's down on the farm.

"Tell him there's been an accident, and one of my drivers was killed. Ask him if he could come home today instead of tomorrow, and tell him to leave the kids down there for the time being."

After offering condolences Auntie promised to send someone to find Richard and relay the message. It was still early; not yet six o'clock. I wondered if Verna had returned from the hospital, and I dialled her number. The phone rang for a long time with no answer and I hung up, assuming she was still at the hospital, although doing what, I had no idea. I wondered where her children were.

I was at a dead end. I didn't know what to do, so I phoned the police station to see if the investigating officer was there. I was told to call back in the evening as he was on the night shift. I asked if anyone else could give me details of the accident which had occurred on Darlington Drive. I was told to call back in the evening. Typical.

Lurline arrived at seven-thirty, and at eight o'clock I called Verna's number again. There was still no answer. I

The Missing Years

decided to go to work; Verna lived at Old Harbour Bay and would have to pass SmallRock on her way home from the hospital. If she called at *Sweet Home* Lurline would give her the note I had left for her telling her to either phone me or visit me at the office. I also told the Bay taxi drivers, whose stand was in front of the Tax Office, to ask her to come and see me if they saw her.

There was nothing more I could do for the moment. I tried to concentrate on work, but could not. I kept seeing Lizard in my mind; a serious, bespectacled young man who was a practising Christian and went to church with his family every Sunday. I could not believe I would never see him again.

I drafted an obituary for the next edition of the paper, including a glowing tribute to Lizard. I hoped his wife had a good photo of him that we could use. He deserved to be recognised. He had been a good man, a trusted employee and a loving husband and father.

Richard finally called. Auntie had told him what happened, and he did not waste time questioning me, but said he was leaving immediately and would be with me in a couple of hours. I felt a wave of relief wash over me. Richard would come and take charge. I had not realised how much I needed him to be with me.

I kept trying Verna's number without any response. I knew she could not still be at the hospital so I assumed she had gone home with her mother. I sent George to the taxi stand to ask amongst the drivers if they knew where either Lizard's or Verna's parents lived. He returned with the information a short while later.

As soon as Richard arrived I filled him in on everything

that had happened and told him I was anxious to see Verna. George had furnished me with directions to both her and Lizard's parents' homes. Before we could leave, however, Denise, the receptionist phoned through to say that Verna was in reception.

She was escorted into my office and I went to her and hugged her, giving her my condolences. It was obvious that she had been crying, but now she presented a dignified front.

I reassured her that I would do everything I could to assist her and the children, and that I would help with the funeral expenses. I gave her a sum of money to tide her over, and asked Richard to drive her home.

Later in the evening Richard and I visited the police station to try and see the investigating officer and to pick up the accident report form for the insurance. We were told that the officer was "on the road" and that the best time to see him would be around six in the morning before he went off duty. Frustrated, but defeated, I wearily went home.

Richard told me that Adele and Donovan, our two children were upset at being left at Walker's Wood, and I suddenly wished I had not told him to leave them. There was no earthly reason why they could not have come home. There were plenty of people to look after them; Lurline, Mavis, and if it came to that, they could always go to Country.

But I had an aversion to death and I wanted to shield my children from it as much as possible. I decided I would leave them at Walker's Wood until the weekend.

Richard and I were again at the police station at five-thirty Wednesday morning. This time we were in luck; the officer was actually in the building. His name was Sergeant Devlin, and he was a short stocky little man with an arrogant manner. I knew several of the officers at the station, but there seemed to be a constant change of personnel, and I was not familiar with Devlin, who had recently been assigned there.

Richard and I sat patiently in the small cubby-hole which passed for the Traffic Office, while Devlin made phone calls and doodled, keeping us waiting for over twenty minutes, although it was obvious that he was doing nothing important. He finally stopped shuffling the papers on his desk, and gave us his attention.

I explained why we were there and asked for the name and address of the other driver for insurance purposes. I also needed an official accident report to submit with the claim. He took details from me regarding my car and driver, and said the accident report would take a few weeks because he had to interview the other driver who was still in a serious condition in hospital.

I asked him for his take on the accident and he said according to a witness it would appear that both cars were speeding. As far as I was concerned Lizard had had the right of way, and even if he had been speeding, which I doubted, that did not excuse the other driver from not giving way at the junction.

I asked the officer if he had been able to ascertain the blood alcohol level of the other driver, or measured the skid marks, and he replied in the negative to both questions. I asked him if he had even visited the scene of the accident and he said that there had been no need since the victims had been removed to hospital before he was notified.

I looked at Richard and shook my head. I was no longer surprised at the sheer incompetence and the "don't care" attitude of the local police. I told the Sergeant that I would like to see the vehicles, and he directed me to a garage on Darlington Drive where they had been taken.

Before viewing the vehicles, Richard and I went to see the accident site. I did not really want to see it, but Richard did, and I remained in the car and busied my mind with trivial and mundane things pertaining to the office, just so I wouldn't have to think about Lizard.

But my mind refused to behave itself, and I found myself wondering if Lizard, from beyond death, could see us. Some people said that wherever death occurred the spirit remained there, and I shivered at the thought that Lizard might be observing us examining his death scene.

I was not a superstitious or religious person; did not really believe in God or life after death, but when one lives among people who swear by the Bible and take it literally word for word, it is hard not to wonder sometimes if there might not be a grain of truth in there somewhere.

Finally, and much to my relief, Richard returned to the Range Rover and we proceeded back down to the garage at Darlington Drive to look at the vehicles.

Both vehicles were there; usually crashed vehicles were kept in the yard at the back of the police station, or parked along the roadway outside the station, but if there was no space available they would be sent to a local garage to await inspection by the official Examiner.

When I saw the condition of the other vehicle, a Honda Civic, I was surprised that both occupants had not been killed outright. The entire front of the vehicle had been pushed almost into the back.

My own car, a 1989 Lada, had gotten off surprisingly

lightly. Only the driver's side had been severely impacted; the passenger side had been pushed up against a high curb wall which had broken the impact, but the damage was not that severe.

Looking at both cars it would have been easy to assume that the deceased had been in the Honda Civic, which looked a total write-off, instead of the Lada which did not seem as badly damaged.

I was disgusted to learn from the proprietor of the garage that there was a daily storage fee for keeping the vehicle on his premises. I wanted to remove it to *Sweet Home* but was told it could not be moved until the Examiner had inspected it for the accident report. I was not happy, but could do nothing about it.

Three weeks later, the car was still there; the Examiner had still not made his inspection, and the daily fees were accruing. When I called the Examiner at the examination depot in Spanish Town I was told they had not had a request from the Old Harbour police, and would only be able to conduct the examination when this was forthcoming.

Richard and I made frequent visits to the station, sometimes together, sometimes separately, in attempts to have the examination expedited, but kept on getting the run-around. Sergeant Devlin seemed to have developed a dislike for me; perhaps because I was not impressed with his self-importance and was not intimidated by him, but looked him straight in the eye and spoke up forcefully. Or maybe it was just that he did not like women who were taller than him.

I had noticed before this that the local police officers did not like people who knew their rights, and who were not afraid of, or intimidated by them. For some reason the officers seemed threatened by sensible, intelligent, and confident people.

Then I learned that Sergeant Devlin and the owner of the garage where my vehicle was being kept were bosom buddies, and that all the crashed cars in the area were sent there for storage, while they awaited the Examiners' pleasure. I learned that by the time some owners were able to remove their vehicles the accumulated fees were so high that many of them forfeited the vehicle to the garage proprietor.

I began to suspect that Devlin was in collusion with the garage owner, and I decided to go to the station to confront him with my suspicions. Before going to see him I had visited the depot at Walks Road in Spanish Town and spoken to the Chief Examiner, giving full details of the accident. He had confirmed that there had been no notification or request from Old Harbour. I wondered if he and his staff too were a part of the suspected conspiracy to milk money from the victims of road accidents.

However, he had told me that he would be passing through Old Harbour on his way to May Pen later in the week, and he would stop by and do the examination, pending receipt of the request from Devlin. I had thanked him, and gone to see Devlin.

I did not accuse him; I merely said I could not understand why it was taking so long for him to notify the Examiner's Department. He claimed he had notified them weeks ago, and that they would get around to it when they were able.

I did not tell him that the Examiner would be looking at the vehicle pending the paperwork; I only told him that I had visited the depot and the Examiner had confirmed that they had not received a request for the examination of my vehicle. I requested that he give me the paperwork to take to the depot myself, intending to give it to the Examiner when he came to inspect the car.

Devlin declined to give it to me, saying they had their systems and procedures. I suggested to him that if that was the case it would behove them well to implement them, otherwise someone might be inclined to think there was some sort of conspiracy to milk poor motorists out of their money or their vehicles. I added that I noticed that crashed cars were no longer being parked at the station, where they incurred no fee, but that all vehicles were being sent to "your friend's" garage.

I have never read such raw savage anger and hatred in another's face toward me. Devlin's eyes narrowed to mere slits in his dark face, and he seemed to have to clench his fists to prevent himself from going for his firearm. I felt a little flutter of apprehension; although I was not exactly afraid of him, it did not do to blatantly antagonise a gun-bearing person, law officer or not.

"Yu mekkin' some kine-a accusation, Mam?" he snarled at me.

"No," I replied calmly, "merely voicing a suspicion." I *absolutely hated* to be called "Mam."

We stared at each other in silence for an eternity, each being unwilling to be the first to look away. Finally, he stood up from around his desk and said, "Dat's why A doan like oonu farrinahs y'nuh. Oonu come fram farrin wid oonu money an oonu show-off self come-a eggs-up oonuself pon people. All dah dutty Rasta-man weh yu deh wid, him fi dead.

Claudette Beckford-Brady

A don't like dem dutty Rasta people dem. Di whole a dem fi dead!"

Now Richard could by no means be described as a "dutty" Rasta. He was always impeccably – not to mention expensively – dressed, and his dreadlocks were always clean, tidy, and well maintained.

Normally, when insults are hurled at me, I would ignore them and the hurler, and walk away in a dignified manner, without belittling myself to make a response. But these insults were not aimed at me; if they had been, I might just have walked out – but they were aimed at my beloved Richard, who was *not even* a Rasta, despite his dreadlocks, and who was not there to defend himself.

I drew myself up to my full height and looked down on the short stocky Sergeant. "First of all, *you*, yu arrogant, jumped up, pompous little ass, are a public servant. *I* am your boss; my taxes pay your salary and don't you forget it!

"Second of all, I am no foreigner. I was born right here on my island, at Gravel Hill, not eight miles from here! SHUT UP! I haven't finished," I shouted, as he tried to interrupt me.

"And third of all, I will be making a written report of your conduct and your insulting words to your superior officer and also to the Police Complaints Authority, although I doubt very much if that will serve any purpose, since they are your colleagues and you all stick together.

"But you would be wise to remember that I *own and run* a newspaper, and I can write damning editorials and bring unwanted focus and attention on certain police practices and inefficiencies, and if you think you can shoot me, or hire someone to do it for you, then go right ahead. I dare you!"

And without waiting for his response, I stalked out of his

office without looking back. I did not take the time to see his response to my outburst.

Later when I told Richard about it, he chided me and told me I should not antagonise the police.

"I'm not afraid of them!" I said. "I'm not like these poor locals who don't know their rights and are intimidated by the uniform and the gun."

Richard, who hardly ever got angry, and never raised his voice even when he was, replied exasperatedly, "Yu too volatile, by far, Michelle," and I felt a little shiver at how *very much* like Clive he sounded.

Clive; my first love, who had been killed in 1978, fifteen years before, but whose memory was still very much alive in my heart. It was uncanny how alike he and Richard really were, and sometimes Richard would say something, and I would be certain it was Clive.

But secretly I was a little worried that I might have gone too far with Devlin, and although I could make sure that if anything happened to me, Devlin would be top of the list of suspects, it was no real consolation; murders were rarely solved in Jamaica and mere suspicion alone would not convict him.

Richard told me to forget about making a report to the Complaints Authority, and although I was still stewing and wanted the book thrown at Devlin, I complied.

Finally, two days later, the Examiner phoned me at work and said he was on his way, and I should meet him at the garage, which I did. I arrived before him, and noticed the garage owner's surprise when I told him the Examiner was on his way. He said that could not be, because he had not been told to expect him. I told him that Devlin was not the only one who could decide when, or if, I got my vehicle.

"But him kyaan come till him get di paperwork," the garage owner insisted. I replied that he seemed to be privy to information that only the police and Examiner should have.

"How yu know seh him nuh get di paperwork? Yu an yu frien' Devlin eena collusion?" I asked him. I deliberately spoke patois.

The proprietor, Zekel, by name, went inside his office and I lurked near the open window to eavesdrop on the phone call I knew he was going to make. Sure enough he phoned Devlin and told him that "Di newspaper ooman deh here, and seh di Examina deh pon him way." I could not hear the response from the other end, of course, but I was gratified to see and hear that Zekel was agitated.

"Afta mi nuh know!" I heard him exclaim. "All mi know, shi seh him deh pon him way…. Stop dem? How *me* fi stap dem? *Me* fi tell examina seh him kyaan inspeck di veekle….? Yu know wha'? *You* come tell him!"

I saw a vehicle coming in through the gate and, wondering if it was the examiner, I moved from under the window and went towards the newcomer. He stepped out of the car and said, "Hello, Mrs Armstrong. We meet again."

"Yes sir," I replied. "Thank you for taking time out to deal with this matter for me."

He looked me up and down appraisingly, as he had done when I visited the depot. I could tell he liked what he saw. He smiled. "Yu welcome, Mam. A was passing dis way, anyway. Which veekle is your own?"

I wanted to tell him that I hated to be called "Mam" but I didn't bother. Zekel had come out of the office and was coming over to us. The examiner was already inspecting the

The Missing Years

vehicle and making notes. Zekel seemed uncomfortable, and shifted from one foot to the other. He kept glancing at me, but I ignored him totally.

Finally the Examiner looked up and said, "Ahright, Mrs Armstrong, A wi' stop at di station and wrap up di paperwork and mek yu get di report." Then he glanced at Zekel and said, "Yu soon won't have nuh space inside here if yu nuh get some-a dem kyar here move."

After he had left, I told Zekel that I would be moving the vehicle immediately and asked him to give me the bill for the storage. I had already made the calculations myself, but I wanted to see how much he was going to charge me. He told me I could hire his wrecker (tow-truck) to move the vehicle. I declined, telling him that my husband had made arrangements and would be there directly.

He went into the office, sulkily, I thought, and returned a little while later with the bill. As I had known he would, he had calculated for one day more than was due. I pointed it out to him, and handed him the correct amount, asking for a receipt. He went back into the office and wrote it without protest and brought it back out to me.

The tow truck that Richard had hired arrived and they loaded the car and took it away to the garage at Church Pen where it would be repaired. The insurance company had already examined and photographed it and given the go-ahead for the repairs.

Meantime, Lizard's funeral had taken place and he had been interred in the Church Pen cemetery. I had visited his relatives – his wife and kids, and his parents – and made my contribution to the funeral expenses. I had also given Verna a small financial settlement, although, as I belatedly discovered, drivers were not covered under the Public Passenger insurance; only the passengers themselves, along with the vehicle, which I thought rather stupid.

At the end of September, some six weeks after the accident, and three weeks after the funeral, I finally obtained the police report, which claimed that the driver of the other vehicle had fallen asleep at the wheel.

There was no mention of the fact that he had been totally inebriated at the time of the accident, and I assumed that if Devlin could have gotten away with it, he would have claimed that it was *my driver* who had caused the accident, but of course my driver had been on his right of way, and there was no disputing that. But he did claim that my driver's speed contributed to the magnitude of the impact.

The other driver was charged with two counts of manslaughter – his passenger had subsequently succumbed to her injuries – but was not charged for his drunkenness, which would have made the charges more serious.

I was convinced that cash had changed hands, and that Devlin had been "persuaded" to make the charges lesser. I wanted to take him to task over this, even going so far as to get Frank to try and legally obtain a hospital report which might indicate the man's blood alcohol level at the time of his admission.

But Richard, Daddy, and especially Mavis, told me to leave it alone; nothing could bring back Lizard and I was only going to succeed in making enemies out of the police, which would not be a good thing. I told them that this was the reason that these things could happen with impunity, because no-one was willing to make a stand and take the corrupt cops to task.

The Missing Years

However, I allowed myself to be persuaded, and did not muddy any waters, but waited for the outcome of the court case, to see what (inadequate) punishment would be imposed for the taking of two lives and depriving a family of husband, father, and breadwinner, contenting myself with doing what I could for Verna and her children.

I had been horrified to discover that my Public Passenger insurance, for which I had to pay through the nose, did not cover my driver, only the passengers. I had not bothered to read the fine print, and so had had no idea. I immediately set about purchasing separate cover for my remaining drivers, while setting up a means of steady income for Verna and the kids.

The car had been repaired and I suggested to Richard that I should just deed it over to Verna; it would give her a start in providing for herself and her kids, always supposing she could find a steady decent driver. Richard, always intuitive and empathetic, suggested that it might give her unpleasant memories, even though it had been expertly repaired and repainted, and said he would buy her one.

I loved him for it, but declined his offer and promptly swapped cars with Shortman, giving Verna the one he was driving and giving him Lizard's former car. At first he was against it, saying that it was a "bad-luck`ed" car, but I finally persuaded him that he was just being superstitious. I bribed him by telling him that in a year or so we would sell it and buy him a different one, since I had already gotten four years good service out of it. So we changed all the paperwork and Verna now had a means of survival, and I could stop worrying about her.

It was now October and my daughter, Adelaine, who

would be five next January, had started Prep school in May Pen and was loving it. She was taken there every morning by Wilbert, my longest serving driver whom I trusted implicitly, and picked up again in the afternoon. She would come home and teach her brother Donovan what she had learned each day.

I had accompanied her to school on the first day of term, and had intended to do so for a full week, but after the second day she said to me, "Mummy, yu don't need to come. I'm not scared. I like school." And so I had left Wilbert to the daily task.

Donovan was now three. He had recently started to attend a day nursery, but was not as outgoing and gregarious as his sister, and frequently cried when Lurline left him at the nursery.

He did not really have to go to the nursery at all; Lurline was used to looking after both children as well as taking care of the housework. But I wanted him to socialise with other children and hopefully grow to be a bit more self-assured and able to fend for himself. He was far too timid for a boy, I thought, and I wanted to prepare him for the day when he too would start school proper.

Meantime, my third child continued to grow in my stomach while I waited impatiently for his or her arrival in November, thankful that he would be born before Christmas, when the entire extended family would be arriving on the island for the festive season and the Campbell family reunion.

CHAPTER THREE

My Own Line, and a Happy Grandma

The new baby was a girl, much to Adele's delight, and my relief. She already had three brothers and I had sort of half-promised her a sister. I do not know how I would have explained or consoled her had this one turned out to be another boy. But thankfully, I did not have to.

We named her Estelle for Richard's deceased mother, and Miriam for my grandma. Richard suggested we could call her Delisia, for my own biological mother, but I declined; Delisia and I had a long way to go before I would feel like naming my child after her – in any case it was Mavis who had mothered me, so if anything I would rather call the child after her, I said.

Richard was horrified. "Over my dead body will yu inflict a child of mine with a name like *Mavis!*" he exclaimed.

I knew what he meant, but I had to tease him. "Mum will be *so hurt* when she hears how you are denigrating her name. *She* doesn't find anything wrong with it."

Claudette Beckford-Brady

He was unfazed. "Mavis will understand what A mean and not tek offence. She's a sensible intelligent woman."

When I was younger I had always been mildly surprised at Mavis' intelligence and plain common sense. She had only had an elementary education, but sometimes she would make really sage remarks, or use words I had no idea she even knew. My first boyfriend, Clive, used to accuse me of being patronising whenever I had shown surprise at something Mavis had said.

We were all staying over at the Big House with Daddy and Mavis. The extension which we had decided to add on to *Sweet Home* to accommodate our growing family was complete and in the process of being painted, and I had to get away from the smell of paint. We could have just moved across to Mummy Myrtle and Daddy Wilf's side of the house, but Mavis and Daddy insisted that we stay with them.

A large playroom with its own veranda had been added downstairs, adjoining my own living room and veranda, and two more bedrooms and an additional bathroom had been built on top of that. I had had to lose a part of my flower garden and several fruit trees, much to my regret, but we needed the additional rooms.

The family in England was growing also and we wanted to be able to accommodate everyone, especially with the Campbell family reunion coming up, which every member of the UK family would be attending, including, for the first time, the twins' husbands, Tony and Roy.

Traditionally, at the family reunion, the head of each family unit would have his family lined up behind him, and in previous years I had been attached to Uncle Keith's line. I had decided that this year I would form my own line, and include all my immediate Freeman relatives in it, rationalising that if they were my relatives, that also made them Campbell relatives – after all, not all the extended family members were named Campbell – and so I wanted as many of my Freeman family members as possible to be in attendance.

My brother Delroy, and his wife, Joy had three children; Clivey, who was almost ten; Kieran, aged six, and their youngest and only girl, Vashti, who was approaching two years old.

The twins, Rachel and Rebecca, had two children each. Rachel's two girls, Chelsey and Ishia, were four and two, respectively, while Rebecca's two boys, Gregory and Stefan, were aged two and three. My youngest sister, Samantha, was eighteen, and still at school.

I had received a letter from Delisia in September saying how glad she was that we had established a line of communication, and that she was looking forward to the family reunion in December. I grudgingly thought that she would be the one heading up my line, instead of Richard, but after all, I reluctantly acknowledged, she was the Campbell head of our branch of the Tree. I peevishly did not respond to her letter for several weeks.

After Estelle's birth in November I relented sufficiently to finally write her back, telling her about the birth of her latest granddaughter, and sending her photos of all the kids. I still had mixed feelings about her; in fact I was not quite sure how I felt about her. In one sense I was happy that she had been found and that we were communicating, but I still incubated a sense of abandonment, and still felt as if she did not deserve to share fully in my children; not to mention the fact that I was jealous of the attention being lavished on her

Claudette Beckford-Brady

by my beloved Grandma.

Since 1978 I had easily been the most important person in Grandma Miriam's life, and was unreasonably proprietorial toward her. Now I was beginning to feel that Delisia was usurping my position; as if I had only been keeping the place warm for her, and now that she was back in Grandma's life I would have to move over.

I did not share these feelings with Richard, who I knew would say I was being fanciful and ridiculous. Of course I knew deep down that I *was* being unreasonable; there was no difference in the way Grandma felt about me, and no difference in her treatment of me.

In actual fact, having Delisia back made Grandma want to draw me and my children into a close knit family group with her, and she kept referring to Delisia as my "mother" and my children's "grandmother." She seemed, at times, to have totally forgotten the existence of Mavis, who in my mind was my "real" mother, despite the fact that Delisia had birthed me.

I knew that Grandma did not mean to slight Mavis, whom she liked and respected, and I suppose one could not really blame her for wanting her daughter and granddaughter to be close. For her sake I would maintain the fiction of being a family with Delisia, but in my mind, the only thing we could ever really be to each other would be friends, if we could overcome the entire past and move on.

And we had yet to clear that past, for even though we had had a good and friendly conversation there were unresolved issues still between us.

Richard, the children, and I returned to *Sweet Home* the first week in December. The new addition was all painted and

The Missing Years

furnished. I moved Adele and Donovan out of my old study and into one of the new rooms, and turned the study into a nursery for Estelle. When they were old enough the two girls would share a room, and I could have my study back, because I was currently using the living room, which was not ideal.

I was working on my second novel, in between running my business and being a wife and mother. I had a pretty good routine worked out, and Lurline was a tremendous asset. I was extremely lucky to have found her.

I had continued working throughout my pregnancy, and now I took Estelle to work with me so I could breast feed without having to express my milk. There was no shortage of volunteers to change her nappy and console her when she cried, which was rare, for, like Adele, she was a very contented child.

Both the *Districk Bell* and *Jamaican Woman* were doing well – locally and overseas. We had worked hard to convince Jamaicans in the wider Diaspora to subscribe to both, and it was these overseas sales and advertising which helped to cushion us and keep us from high interest bank loans.

My partner, Barbara Brown-Davies, previously a roving reporter, was now News and Features Editor, while I concentrated on the day to day running of the business as Managing Director, as well as writing my own weekly column. Our other partner, Cecile Jakes, aka Cee Jay was editor of the magazine, and we had employed several more writers and reporters.

At the beginning of December family members began arriving on the island from all over the world. Because of the numbers expected, and from previous years' experience, the majority of the extended diasporal family had booked hotel accommodation; some in Kingston, some in Ocho Rios, and a few even in Old Harbour, for Christmas and Boxing nights.

My siblings and their families, and Mummy Myrtle and Daddy Wilf, had arrived on December eighth, and they were followed on the twentieth by Uncle Keith and his family. Delisia arrived on Christmas Eve.

Uncle Kenneth and the few other members of the North American family who would be accommodated locally also arrived, and everyone, including Delisia, stopped at *Sweet Home* for a brief visit before going on to their appointed places – Delisia to Country and Uncle Kenneth and family to Cousin Daniel's at Colbeck.

Uncle Keith and Aunt Vilma would also be staying at Gravel Hill, but my cousins Veronica, Joseph, Elaine and Jennifer would all be staying with us at Island Farm. Accommodations would be tight, but with my new rooms and Mummy Myrtle's guest rooms we would manage.

Christmas morning 1992 dawned bright and sunny and we all packed ourselves into the coaster bus that Richard had hired, and Richard's Range Rover, and headed up to Gravel Hill. We did not have breakfast at home because we knew there would be a mountain of food at Country, and with so many people to cater for it would have been a hassle, especially owing to the fact that neither Lurline nor Miss Pearl, Mavis' helper, were working today, it being Christmas.

Grandma Miriam was in her element as matriarch of the clan. Her beaming smiles were in evidence throughout the day; this reunion was not being overshadowed by Delisia's absence and unknown whereabouts, and I hid my resentment and tried to be genuinely happy for Grandma, who kept referring to the fact that this could be her last family reunion,

The Missing Years

given her age.

I do not know why Grandma was always so preoccupied with her mortality; I kept telling her she could live to be a hundred, given the fact that she had no medical problems, and was still fit and strong for her age. But of course the future is always uncertain and I suppose five years was a long time when looked at from her perspective. Still, she was remarkably happy, and I was glad that Delisia's presence had done that for her.

After we had eaten breakfast Delisia called me into the house and produced a load of packages and several envelopes. I did not really believe in Christmas and gift-giving. I was trying to teach my children that giving a gift was something done spontaneously from the heart at any time, and did not need an occasion like Christmas to validate it.

In my mind Christmas was something that had been invented by the capitalist society in order to get rich at the expense of poor people. I gave my employees Christmas bonuses because I knew that it was a time of year when more money was needed, and there were a few persons in the local community that I sent parcels of food or gave a little money to, because I knew they needed it. But I never bought Christmas cards and I never gift-wrapped presents.

I knew my children were too young to understand my reasoning, and I did not stop them from accepting Christmas gifts when they were given. My friend Lynette Barrington thought I was wicked to deprive my kids of the fun of a Christmas tree and the opening of Christmas presents, but I was not swayed; they got plenty of fun opening gift-wrapped presents from other people.

Delisia had brought gifts for me, Richard, Daddy and

Mavis, as well as the children. I thanked her and told her we would open them when we got home, but I did look inside the envelopes. There were three, each one labelled with one of the children's name. She had set up trust funds for each of them.

I did not know how to respond. I suppose she had a right, if she wanted to; after all they *were* her grandchildren, and *I* had no right to refuse on their behalf. And indeed, why should I? I told her I was overwhelmed by her generosity and thanked her on behalf of the children.

As the morning progressed, more and more people arrived and in a short while the roadway leading down into the yard, and the road above it, were filled with parked vehicles, some of them parked so badly that persons who had parked earlier who wanted to get out could not, without a major shifting of vehicles. This is why our vehicles had been parked in Miss May's yard, up the road.

Around midday a bell was rung and the entire family gathered in front of Grandma's house and on the babbeque for the usual formalities. Uncle Kenneth, as usual, being the eldest male, took office.

He had aged considerably in the last five years. At sixty-seven, his short-cropped hair was completely white, and he did not move as briskly as he used to. His voice, though, had lost none of its resonance.

As he always did, he began with a prayer. The Christians among us supported him with "Amens" and "Yes Lords" while the rest of us suffered patiently until he had finished. This year's prayer seemed interminable as he gave special thanks for Delisia's safe homecoming and reconciliation with her family, but at last it came to an end to a chorus of relieved

The Missing Years

"Amens."

Then came the obituaries of loved ones who had passed on since the last reunion, including Uncle Kingsley who had died earlier in the year. After that, speeches and accolades, and finally, what I had been waiting for, the call for the family to line up for inspection.

I organised my family's line, but noticed that Delisia had remained on the veranda where she had been sitting with Grandma, Great-Aunt Zoë, and Uncle Kenneth. It didn't matter to me, but Richard obviously thought she should be with us, and went and got her. It seemed to me that she came reluctantly, but she came anyhow, and stood at the head of our line.

I was slightly amused to see that my line was now longer than Uncle Keith's. His line consisted of himself and Aunt Vilma plus their four children, Veronica and Joseph's spouses and four grandchildren, a total of twelve.

Mine consisted of Delisia, myself and Richard with our three children, plus Daddy and Mavis, my four siblings and their spouses, and all their kids, even Mummy Myrtle and Daddy Wilf. I looked across at Uncle Keith and said, "What a short little line! Is loaf oonu a loaf!" Uncle Keith replied that I was cheating by padding my line with Freemans, and we all had a good laugh.

It was a great reunion. Mamma and Pappa Freeman and the rest of my paternal relatives had all been invited and when I looked at the large number of persons, many of whom I didn't even know, and realised that I was in some way related to all of them, I was overawed. We spent a good hour taking photographs and recording videos.

At some point, a group of around thirty young people,

including Samantha, the twins and their spouses, set out on a trek to the river. I watched them go with envy, feeling like a mature matron who was long past fun excursions to the river. Richard must have seen the wistful look on my face as I watched them go, for he said, "Why yu don't guh with them? Yu have more baby-sitters than yu need," but I declined, saying that their energy made me feel old and decrepit.

Later in the afternoon Grandma Miriam called me, and she, Delisia and I walked up to the sunrise hilltop. We paused at the pimento walk and examined our navel string trees, crushing and smelling the aromatic fragrance of the pimento leaves.

I had wanted to plant my children's navel strings here too, along with pimento suckers, but Richard said that the place to plant them was at *Sweet Home* and so we had planted an Ortanique orange tree for Adele, a coconut tree for Donovan, and a tangerine tree for Estelle. I told Delisia about them.

Delisia was happy and smiling. She admitted to us that she had been full of trepidation at the prospect of being the centre of attention, but to her relief everyone had acted as if she had always been among us and was just another family member attending the reunion. Apart from the mention in Uncle Kenneth's prayer, and a "welcome home, Delisia" address, she had not been singled out in any way – her achievements were chronicled along with other family members.

She had, of course, been taken aside by individuals, her siblings included, and interrogated, but she had not been condemned or vilified, and she was inordinately relieved that the perceived ordeal had not materialised. She had returned and claimed her place in the family and it was almost as if she had never been "lost."

The house on the hilltop had been given a new coat of paint, and glistened whitely in the late afternoon sunlight. Maisie's garden and food grung were flourishing; corn, and gungu peas, cucumbers, okra, and ripe red tomatoes, as well as yam, sweet potato, banana and plantains.

Delisia had of course visited the hilltop and seen the house before this visit with me and Grandma, but this was the first time we were both visiting it together. I was curious to know her thoughts regarding the house and the hilltop, but did not want to bring up the subject of ownership myself. As it turned out, I didn't have to.

Delisia herself brought up the subject. "Y'know, when I was a girl I always imagined this hilltop with a house – *my house* – on it. And then when I was carrying you, Michelle, I fantasised about living here with you. Me and my baby, in our own little house on our own little hilltop." The Californian twang was evident in her voice.

She paused, and I remained silent, not knowing what to say. At least she referred to it as *our* hilltop, and not *her* hilltop. Before I could think of a response, she continued. "I'm glad Mamma gave it to you; that way I can still feel connected to it, through you."

Grandma had obviously told her about giving me the hilltop. I wondered if she had mentioned to Delisia that I had been concerned about its ownership since her return.

Maisie and her children were down at the yard with the extended family, but the house was not locked. We sat on the veranda and looked out over the hills and valleys of St. Catherine. Other than the time at Cousin Daniel's house when Delisia had first arrived, this was the first time she and Grandma and I were absolutely alone together.

That other time had been very uncomfortable – Delisia had been annoyed that I had sprung Grandma on her without warning and had been on the defensive. Also at that time she and I were still antagonistic toward each other. This time we were all comfortable in each other's presence, and I could see that Grandma was the happiest she had been in years.

She kept looking at me and Delisia and nodding and smiling to herself. She was not very talkative today, but we could see how happy she was. I think she was keeping quiet because she wanted me and Delisia to talk to each other more. I broke the silence which had been lengthening since Delisia's last statement.

"Grandma looks like the cat that's got the cream, or the canary, or both," I said to Delisia. "Look at that smug look on her face."

"I see it," Delisia said. "But it lights up her face and enhances her beauty, don't you think?"

"It sure does," I answered, "and isn't she a beauty for such an old girl?"

"Aint she though?" Delisia replied and we laughed, Grandma joining in.

"A don't feel old todeh," she said happily. "Yu know how many times over the years A imagine this moment? Michelle, is a pity wi never think to bring the girls up here; then I could look at four generations of Campbell women all together in one place."

"You've done that already, Grandma. Several times."

"Yes, but always with other people around. A muss get some picture tek with the four generation of us.

The Missing Years

"A feel suh proud when A look pon oonu; mi daughter, granddaughter, and great-granddaughters; a set of strong, feisty, spirited and independent women. The Campbell Women. Yu should write a book about us, Michelle."

"I just might, Grandma, I just might."

We spent an hour on the hill making light conversation. There would be plenty of time for me and Delisia to deal with whatever issues we had to deal with; today was Grandma's day, and so I bent over backwards not to let any little feelings of awkwardness creep in and spoil the occasion.

It was late afternoon, and the December sun had travelled westward across St. Catherine and over the Clarendon hills. It was now well on its way to setting, and my breasts were beginning to feel rather full; it was time to feed Estelle. As the thought entered my mind I heard someone calling my name and I looked up to see my nephew, Clivey. He had been sent to tell me that Estelle was awake and fretting.

Clivey was almost ten. Like his father, my brother Delroy, he had a quiet and tranquil personality, but he could also be boisterous at times. He was going to be tall, too, like his father and grandfather who were both over six feet tall. And he was very outspoken, and not very tactful.

He knew Grandma, of course, although he had not spent any time with her one on one; the last time he had been on the island he had been only five, but Delisia he did not know at all. He knew the story of my "other mother" as they all did, and now I noticed him looking at Delisia with frank curiosity, not bothering to disguise his interest.

"Gosh, Aunt Michelle," he ejaculated, "your other Mum looks just like you! You could be twins."

Claudette Beckford-Brady

I scratched the top of his head. "It's the other way around, Clivey. *I* am the one who looks like *her*; she was here first. Anyway, her name is Aunt Delisia to you, okay?"

"'Kay. You coming down?" I nodded, and got up from the veranda chair. Grandma and Delisia got up too, and we started back down the hill to the yard, with Clivey running on ahead.

The sun had set, and dusk had fallen, and then suddenly it was night. It still surprised me how quickly evening turned to night here in the Caribbean. By the time we got back to the yard it was full dark, although it had taken us no more than ten minutes, and that only because Grandma moved slowly.

In the yard a party was in full swing with music thumping out from Cousin Bulla's sound system, liquor flowing copiously from the back of Cousin Daniel's pick-up, and smoke bellowing out from the many spliffs and cigarettes. Periodically there would be the sharp explosion of a firecracker, or cribs, being let off.

A group of elders and some of the younger children were on the babbeque, but if it was a story they were wanting, there was no chance of them hearing one over the music. I told the story-master, Uncle Cornell, that if he was intent on story-telling, he had best take the kids and go up to the hilltop. The moon would be up full and bright in a little while, and they could always turn on the veranda light if necessary. They would still be able to hear the music, but they would also be able to hear the story being told.

In a few minutes I was gratified to notice a line of youngsters, Pied Piper fashion, following after Uncle Cornell, Adele and some of my nieces and nephews amongst them. They headed off around the house toward the pimento walk

The Missing Years

and hilltop and I noted with a measure of relief that Joy and Mummy Myrtle were accompanying them.

Uncle Cornell loved to tell a story. Anancy stories, duppy (ghost) stories, even fairy stories and foreign legends, suitably adapted for the Jamaican audience. I remembered how one year he had told the story of the Headless Horseman by Washington Irvin, and played a trick on everyone, with my cousin Levi riding Marcus the mule and draped in a white sheet with a black cloth over his head. I have to admit; he had made a very credible headless horseman, and had sparked real fright among some of the younger children.

I fed and changed Estelle and put her back down on Grandma's bed, where she promptly fell asleep again. Although full dark, it was only just six o'clock and the party was likely to go on till the small hours. We would probably stay till around ten, or till the kids started to fret, and then make our way home, leaving the rest to party till they stopped or dropped.

When I came back out from putting Estelle down Richard and Delisia were in conversation. I felt a small flicker of irritation, and circumvented them, going on to the babbeque where some of the elders were gathered.

Around ten-thirty we started rounding up the kids in preparation for leaving. Some of them had already, or were on the verge of, falling asleep. The twins and their husbands were not ready, and said they would stay at Country overnight and find their way down in the morning. Richard and Joseph left to go up to Miss May's to pick up the bus and the Range Rover, and returned in a short while. We boarded the vehicles and proceeded down Gravel Hill towards Old Harbour.

Claudette Beckford-Brady

The car was in front with Richard, me and the kids, and Mummy Myrtle. We passed Free Marlie and Bois Content and were travelling along the part of the road known as Long Level, when Richard slowed right down and kept the vehicle at a crawl, constantly checking the rear view mirror. I assumed he was waiting for the bus to close with us.

After a few more minutes and the bus had not come into sight, he pulled over and cut the engine. I noticed he was frowning. "What's wrong?" I asked, but he held up a hand and said, "Shh."

The children were all asleep, even Adele. She had had the time of her life and was literally exhausted. Mummy Myrtle had been about to say something, but at Richard's gesture she changed her mind.

Richard had gotten out of the vehicle and was in a listening pose, staring back up the road. I too strained my ears for the sound of the bus, but encountered only silence. It was a still, quiet night. There were no traffic noises on this little country road, and most of the houses we passed had been in darkness. It was not a busy road at the best of times, and it being Christmas night, and late, not many people were abroad.

Sound generally carried a long way in these quiet country parts, and the bus had been right behind us when we turned the corner at Bois. We should be able to hear it. It must have stopped. Various scenarios flashed through my mind. They may have picked up a puncture; someone may have wanted to urinate...

Richard returned to the vehicle and started the engine. He began to reverse slowly, listening intently all the while and looking for the bus' headlights. When we had gone back about five hundred yards he stopped the vehicle again, and listened. Silence. He turned the car around and we drove back the way we had come.

As we rounded a corner the headlights picked out the bus, which was stationary in the middle of the road. Everyone seemed to be aboard; I could see Joseph in the driver's seat and the silhouettes of the others. Then everything seemed to happen at once, and in slow motion.

In the same instant that I registered that all was not right, Richard drew sharp brakes, thrust the vehicle into reverse and screeched backwards around the corner. But not before I had noticed several things.

Simultaneously I saw a white Lada station wagon beside the bus, facing back toward Bois, with two men just entering it. Two other men leapt from the bus and ran for the Lada. One of them raised his arm and pointed towards us and I heard two sharp pops which sounded rather like firecrackers.

Only they weren't. They were gunshots.

CHAPTER FOUR

Robbery under Arms

I had never before in my life known such stark terror. Richard gassed the car in reverse and shot around the corner and back down the road. Then he stopped the car and jumped out, and I saw to my shock, horror and surprise that there was a *gun* in his hand. Before I could react, he hissed at me, "Gi Estelle to Myrtle and drive fast as yu can fi di police!" and he was off up the road at a running crouch.

I sat in stunned shock, not knowing what to do. It would take at least thirty minutes to get into Old Harbour on these potholed roads – and I could only drive so fast with my kids in the car. Another twenty or thirty minutes for the police to mobilise and get to the scene. By that time Richard could very well be dead.

And what about the rest of my family in the bus? Were any of them hurt? Injured? Dead?

My skin began to crawl with goose bumps and I started to shake. I could not handle death. What was I to do? Richard had said drive for the police but I didn't see how that was going to help the present situation – they would not, could not, be in time to be of any use.

I realised that Mummy Myrtle was taking the sleeping Estelle from my arms. Donovan was sleeping soundly and Adele had woken up and was sitting up on the seat, her eyes wide open, wanting to know what was happening. Mummy Myrtle nudged me and told me to get into the driver's seat, which I did mechanically, while she held Estelle and put her arm around Adele, hushing her.

And still I did not move the vehicle. I could not abandon my entire family to the mercy of gunmen on a lonely country road. But what was I to do? A few dwellings were scattered at intervals along the road and on the hillsides, but even if the occupants were not in their beds, who amongst them could help us? You could not face gunmen with machetes and hoes.

No one had heard the two gunshots, or if they had they were playing it safe and staying in their homes. Or perhaps they thought they were firecrackers. Telephones had not reached these parts yet, although it was almost 1993. I had no choice – I had to drive for the police.

But still I hesitated. My mind was beginning to calm down and I began to think more clearly. The gunmen had been actually getting into their car which was facing away from us. It seemed to me that when we happened upon them they had been preparing to leave the scene. I had heard no shots other than the two which had been fired toward us and which had fallen short.

They must have heard the approach of our vehicle and ran for their car, throwing out the two shots to keep us at our distance. I felt, I hoped, that they had driven away at top speed and was past Bellas Gate by now. Any minute now I would see the bus coming around the corner with Richard aboard.

And then my heart plummeted to the bottom of my stomach as I heard the distinct crack-crack of a firearm being discharged and then several more crack-cracks. I heard the sound of a car door being slammed and a car driving off at high speed, the sound receding into the distance – and then – deathly silence.

Taking complete leave of my senses, I threw open the door of the car and jumped out, ignoring Adele's cries and Mummy Myrtle's pleas to come back, running up the road as fast as I could. As I approached the corner I slowed down and keeping as close to the banking as I could, I inched my way around it at a crouch until I could see the bus. It was on a stretch of road which was totally devoid of street lighting, but the moon was high and full and the bus' headlights were full on, enabling me to see the scene clearly.

A prostrate form lay on the ground in front of the bus, and another form stood over it, looking down and pointing a gun at it. I noted with relief that the person standing over the prostrate form was Richard. He appeared to be unhurt and in control. Every now and then he glanced back up the road as if he expected to see the white Lada coming back.

The people in the bus were all now crowding forward, and Daddy was stepping down, followed by Delroy and the other men, all of them, I noticed, minus their shoes. Richard bent down to examine the injured man, and feel for a pulse. When he stood up he did not indicate whether the man was dead or alive.

The look on his face was terrible to see. It was a look of

burning anger; I wanted to run to him and hug him, thankful that he was okay, but I was afraid of him – of the look on his face. Me – afraid – and of my own beloved, gentle Richard. Instead I ran to Daddy and clung to him.

All of a sudden, and from out of nowhere, people, some of them in nightwear, started arriving and stood looking down at the figure of the young man lying on the ground. He was lying face up and I noticed for the first time that there was a large red patch spread out across his chest. I heard someone say, "Him dead?" and someone else reply, "It look suh."

Despite myself, and my hatred of anything to do with death, I was drawn by a morbid curiosity to look more closely at the young man lying prone on a country road at eleven o'clock on a Christmas night. He could not have been more than nineteen or twenty, and I turned away quickly as his lifeless eyes stared up at me in stunned surprise.

Daddy Wilf and Delroy were trying to keep the women and children from seeing the body, but they had crowded up to the front and were peering through the open door, chattering excitedly, and some of the children crying. I climbed into the bus and hugged and kissed everyone and we all tried to talk at once.

Then Richard looked into the bus and saw me, and the anger which was characterising his features as he stood over his victim increased tenfold. He strode over to the open door of the bus and said, in a voice which filled me with trepidation and embarrassment, "Michelle, what yu doing here? A didn't tell yu to drive into Old Harbour and get the police? Why, for once in yu life yu can't obey mi, eeh?" Then he turned his back on me and started giving orders.

Claudette Beckford-Brady

"Everybody get back into the bus. Oonu drive to the station and tell them what happen. Pick up Myrtle and the children down the road. A wi stay here suh till the police come."

Everyone got back into the bus except Delroy, who said he would wait with Richard. I did not get into the bus either. Richard barely glanced at me as he said, "Yu gwaan too, Michelle."

I did not want to go, but the anger in him was too much for me to oppose. This was not the time for a contest of wills, so I meekly – well, perhaps not meekly – got into the bus. Joseph was still a bit shaken up, so Daddy took over the driving and we proceeded down the road to where Mummy Myrtle waited impatiently to be made aware of what was going on. She was quickly reassured that no member of the family had been hurt.

So we headed for Old Harbour, leaving Richard and Delroy, plus a crowd of curious onlookers who had materialised from out of the thickets and bushes which characterised the area.

On the way down, Mummy Myrtle and I were given details of the robbery. As the bus had turned the corner at Bois, a car had come up so close behind them that Joseph, who was driving on this road for the first time, was intimidated and had pulled right over to let it pass. The car passed them and drove off and they resumed their journey. Half mile down the road, and just before a bend in the road, the car was waiting for them, sitting in the middle of the road and facing in the direction from which it had come.

There was no way around, and when Joseph stopped the bus, two gun-toting youths boarded it while two others

The Missing Years

kept watch up and down the road. One of the gunmen on the bus stuck the gun into Joseph's side and told everyone that if anyone tried anything they would kill him instantly. He ordered everyone to take off their jewellery and bring out their money.

The other one started collecting watches, rings, gold chains, and whatever other valuables were to be had. There was little cash; there had been no need to take money to Country – there was nowhere to spend it.

To satisfy himself that he was not being cheated, the gunman searched the women's bags and went through the men's pockets. They even made the men take off their shoes, which they threw to one of their accomplices outside the bus who then threw them into the waiting car.

There were nine adults and eleven children in the bus. The twins and their husbands, Verr's husband, Samantha, Jennifer and Elaine had remained at Country, fortunately for them. The gunman only had Daddy and Joseph in the front of the bus left to search when Richard had rounded the corner and come upon them.

The lookout had not been doing a good job; did not appear to have even heard the sound of our approaching vehicle, and they seemed as surprised as we were when the lights hit them. The two lookouts jumped into the car, followed rapidly by the two who had jumped off the bus, one of whom fired at us before getting into the car and speeding away.

But they had apparently not gone very far. They must have decided that whoever had come upon them must be halfway to Old Harbour by now, and deduced that they would have time to come back and clean out Daddy and Joseph before the police could get there. For whatever reason, they returned to the bus and finished robbing my still-bemused family members.

But little did they know that Richard had not sped off to get the police, and I supposed they felt invincible with their guns, and comfortable in the knowledge that the police could not get there for at least forty-five minutes at the soonest.

But Richard had armed himself and crept back to see what was happening. He had heard the Lada reversing back down the road and had been just in time to see the gunmen re-board the bus. He waited until they finished with Daddy and Joseph and had stepped out of the bus and was on their way back to their waiting car, walking backwards with guns still pointed at the bus.

He fired, dropping one and wounding another. The wounded man made no attempt to return fire but dashed for the car where he managed to get inside before his partners-in-crime sped away, leaving the other one bleeding out his life on the ground.

Joy said the robbers had been laughing and speculating about whether to kidnap one or more of the women. One had been all for it, but the other one had said it would be too much trouble and would cause the police to hunt them more seriously. She said she didn't believe any of the gunmen had reached their twentieth birthday.

I couldn't understand why Joseph had not gunned the engine and sped away the minute the gunmen's car had left the scene the first time, but Daddy said they had all been in shock and Joseph was shaking so much he did not think he would be able to drive. After all, he had actually been in intimate contact with the gun which had been pressed

The Missing Years

painfully into his side the whole time and he had been afraid to even *breathe*.

And then of course it did not occur to them that the gunmen would come back, and Daddy had been preparing to take over the driving when they had returned.

We made the report at the police station and then drove home. Daddy changed his socks and put on another pair of shoes and left in his own car, saying he was going back up there. I would have rather he stayed with us, but I said nothing. Daddy Wilf went with him, taking a pair of shoes for Delroy.

We made hot drinks to settle the children who were all over-excited. Most of them were too young to really understand fully what had taken place and were only fretful because they picked up on the adult vibes, but some of them did. Clivey was the eldest child, and now that the danger was over, he was full of excitement. He couldn't wait to get back to England so he could tell his friends about his exciting adventure.

Eventually we got them all calmed down and into bed at the Big House, and then we made coffee and sat waiting for Richard and the others to arrive. Mummy Myrtle and I had been pumping Mavis, Joy and Veronica for more details, but they said Daddy had more or less told everything.

Mavis, Veronica, and Joseph's wife Bernice, seemed to have handled the ordeal okay. They were understandably shaken and upset, but otherwise fine. Joy, on the other hand, seemed somehow detached from the whole thing; she spoke unemotionally, and put me in mind of myself when Clive had died so many years ago. It suddenly occurred to me that she must be in a deep state of shock.

Claudette Beckford-Brady

And why wouldn't she be? *I* lived in a country where this sort of thing was a fairly common occurrence, and so I should not have been all that shocked; after all I reported things of this nature on a regular basis in my newspaper. But I had never dreamed of anything like that actually happening to me or anyone I knew personally. After all, these things only happened to "other people."

But Joy lived in England where things like that just did not happen at all, except on the movie or TV screens. I wondered if she realised how easily one or more of the family could have been shot. Some of these gunmen were only opportunists, others were "crack-head" junkies and were only interested in getting their cocaine money, but others were cruel and viciously brutal, killing for the fun of it, or to enhance their underworld reputations. Our family had been remarkably lucky tonight.

And then I thought of Richard standing over the body of the young man with the gun in his hand, and suddenly, I wanted to cry. Me, who had prided myself, since girlhood, on not being a crying sort of person.

I had not even seen where Richard had taken the gun from. One minute he was reversing rapidly around the corner and down the stretch of Long Level, and the next he was out of the car with a gun in his hand acting like a damned commando.

I'd had *no idea* he even *owned* a gun, let alone carried one on his person when travelling with his family. I did not like it, not one bit. But there was no denying that it had served a purpose tonight – a deadly purpose.

I speculated on whether it was an illegal gun or a properly licensed firearm, but quickly came to the conclusion that it must indeed be legal. Richard was not the sort to carry an illegal weapon, and as a prominent businessman I supposed he would meet the criteria for obtaining a firearm licence. And his order to summon the police further assured me that he was within his rights to use force of arms to defend his family.

But still I did not like it. He had killed a man; taken a young life. Yes, it was a criminal he had killed, but it was somebody's son, brother, possibly even someone's father, although he seemed little more than a boy.

And I had not even known that my own husband possessed a weapon of death.

Where did he keep it? Was it on his person at all times? Did he sometimes leave it in the house? Could one of the children inadvertently find it?

My thoughts were interrupted by Joy suddenly bursting out, "Shellie, tell me we *weren't* held up by gunmen tonight! It wasn't *real*, was it? Richard didn't *kill* someone, did he?"

It had finally hit her. I wished Richard and the others would arrive home. Joy needed Delroy. It seemed like hours since Daddy had dropped us off. Where were they?

Joy had gotten up from the armchair she had been sitting in and started wandering distractedly around the living room. Mummy Myrtle had gone to make more coffee and Mavis was tending to one of the children who seemed to be fretting. I spoke to Joy.

"We were very lucky tonight. It could have ended differently. At least none of you were hurt. Shoes, watches and chains can be easily replaced." I didn't know what other comforting statement I could make. I was surprised by Joy's response.

"Richard didn't have to *kill* him," she said. "He was so young."

I stared at her in puzzlement. "He *robbed* you, Joy. He could just as easily have killed you, or one of your children or anyone on the bus. He might have killed many people in the future; at least he will never kill anybody now."

"But they were leaving, and they didn't hurt anybody. If Richard had to shoot he could have just wounded him," Joy insisted.

"And give him a chance to shoot back? Richard did the only thing he could, Joy."

But she had put into words the little disquiet which had been creeping up on me. Privately I felt the same way she did. They had finished robbing and were preparing to leave the scene. They had physically hurt no-one. Richard could easily have just let them leave.

But I knew Richard would not let a threat or hurt to his family go unpunished. He was a gentle loving husband and father, but was fiercely protective where his family was concerned. And the deed was done; the youth had reaped what he had sown; he had lived by the gun and had died by the gun.

Joseph had drunk too large white rums and was now fairly calm, although every now and again he shook his head to himself. Bernice sat beside him on the sofa and held his hand, not saying anything but offering silent comfort. Now he made his contribution to the conversation.

"Richard should have killed them all!" he ejaculated forcefully. "They should abolish prisons and summarily execute *all* criminals! *That* is the only deterrent."

I looked at him in surprise. This was so unlike Joseph,

who was a bespectacled bookworm, and generally very placid. But he had had a gun thrust into his side, and been robbed, after all.

We fell silent. Now was not the time for a political debate on criminal justice. The night seemed interminable. At two-thirty I had just about decided to phone Wilbert to come and take me to see what was happening, when we heard the cars pulling into the driveway. We rushed out to the veranda and I unlocked the grille which Daddy had locked before he left. I saw a flashing blue light and realised they had been given a police escort.

It was Sergeant Newell, one of the few decent police officers currently serving the Old Harbour Division. He wanted to question the occupants of the bus, but said he required a signed statement only from Joseph, as the driver, and one other corroborating witness.

He assured us that he would alert the police in all the surrounding districts – Bellas Gate, Connors, Ginger Ridge, Browns Hall, etc. – to look out for the criminals, and have patrols along the road to ensure the safety of others coming down from the reunion tomorrow night. He also agreed to send an officer to the yard at Gravel Hill to let them know what had happened, and for them to be on their guard.

Cousin Daniel and his family had come upon the scene while Richard and Delroy were waiting for the police, and had waited with them. They had seen no sign of the white Lada on their way down, speculating that it had probably passed Gravel Hill before they had left the yard.

After Sergeant Newell had left I got one more surprise for the night. Richard, whom I had never known to drink anything stronger than wine or a lite beer poured himself a large rum and knocked it back without chasing it. It seemed to me that he was studiously ignoring me – his angry expression had not relaxed much.

Now that everyone was home and safe Mavis said she was going to find somewhere to lay her weary bones, since her bed was currently accommodating four children. Mummy Myrtle and Veronica had walked across to *Sweet Home,* leaving Veronica's sleeping children. Joy too had gone upstairs, leaving me and Bernice with the men.

I was waiting for Richard so we could walk across to *Sweet Home* together, but he did not appear to be ready, as he poured another drink and passed the bottle to Daddy Wilf, and they began to discuss the events of the night.

Bernice and I sat quietly listening to them as they talked. I watched Richard closely, trying to get a clue as to his state of mind. He had just killed a fellow human being. How did that make him feel? Was it the first time; had he killed before?

The only thing I could deduce from his manner and expression was that he was still very angry, but it was a tightly contained anger. He still had not spoken to me – had hardly even glanced my way. Was he still that angry with me for not going for the police?

He was speaking. "Damned stupid little fools! Look how easy the boy give away him life, eeh? It probably never occurred to them that they could die; the gun made them feel invincible."

Joseph repeated his earlier sentiments, wishing that Richard had managed to kill all of them. "After all," he said, "why should people study so long and work so hard to give themselves a good quality of life, only to have some lazy good

The Missing Years

for nothing loafer come along and *demand* their possessions as if they had every right! Pushing that damn gun into my side and taking away my brand new hundred pound Clarks!"

Richard's face lost some of the anger and his voice took on a resigned weariness as he replied to Joseph. "They're products of their environment, Joe. They want the good life too, but can see no legitimate way to get it. They lack the educational opportunities; the schools lack resources, and even if they manage to leave school with a decent education, employment is hard to come by, and generally poorly paid."

Joseph was not sympathetic. "That is no excuse. Plenty of poor people lack resources and opportunity but they don't go around robbing people and sticking guns into their sides!"

He had really been shaken up by that gun. I think he would perhaps not be so vehement if they had not actually *touched* him with the gun.

Seeing that Richard was beginning to lose that terse angry look, I relaxed sufficiently to fall asleep. When I woke up, still sitting in the armchair, it was to find that everyone else had disappeared and Richard was standing over me with a mewling Estelle in his arms.

I nursed and changed her and she went straight back to sleep, little angel that she was. Richard wrapped her up in a blanket and I found something to throw over my shoulders against the chill December morning, and we left Adele and Donovan sleeping and walked across to our own house.

It wasn't quite six, and still very dark, but the outside and back veranda lights were on. I held the baby while Richard unlocked the back grille and we went in. I put Estelle into her cot and dropped onto my bed fully clothed, and went out like a light.

CHAPTER FIVE

Where is Richard?

"Are you awake, Michelle?"

"Hmm? N'yet. Wassamatta?" I opened my eyes reluctantly and peered bleary-eyed up at Richard. "Wha'time'zit?"

Before he could reply, the events of the previous night came flooding back into my memory. I sat up abruptly and stared at him. "Are you okay? Did you get some sleep?" He nodded and handed me a cup of mint tea, which I accepted gratefully. I eyed him surreptitiously over the rim of the cup. His face had lost that fierce angry look, but he seemed tired and distracted.

"Yu mother and grandma downstairs."

"What?" His statement threw me for a moment, and then I realised that he must be referring to Delisia. I frowned; he knew I hated it when she was referred to as my mother. But I was so surprised at the fact that Grandma was here that I let it ride. "Grandma's *here*?"

The Missing Years

Grandma never went anywhere. She had been schooled in Canada, and had visited the United States and England several times in past decades, but had only left Country once in recent years – five months ago when she had come down to Cousin Daniel's to see Delisia.

Now here she was "down-a low" again. I was always glad to see my Grandma of course, but I did not think the events of last night required her to go so far out of her way; after all, *I* had not been in any danger.

And the timing was off – I had wanted to spend quality time with Richard this morning; I needed to know how he felt about what had happened and the fact that he had taken someone's life. I needed to make sure he was okay and had not been traumatised by the experience.

Still, Grandma was here already. And Delisia too. I sighed wearily. I had not had nearly enough sleep. It was a good thing that Estelle was such a contented child who slept for four or more hours at a time. I glanced at the clock and saw that it was just after nine. I had been asleep for less than three hours, not counting the puss-nap I had taken in the armchair at the Big House.

I needed a long relaxing bath; Grandma and Delisia were going to have to be patient. I told Richard to tell them that I would be down in a while, and then I looked in on Estelle, who was still sleeping soundly, before setting the bath and adding a quarter bottle of *Fenjal*.

Forty five minutes later, rejuvenated by my *Fenjal* bath, and clutching a just bathed and fed Estelle, I descended the stairs, not even feeling guilty at having kept them waiting so long.

They were sitting on the veranda talking quietly with

Claudette Beckford-Brady

Mummy Myrtle when I came through the door, and at sight of me Delisia jumped up, and for a brief moment I thought she was going to hug me, but then she seemed to think better of it and said in an agitated voice, "My God, Michelle! I can't believe it! Thank God you're all okay!"

I smiled a weak smile of acknowledgement, gave Estelle to Mummy Myrtle and kissed Grandma, who clung to me for a moment and then said, "Is a mercy none of oonu nevah get hurt. Is Miss Esme grandson an him crony-dem; di police have two a-dem, but one get weh. One a dem deh-a hospital inna serious condition under police guard. Likkle bit a bwoy dem. Is which part dem could-a get gun from, eeh?"

Her liberal use of the patois dialect showed her state of agitation, although outwardly she seemed calm enough. At least her heart had been strong enough to withstand the shock, I thought.

But I was surprised to hear that two of them had been apprehended already. The police must have really done their work last night for a change. It was fortunate that Sergeant Newell had been on duty – he was the type of officer the Force needed more of. I shuddered to think what if it had been Sergeant Devlin. Good thing he was assigned to Traffic and not crime investigation.

I wanted to get over to the Big House. Adele and Donovan had spent the night over there and must be awake by now. I knew they would be taken care of; washed and fed, and they had hordes of company to play with – they wouldn't be missing me a bit, but I wanted to see them, not to mention the fact that I was extremely hungry.

I wanted to see Richard too. I had no idea where he had gone. I had left him in the bedroom when I went to take my

The Missing Years

bath, and when I returned he had gone. Maybe he was at the Big House. I said I was hungry, and suggested we all go over.

It was Boxing Day and I was not expecting Lurline; in fact we had been planning to return to Country for the second day of the reunion. Well, the others could go if they wanted to, but I was staying home today. I just was not up to the excitement of relating the story over and over to thrill seekers. Let them read about it in the *Districk Bell's* next issue.

But I discovered on arrival at the Big House that Country had come to Island Farm, and Richard was not there, and I immediately regretted the fact that I had walked over. What Grandma and Delisia had failed to tell me was that they had not come alone.

There were vehicles parked in the driveway and on the road outside the house. The twins and Samantha, and the others who had stayed at Country last night had come home, and my father's two brothers, Linval and Bertie were there, as were the seven Campbell uncles along with some of their spouses, and several cousins, including Daniel and his wife Darlene.

As I greeted them all half-heartedly I was further dismayed to find that more people seemed to be arriving. I excused myself and went to find my children, who, although glad to see me, were impatient to get back to their play, and squirmed when I tried to hug them. I let them go and helped myself to liver and green bananas and chocolate tea.

No-one had seen Richard. His car was still in Daddy's driveway where it had been left last night. I was beginning to get worried; I did not know what his state of mind was.

More people had arrived and I noticed with surprise

that it was Richard's family from Walker's Wood. I had completely forgotten that they were due today to accompany us to Country; they had gone to *Sweet Home* first, and getting no answer to the gate buzzer they had driven around and come to the Big House.

Richard had obviously not phoned them about the incident because they were horrified when they heard about it, especially when they learned that he had killed a youth and injured another. They all wanted to see him straight away, of course, but he was nowhere to be found.

I reasoned that since his car was still here, he could not be too far away. Perhaps he hadn't felt up to facing all these people and reliving the incident; perhaps he had walked down to the back-end of the farm, down to the river's edge. I decided to go and look for him, but didn't tell anyone except the Armstrongs, and I asked Specky, Richard's brother-in-law, to accompany me.

"Specky" was short for Inspector, but in fact he was now a Senior Superintendent of Police (SSP), however, the name Specky had stuck despite his repeated reminders to us that he was now "Supe." I specifically wanted him with me because he had supervised officers who had killed in the line of duty and might be able to offer Richard some counselling or advice if we found him.

Specky was a very large man; tall – at least six-five, and a large frame. He looked intimidating but was in fact a jovial fun-loving man, although at work he was by all accounts feared and respected.

As we were slipping away, Richard's two sons from his former marriage, Richie and David, who were spending Christmas on the island, asked if they could come too, and

The Missing Years

the four of us went out the back door and started to walk out the farm.

With Daddy's ten acres and our five, it was quite a bit of ground to cover, but I thought I might have an idea where he would be if he was out here. I guided the others through the cash crops; calalloo, pak choy and okra, cucumber and tomatoes; through the gungu and corn-field, past the tree crops and down to the river bank where a giant gwangu tree stood, its widespread branches creating a shady canopy under which we often sat and dangled our feet in the river.

He was not there. We separated and went in different directions, calling his name as we went. An hour later, without Richard, we returned to the house. I was now beginning to get really worried. It was not like Richard at all. He was always so considerate; surely he must know that I would be worried by his absence?

Apart from Mummy Myrtle, and Grandma and Delisia whom he had let in this morning, no one had seen him. I did not know what to do, and the houseful of people was beginning to get on my nerves.

And it looked like they were there for the long haul, because food had miraculously appeared from somewhere – no preparations had been made for cooking, apart from breakfast, since we were all supposed to be at Country today.

But a big pot of curry goat was bubbling outside on a wood fire, next door to half dozen roasting breadfruit, next door to fish and chicken that was being fried. Inside the kitchen carrots and cabbage was being shredded and tomatoes sliced, while the peas were being cooked for the rice. They had brought the reunion to us.

I couldn't deal with it. I told everyone that I was going

Claudette Beckford-Brady

back over to *Sweet Home* for some peace and quiet, and told my in-laws that they could either come with me, or come over when they wanted to. I think they must have sensed that I wanted to be alone, for they all said they would stay where they were, or maybe it was because the night's incident was still being discussed and they wanted to hear everything.

The phone was ringing as I came through the back door and I picked up the kitchen extension. It was Frank Barrington, my friend and lawyer. "Shellie, thank God oonu ahright! A been calling all morning – A couldn't find yu mother's number – I assume that's where oonu was? How oonu do? Is everybody okay?"

The phone at the Big House had been ringing all morning too, but I had told the family to tell all callers that I was not available. I had called both Cee Jay and Barbara and given them the story so one of them could write it up for the paper, although it would be late news as the next issue was not due out for several days. The national press would probably carry the story before my own paper did; indeed, I had authorised Barbara to get the story out to the media, giving her Sgt. Newell's name and number for the police report.

I responded to Frank's queries. "Yes, thank you Frankie, we're all fine, but I'm really worried about Richard. He's disappeared; been gone all morning without a word to anyone, and his car is still here. I've walked out the entire farm and he's nowhere around. I'm really worried."

Frankie's tone was reassuring. "Don't worry about Richard, him mek out-a stern stuff. Him prob'ly gone cool out him head; it must be a very hard thing to deal with when yu have to tek another person's life, especially for a decent man like Richard. Him need to come to terms with his action and his feelings. When him sort those out, him will come home."

"But where could he have gone without his car? And how long will he take to sort them out, and why couldn't he have told me he was going to cool out? I'm his *wife* for Chrise-sakes!" I was beginning to feel a slight anger towards Richard. Frank heard it, and said, "Give him space, Shellie. That's the best thing yu can do for him right now; is a big burden him-a carry and him have to deal with it in him own way in him own time."

He said Lynette wanted to talk to me, and I told him I would call her in a few minutes as I wanted to go and put down Estelle who was still in my arms. As I replaced the receiver the phone rang again, but I ignored it. Let the answering machine get it.

I put Estelle in the bassinette near the open veranda door, and Vivaldi's *Four Seasons (Winter)* into the tape deck. Then I turned on my computer and began to write. I remembered that I had promised to call Lynette, Frank's wife, but I did not feel like it, so I didn't. And the answering machine tape was full and accepting no more messages.

I did not care. I took the phone off the hook and turned off the outside world and entered the world of my writing, the most therapeutic place I knew.

Several hours later, which only seemed like several minutes, I heard voices and realised that I was going to be denied my solitude. But it was only Grandma and Delisia come to bring me some food and to say they were returning to Country with Uncle Cornell. They left, and I fed and changed Estelle and put her back down.

My concentration had been broken, though, and I could not pick up the thread of my story, so I shut down the computer, ate the fried fish and bread with some salad, and decided to go upstairs for a nap. I had not had my full quota of sleep last night.

I picked up the still sleeping Estelle and went up to my bedroom, and there, sprawled out on his back on the bed with his eyes wide open and staring at the ceiling, was my missing husband, Richard.

My relief was overwhelming. I wanted to hold him; I wanted *him* to hold *me*. But I suddenly felt as if I were intruding on him.

He gave no indication that he was aware of my entry; his eyes remained focused on the ceiling fan above the bed. I hesitated, not quite sure if I should go away and leave him alone, or make an attempt to get him to talk to me. I put Estelle down in the nursery and returned to the bedroom where I stood looking down at Richard lying on the bed. He was still ignoring my presence.

I wondered if he was still angry with me for not having gone for the police at his instruction last night. Finally I sat beside him on the bed and said tentatively, "Can I go and get you something to eat?"

"No." His voice sounded hoarse. "Well how about a drink?"

"No."

I sighed, not knowing what to say next. Eventually I said, "Can you tell me how you feel?"

"Like not talking."

I remembered what Frank had said about giving him space, but it was no good him brooding and keeping everything bottled up inside. Richard himself had told me the same thing when I had been stewing over Delisia's treatment of me. Still, I decided not to rush him. I quietly left the room and went back downstairs where I picked up the phone and called Daddy's number. I asked to speak to Specky, and told him that Richard was at home and seemed to be depressed.

"He's being very uncommunicative," I said. "Do you think I should press him to talk?"

"Aahm...A don't think suh. Maybe yu will have to at some point, but geem a likkle more time."

"Do you think it would help if you or his father and sister came over? He knows you were expected today."

"It's obvious him don't want a crowd. Wi okay over here suh; wi been fed and watered," Specky said.

"Well, tell the others he's been found," I said. "I'll see you later."

I went back upstairs. Richard was in the exact same position I had left him in. I wanted so much to help him, but I didn't know what to do. I got onto the bed and positioned myself so that I could lean back against the headboard and put his head on my lap. He didn't protest, and I began to gently massage his temples, not saying anything.

I massaged his entire head, working my fingers deep into his thick dreadlocks until I reached the scalp, and then I moved the hair out of the way and began to work on his neck and shoulders. It seemed I was doing the right thing, because he accommodated himself to me by shifting position to facilitate the rubbing, and from time to time he gave a deep sigh.

I did not press him to talk; all this time I said not a word, giving him space, and the opportunity to initiate a conversation if he wanted to. I felt some of the tension ease out of him, and he lay there with his eyes closed. I thought he had dozed off, and gently eased myself away from him, and slid a pillow under his head, but as I made to leave the room, he spoke.

"Don't leave, Shellie."

Well, you could have knocked me down with a feather! Richard had never, in our entire relationship, called me "Shellie." He mostly called me "Baby" or "Honey" or used my full name, with different intonations depending on whether he was happy, annoyed, or exasperated (he never got angry) with me, but very occasionally when he was feeling particularly good or playful he would call me "Cheree."

But here he was now, calling me "Shellie." That must speak, somehow, to his state of mind.

I retraced my steps to the bed and sat down. I did not know if he wanted to talk, or if he just wanted my company, so I just sat quietly stroking his face while the minutes ticked by. After a long while he spoke again.

"I feel like a murderer."

That was good; he was beginning to talk, but I wished Specky was here, because I was not sure I would know the right responses to make. I mean, should I just keep silent and let him talk out his feelings or what?

But no; how could I keep silent when his words and the plaintive way in which they were spoken cut deep into my soul, and drew me into him, making me feel exactly what he was feeling. I recognised that he was crying out for reassurance, for absolution, and I needed to say the right words in order to allay his guilt.

I was no psychologist, but I recognised that empty

platitudes and reassurances would do no good, and Richard was far too intelligent a man to insult with them. I prayed my instincts would lead me to say the right thing in the right way.

"Honey, you were protecting your family; that's the same as self-defence – you did what you had to do. It's a good thing you possess the presence of mind and the skill to do what had to be done; a lesser man might have bungled it and placed us in even more danger. I'm really proud of you – the whole family is proud and grateful."

I hoped the doubts I had felt about the necessity of killing the youth did not creep into my voice, and indeed, as I spoke I realised that I really did believe that he had done what he had to do. But he put my earlier doubts into words.

"I could have just let them go. They had finished robbing and were leaving the scene. They were just kids – Ritchie's age – I could have just let them go..." His voice trailed off.

"Honey, you were running on adrenaline and acting instinctively. You hardly had time to think – you had gone into protective mode because your family was under threat. I don't see what else you could have done, under the circumstances. What do the police think? Will there be charges arising?"

"No; I've been absolved, but that's not the point..."

"That is exactly the point. Any room for doubt and they would have locked you up. Stop beating up yuself." I reiterated; "You did what you had to do, what anyone trying to protect their family would have done."

He did not immediately reply, and my mind jumped to the subject of the gun. There were no charges arising, which meant that the gun was legal and licensed. I was still shocked at the thought of him actually possessing a gun, and felt I should have been made aware of it. I would tackle him about that at some time in the future, but now was definitely not the time. He broke into my thoughts.

"Yu right, up to a point, but A think A wanted to punish them for daring to attack *my* family. A think I summarily appointed myself their executioner. I had no right."

That was my husband. I smiled inwardly as I thought about the negative stereotypical image the world (and indeed many Jamaicans) had of the Jamaican male psyche, especially the ones with dreadlocks.

Violent, lazy, worthless, good-for-nothing; drug dealers, pimps and gunmen was the way I had heard a white British police officer describe Jamaican men in general; he had had more vitriolic things to say about Rastas – a title he attributed to *all* dreadlocked men, regardless of whether they were actually Rastas or not.

I suspected that Richard was probably right in his self-assessment, and it was no point me denying it; but I sought to put it into perspective. "Well, I think *anybody* in your position would have done exactly the same, and I'm sure you didn't have time to say to yourself, *"Shall I kill him? Yes I think I will."* I'm sure you acted purely from instinct – to protect and preserve your family – and who can fault you for that?"

And the more I sought to reassure him, the more I felt that what I was saying was right. My earlier disquietude had evaporated and I was now quite angry at the youths. They may not have physically harmed anyone, but their actions had caused trauma and left repercussions, not just to us but to their own families too.

They themselves had caused death and injury; *they* had

instigated the chain of events; *they alone* were culpable. My husband was innocent.

I kissed his forehead and said coaxingly, "Come on, go have a shower and get changed. Your family arrived some time ago; they're over at the Big House. I'll go get them while you freshen up, okay?"

He gave a deep sigh and said, "Yes, A better pull miself together – this is doing no-one any good." He got up and headed for the bathroom without further comment.

I decided not to go over to the Big House but picked up the phone instead. My brother Delroy answered. "Wotcha, Shell, yu okay? We been worried bout you. Is Richard all right?"

"Thanks, Del, we're both okay; he just needed some quiet time to reflect and come to terms with himself. I think he's okay now, but doesn't need the crowd; just his immediate family. Could you tell Daddy Armstrong and the rest to come on over? Oh, and ask them to bring over some food, will ya?"

We chatted a while longer and I spoke to Mavis and Joy before hanging up. Most of the uncles had gone back to Country leaving only Uncles Kenneth, Keith, Linval and Bertie, along with Daniel and Darlene.

When I came off the phone Richard was back from his shower. He gave me a shadow of a smile and I hugged him, and then we kissed a long deep kiss. Everything was going to be alright.

I got Estelle from the nursery, and leaving Richard to get dressed, I went downstairs to wait for the family. They arrived in short order and while we waited for Richard to come down I quickly briefed them on his state of mind and gave them a synopsis of our conversation.

Richard's family consisted of his widowed father, David, who was a retired ophthalmologist; his father's sister whom everyone called Auntie; his sister, Rachel, who was his twin and a practising paediatrician; Rachel's husband, Senior Superintendent of Police Constantine Grant, affectionately known as Specky from his days as an Inspector, and their four children, Trevor, Stacy-Ann, Neville, and Grace.

Then of course there were Richard's two sons from his former marriage, Richie (Richard Junior), and David, named for Richard's father.

Being surrounded by his family turned out to be the best thing for Richard. When he came downstairs he was hit by a barrage of bodies as the females flung themselves at him with varying degrees of force.

Seventeen year old Stacy-Ann, who hated to be referred to as just 'Stacy' burst into a fit of weeping while she clung to him, which set off seven year old Grace. Auntie, whose bark was much worse than her bite scolded them mock-severely, saying, "Stop the foolishness! What you all crying for? You don't si that Richard is quite fine?"

Nevertheless she sounded emotional and as soon as she was able she too hugged him tightly, surreptitiously wiping away a tear of her own. His twin Rachel hugged him wordlessly.

The men had their turn, shaking hands and embracing him, while I organised a plate of food for him and asked Stacy-Ann to go and pick some limes to make lemonade. I hovered to make sure he ate the food, and although at first he said he wasn't hungry, after the first few mouthfuls he tucked in like a ravenous bear and asked for seconds, much to my delight. His appetite had returned; he was going to be just fine.

By this time it was late afternoon and the December sun was wending his way toward setting. It had not been originally planned that the family would stay overnight, but it was decided that they would stay. Accommodations would be a bit tight but we would manage. Auntie phoned her son Derrick, and gave him a brief outline of what had happened, and letting him know that the family would stay overnight.

We sat out in the garden in the cool of the evening, me in the hammock which was strung between two mango trees, with Estelle in my arms, while the others sat on garden chairs. It was a pleasant evening, with a light breeze and no mosquito nuisance.

Grace said she was bored and wanted to go back to the Big House where all the other children were, and so she and her brother, fourteen year old Neville, walked on over, leaving the rest of us talking.

The conversation did not centre on the events of the previous night, but more on Richard; his wellbeing, his state of mind. Specky said that if Richard wanted to he could arrange for a session with a police psychologist/stress councillor. Richard declined, saying he could resolve his own issues, but thanks all the same.

No one from the Big House came over. I was pretty sure that Mavis had issued orders that we were to be left alone until we indicated differently.

I wanted Adele and Donovan to come over but I knew they, like Grace, would want to be where all the other children were. As I formulated the thought, Richard said, "A suppose our faithless kids abandon the old homestead for the

Big House, eeh?" and then he added, "How's the other kids – the ones who were in the bus?"

I realised belatedly that I had not paid much attention to the state of mind of the children who had been in the bus when the robbers attacked it, but it seemed to me that everyone was fine. If any of them had been traumatised I would have been aware of it, but the usual amount of whooping and hollering which normally filled the yards had not changed.

In fact I had heard Clivey and Kieran discussing it and they couldn't wait to tell their friends back in England all about it. It was the most exciting thing that had ever happened to them, now that the scary part was over. The younger children probably had not fully realised what was happening, and by all accounts the robbers were jovial, and laughing while they went about their dirty deeds.

Before I could answer Richard his father said, "From the amount of shouting and laughing and chasing each other through the house that I have seen, I'd say they are all quite fine. Kids are remarkably resilient, you know, and most of the younger ones had been asleep and were groggy during the incident. It probably seems like something that happened on TV to them."

"For which we should be extremely thankful," Auntie said.

Trevor and Richie, who were both nineteen, and Stacy-Ann and David, both seventeen, brought out the Monopoly and they commenced to play, while the rest of us made idle chatter, talking about everything but the incident.

We stayed out until the moon came up and bathed the garden with its bright golden light which was so reminiscent

The Missing Years

of sunlight. I loved moonshine nights; I had not been able to appreciate moonlight until I came to Jamaica – in England the street lights and brightly lit buildings always negated the effects of the moon.

We finally went inside and sorted out who was going to sleep where. Eventually everyone was settled and Richard and I retired to bed. That night he made love to me so violently that it almost hurt, and I had to remind myself that he was probably trying to expunge the events of the previous twenty-four hours from his system, and so I accommodated him and responded in kind, praying fervently that the sounds of our passion would not be overheard.

CHAPTER SIX

Marital Disquiet

The morning news on the radio carried the report of the robbery and the death of the youth. It had apparently been reported on television the night before, but we had watched no TV.

They reported that the injured youth's condition had been upgraded from critical to serious. One youth was still at large and being sought; his name and address were known – it was just a matter of flushing him out of hiding. He did not possess a passport.

When I checked the messages on the answering machine some of them were from reporters, some of whom I knew well, asking for statements from Richard and me. I erased them; I had already given Barbara statements; she could give the media what she wanted and save what she wanted for exclusive reporting in our own paper.

Sgt. Newell came by and said the police had recovered some pieces of jewellery, but would be keeping them for the time being. However, he would like the owners to come and identify them at some point, but no hurry.

Of the shoes there had been no trace, and I expect some men in the country had "put up" their nice new shoes for a special occasion, or for when the heat had died down. My cousin Joseph was utterly disgusted that his "brand new hundred pound Clarks" had not been recovered.

The youths had been caught pretty quickly and had had no time to sell their booty; however, they had obviously had time to unload the shoes. I told Joseph to be thankful that he was alive and well and to forget about his "hundred pound Clarks" and he admitted that if he had gotten them back, he would probably have given them away, anyway.

Richard went off to his recording studio, against my wishes, and his family departed for Walkers Wood, where we would join them on Thursday for New Year's on Friday. We had excused ourselves from the Barrington's annual barbeque and pool party this year.

It was Christmas Sunday and although not usually church goers, Mavis and Mummy Myrtle decided to go to church with Veronica and Bernice who were both practising Christians and who wanted to go and worship and "give thanks" they said, for safe delivery from the gunmen.

There were many churches in Spring Village, and a Baptist church at Gutters, but both Verr and Bernice worshipped at the New Testament Church of God back home in England, so Daddy drove them into Old Harbour to the church on Darlington Drive.

Joy's parents were Church of God Christians who had disowned her when she had left home to live in sin with my brother Delroy, and prior to that she had been forced to

Claudette Beckford-Brady

attend church almost constantly. She declined to accompany the others, and they didn't even bother to ask me, knowing how I felt about organized religion. The younger women – the twins, Samantha, Jennifer, and Elaine also were not into church, and were sprawled all over the back gardens with books and a blaring radio, while the toddlers toddled or played with toys, and the older children played tag or hide and seek or climbed trees.

The men also had not gone to church, and in a short while Daddy was back from dropping off the others. They set up a domino table on the veranda and commenced their first six, Daddy partnering Joseph, and Daddy Wilf pardying Delroy.

Joy and I were in the kitchen preparing the Christmas Sunday dinner. We had had our fill of ethnic cuisine and were preparing several roast chickens with stuffing, steamed cabbage and broccoli, roast potatoes and Bisto gravy, brought over from England. Mavis actually had some Brussels sprouts growing in her garden, but we all hated them, except her, so we stuck to cabbage.

It was good being able to chat with Joy, one on one. She had been my best friend my entire life, since infant school in England, and I had been overjoyed when she had become my sister-in-law.

She was a few inches shorter than I was, at about five foot five to my five-eight, and she had put on weight and was beginning to look matronly, while I had kept my weight almost constant and had gained only a few pounds during my last pregnancy. Joy was jealous, saying she couldn't understand how I ate so much and yet never gained weight.

Joy had left school without completing A Levels but had

The Missing Years

gotten a good job at Lambeth Council, where she got the opportunity to further herself by doing a course in Personnel Management and Industrial Relations, and was now a Human Resources Manager.

While we worked we spoke of our other best friends, Stephanie and Yvonne. Steph had taken up with a pimping, drug dealing Rastafarian when she was fifteen, had gotten pregnant, and dropped out of school without completing her O and A Levels. She had started growing dreadlocks and become radically vocal about "Babylon's" enslavement and abuse of African peoples.

The guy, Winston, had been violent, and had beaten her, eventually sending her to the hospital with a broken jaw and several broken ribs. Being under age, she and her baby had been taken into care by Social Services, and they had been relocated to a safe house on the other side of London, and eventually placed with a foster family.

Stephanie had again taken up with another Rasta, but this time he was a different breed; an educated civil servant, gently spoken, none-radical, who accepted her son as his own. That son, who had been christened "Nkrumah Neziah" in recognition of his "African Heritage" was now known as "Lion" and was sixteen years old and doing well in school.

Steph and Benji went on to have three more children, and Steph eventual returned to her studies and did her O and A Levels, and finally her Degree. She too was now a civil servant, like Benji, her baby-father. She was the only one of our foursome who was not legally married.

Yvonne was married to Denzil and they had three children. They were both teachers; Yvonne had completed her Bachelor of Education degree at the University of London,

Claudette Beckford-Brady

where I had done my own Media and Mass Communication degree course.

I was glad that Yvonne's marriage seemed to be happy and stable. Yvonne, of all of us, had the most volatile personality, and was not shy to get physically violent if she felt the situation called for it. She had been known to come to fisticuffs with her adversaries, and had sent one ex-boyfriend to hospital for head stitches after he tried to get violent with her.

But she and Denzil seemed eminently compatible and he was a cheerful person with an easy infectious laugh.

Joy said she met up with the girls every so often for a "girls' night out" and I wished I could be a part of it. I missed my friends; I had not seen them since the twins' wedding nearly two years ago. Both Yvonne and Steph kept promising to come to Jamaica but had not gotten around to it as yet.

With everything under control in the kitchen, Joy and I went out to join the others in the back garden. Dominoes were still being slammed on the back veranda, and the radio was blasting out reggae Christmas carols. I thought it a miracle that Estelle, who was in a carrycot in the shade of an almond tree, screened from insects by a mosquito net, could sleep through it. But sleep she did.

At around twelve-thirty Daddy went back to Old Harbour to pick up Mavis and the others from church, and we ate a leisurely dinner and spent the afternoon and evening just kicking back. Richard had not come home for dinner and I had tried calling the studio with no success.

I rounded up a protesting Adele and Donovan who did not want to return to their own home and beds; however, when they realized that Veronica and Bernice's children were coming too they simmered down.

Verr, Bernice and I finally got them all into bed and then the three of us sat out on the veranda till Joseph and Verr's husband, and Mummy Myrtle and Daddy Wilf all came over from the Big House, and then everyone retired to bed. Richard still had not come home and I finally fell asleep waiting for him.

Some sound brought me out of my sleep and I opened my eyes. The room was not full dark – I kept a dim night-light burning – and I could see Richard removing his clothes in preparation for bed. When I looked at the clock I saw with a sense of shock that it was almost three a.m.

Richard did sometimes do late or all-night sessions at the studio, but he always told me when this was on the agenda, or phoned to let me know if it came up unexpectedly. This time he hadn't, and I was peeved. I decided that if he wanted to get amorous I would pretend to be fast asleep and leave him frustrated.

To my chagrin he got into bed, gave a deep sigh, gave me his back, and seemed to instantly fall asleep. I lay there fuming for a long time, before I managed to get back to sleep. When I woke up three hours later he was gone.

I sorted out the kids and then went to the office. There were very few people out and about; tomorrow would be the first official working day after the holiday and only a skeleton staff was at work.

Richard's car was not in the car park, which meant he was not at the studio. I couldn't imagine where he could have gone without telling me. He was never this inconsiderate; what had changed?

I worked distractedly for several hours, reading the

articles which were to be included in this week's issue. Barbara had left a draft of the robbery report on my desk, and I made a few adjustments and passed it for publication. The quotes, supposedly from Richard, had been given by me.

When I got home there was still no sign of Richard. I was beginning to get angry. Where the hell was he, and why couldn't he let me know if he was going somewhere? He was not at Walkers Wood – I had phoned Rachel and no one had seen or heard from him.

I tried his pager number with no success. I phoned Frankie Barrington; not there – hadn't seen or heard from him.

At bedtime Adele said to me, "Mummy, I haven't seen Daddy for a long time; is he gone to the farm?"

"*Has* he gone to the farm, Baby, not *is* he gone. No, he hasn't gone to the farm. I'm not sure exactly where he is but I'm sure he will be home soon."

But he wasn't. I went to bed alone again, and when he came home, again in the small hours, like last night he just dropped into bed and fell asleep, not even bothering to find out if I was awake or not. I was determined that he would not leave in the morning without some explanation.

I tried to force myself to stay awake, so that if he got up early again to leave I would be aware of it, but sleep will not be denied and I could not stay awake.

When I opened my eyes again it was a little after six. Richard, to my relief, was still in the bed, fast asleep and snoring lightly. I got up and began to get ready to go to work. I bathed and fed Estelle before taking my own bath and getting dressed.

Veronica and Bernice were up and about, and so was

The Missing Years

Mummy Myrtle. Joseph and Verr's husband, Tony had already left the house with Daddy Wilf to go and help pick ackee for the canning factory which bought all of our ackee. Daddy had farm workers to do all of that, of course, but the "Farriners-dem" got a kick out of being temporary farm workers.

Lurline arrived for work and set to making breakfast, while Verr and Bernice organised the kids. Now that the holidays were practically over, each household would go back to catering for itself.

I was just finishing a light breakfast when Richard came downstairs, smelling of Imperial Leather and dressed impeccably as usual, his long dreadlocks tied neatly behind his head and hanging down his back.

He gave me a brief "Morning, Honey," sat down at the table and poured himself some freshly squeezed orange juice, put the glass to his mouth and drained it in one go, before refilling it. I wanted to interrogate him about his movements and activities over the last day or two, but decided I should feed him first, since, according to Bob Marley, "a hungry man is an angry man."

"Can I get you some breakfast?" I asked him in a pleasant tone of voice.

"Thanks," he replied briefly.

I got up and went to the kitchen where I dished up callaloo and fried dumplings and returned to the table. I sat and watched him as he ate, his whole attention on the process. For all the attention he paid me, I might not even have been there.

It was past seven-thirty and I should be leaving for work, but I was damned if I was going to go before having words with him about his neglect of me and the kids. I poured myself another glass of juice and sipped it slowly while I waited for him to take the edge off his appetite. Finally, he leaned back in the chair, gave a contented sigh, and wiped his mouth with a paper napkin.

My time now. I looked directly at him and opened my mouth to speak, but he forestalled me. "Wow, Honey, yu look good enough to eat this morning. Yu sure yu have to guh to work?" He leered at me suggestively.

I was caught off-guard. His eyes caressed me warmly and I felt a little flutter of arousal. I was reminded of the first time I had seen him, how his eyes had hypnotised me and drawn me deep into his soul; how my body had awakened sexually for the first time in years.

He was giving me that look again – the one that turned me into jelly and caused me to forget that I wanted to lay into him…

He had gotten up from his chair and come around behind me. He bent down and nuzzled my neck, and I was lost. I turned my face into his kiss, and he pulled me up from the chair and drew me back upstairs. We passed Lurline coming down the stairs and I told her to keep an eye on Estelle who was in the bassinette, not caring if she knew or guessed what Richard and I were up to.

Richard was like a demon. He couldn't seem to get enough of me, and by the time he was sated I was utterly exhausted and ready to sleep again. Not that I hadn't enjoyed it too, of course, but my body felt bruised and sore. Richard was a very passionate man, but I had never before known him to be *quite* so over-ardent.

But no, that was not strictly true. He had been just as

ardent the night after the robbery and shooting, and I had supposed he was trying to exorcise the memory by his rough lovemaking. "Rough" was okay once in a while, but I hoped he would soon return to his usual gentle ways.

Much as I wanted to stay and sleep, I forced myself to re-freshen up and go to work. I had had more time off over the holidays than any of the others, some of whom had even worked Christmas and Boxing days. I left Richard sleeping contentedly, picked up Estelle, who I was taking with me, and left.

When I got home in the evening Richard was again gone, and did not come home till long after I had gone to bed. I had not seen his car in the car park at SmallRock and assumed he had not been to the studio. I made up my mind that I would get to the bottom of his activities this very night, and each hour I reset the alarm to minimise the chances of my being in deep sleep when he came in.

It was shortly before two when he finally came. I had had no real need of the alarm, because I was so pent up and agitated by his mysterious disappearances that sleep was not an immediate requirement. My mind had been jumping all over the place as I racked my brain to wonder where he was or who he was with.

I had briefly considered that he might be having an affair, but had quickly discarded that idea, and his over-zealous lovemaking helped to negate that possibility in my mind, although in conversations with my friends over the years we had agreed that this was one way a guilty and faithless partner might go, to throw the spouse off the scent.

But I was sure there was no other woman; over the nearly six years of our marriage Richard had given me no reason to suspect a rival for his affections. The studio might have kept him busy and out late, but I already knew that was not where he was spending his time. Neither Frankie nor my cousin Daniel, his two closest friends, had seen anything of him in recent days, and had no idea what he might be up to.

I did not pretend to be asleep this time, but sat up in the bed so he would know I was wide awake. He looked a little surprised, but only said, "Sorry, Honey, did I wake yu?"

"No," I said, "you didn't. I was waiting up for you."

"Why? Is something wrong?" He sat on the bed and began removing his shoes and socks.

"Well I don't know," I said. "Why don't *you* tell *me*? I'm curious as to your activities and whereabouts since Sunday; you've not been at the studio all week, and you've been coming home uncharacteristically late and without phoning me, which you always used to do whenever you were going to be out late.

"You disappear for hours on end without leaving any messages, you don't respond to your pager... Even Adele has noticed your scarcity around the place and commented on it. Where have you been spending your time?"

He gave me his full attention, fixing me with that direct stare that seemed to say, "*I can see right inside your soul.*" Then he responded, "Is that an interrogative tone I detect in your voice, or is it an accusatory tone, or perhaps both?"

I sighed. It was late, I was tired, and all I wanted was reassurance. I did not want an argument or a confrontation. "Neither," I said wearily. "We've been through an unusually difficult few days and I think we both need each other more at this particular time. I want to be there for you, and I *need* you to be here for *me*. That's all."

The Missing Years

The weariness was evident in my voice, and he suddenly became contrite. "I'm sorry, Baby; I've been thoughtless and neglectful. But don't worry; I'll be more considerate from now on, okay?"

He had not answered the question, I noticed. Had he deliberately evaded it, or was it that he considered it unimportant enough to ignore? I was still curious, but decided not to press at this time. His next words put me into a blazing temper – at two o'clock in the morning.

"By the way, yu mother will be coming with us to Walkers Wood on Thursday."

"WHAT?!"

I knew immediately he was referring to Delisia and not Mavis, and I was suddenly unreasonably angry. First of all, he knew that I preferred not to have Delisia referred to as my mother, and secondly, he had invited her along without consulting me, or even caring what I thought.

Daddy and Mavis loved it at the farm, and always had a wonderful time there. I did not want Delisia's presence to be a damper for them, although to be truthful, they all seemed comfortable enough in each other's presence. But I used it as a convenient excuse to vent my temper on Richard.

"You had no right to do that without consulting me, Richard. You know how much Mum and Dad love the farm; why would you want to go and spoil it for them by inviting *her* along?"

He looked at me in genuine surprise. "Spoil it fah them? Why on earth would Delisia's presence spoil it fah them? They all seem to get along fine to me. Yu know, Michelle, it's time yu cut yu mother some slack – A really thought you'd gotten past your resentment of her."

Claudette Beckford-Brady

There he was, referring to her as my mother *again*! "She is *not* my mother, and I do not resent her," I said without much conviction, knowing that in my heart of hearts I still did hold some resentment at the fact that she had so easily put me right out of her mind and made no attempt to find and communicate with me over the years, even though she had explained that it was her own guilty conscience which had caused her to put me out of her mind entirely.

Sometimes I found myself wishing that she had stayed "lost" because then I could maintain the fantasy that when she was found we would have a joyful happy tear-filled reunion, instead of the acidic episode at the airport. But if she had stayed lost, Grandma would have been constantly sad as she approached her sunset days. I could not have it both ways.

Richard was responding to my last statement. There was amusement in his voice and it fuelled my anger. "Yu can't use those two 'nots' in the same sentence, Michelle. 'She is *not* my mother and I do *not* resent her' do not go together. They seem to contradict each other." He laughed, and I exploded.

"You had no right to *thrust* her into my family's life! It ought to be *my* decision as to whether she is invited in or not! How dare you take it upon yourself to decide for me?

"I won't have it! I am going to Country tomorrow to tell her that the invitation has been rescinded!"

Richard's voice was calm, but authoritative. "Yu will do nothing of the kind!"

I was not daunted. "Try and stop me!" I was almost shouting, and he responded in a voice into which impatience was beginning to creep. "Why yu don't just wake up everybody in the house and done?" he asked, before getting into the bed and turning out his side of the light.

I lay there stewing in temper. There was no satisfaction in having an argument with Richard – I rarely won. He mostly allowed me to have my own way, but if it was a contest of wills, he usually came out the victor, which was a novel experience for me, who usually came off best in any argument within the family.

He didn't let our disagreement prevent him from sleep; I heard when his breathing changed, and felt him relax in the bed. I lay there stewing in resentment, sleep eluding me despite my body's state of exhaustion.

I had been looking forward to the week at the farm. Once or twice a year, I pretended that I was not a serious minded business woman, and "metamorphosized" into a river-swimming, tree-climbing, jeans-clad tomboy for a day or two. It was generally a time of family fun and frolic, when we let down our hair and did weird and uncharacteristic things. I could not somehow see Delisia fitting into that scenario.

I made up my mind to stay home and let them all go. I had my business; I would be fine. Who needed a vacation, anyway?

I was very cool toward Richard for the few minutes I saw him the next day – not that he seemed to notice or care. He came in late again on Wednesday night, but I said nothing.

On Thursday morning everyone was up bright and early, full of excitement and anticipation. I got the kids ready and packed their bags and by seven-thirty they were ready for the road.

I gathered that Delisia had spent the night at Colbeck and would be making her way out here to join the party, but she had not arrived yet, and the kids were eager to be off. I thought hopefully that she might have changed her mind, in which case I would go, but as the thought was born, there she was, strolling through the open gate with a bright smile on her face, as comfortable as you please.

I felt my temper rise, but kept a tranquil expression on my face, greeted her cordially along with everyone else, and supervised the loading of the overexcited kids onto the bus. I did not tell anyone that I would not be going until the last minute. They had all trooped into the bus, and I gave Donovan and Adele over to Joy's keeping, told them all to have a wonderful time, and exited the bus.

There were a lot of surprised protests, and demands to know why I was not coming. I glanced at Richard, who was studiously ignoring me. I mumbled some excuse about something coming up at work and made a pretend promise that I would try my best to come down later in the week.

Just before they were ready to leave, Richard beckoned me into the house and I went, half hoping he would try to persuade me to change my mind and go with them. He didn't. He looked at me hard and said, "Yu know, Michelle, I've always seen you as being mature beyond your years – until now. If yu can't see for yuself how childish you're being, then I am not going to try and convince you."

Then without another word he strode out of the house, got into the bus (he was leaving his car) and they drove out the gate, turned onto Spring Village Road, and headed for St. Ann, leaving me standing alone with Estelle in my arms, and already feeling bereft, in front of the Big House.

I slowly walked back over to *Sweet Home* where my Campbell Cousins were still staying. They had not accompanied the Freemans to Walkers Wood, since they would be gone a whole week, and the Campbells were intending to spend some time in Ocho Rios with the rest of the North American cousins after New Year's. However, Ochee was only a stone's throw from Walkers Wood, so I expected that they might visit for a day.

I was going to be home alone for a whole week. Both Lurline and Miss Pearl had the whole of next week off, since the families would not be in residence and Verr and the others would all be in Ochee. I was already regretting my childish impulse, and I was hurt and upset that Richard had not tried at all to persuade me to change my mind.

I timed their journey and waited for Richard to call and tell me they had arrived safely, as he usually did when travelling without me, but no call came. I threw myself into my work and stayed late at the office even though it was New Year's Eve. I did not get home till nearly eight o'clock, when I arrived to a deserted house – Verr and the others were welcoming the New Year at Country.

I thought briefly about joining them, but then I decided that since I would not be in St. Ann I might as well attend the Barrington's annual barbeque pool party, so I bathed and put on my party glad-rags, put Estelle in Richard's car and drove into Spring Village where I left her with Lurline.

Wilbert, my driver and Lurline's baby-father, whistled when he saw me. "Whoy, Miss Free, yu look like a worl class maggle, (model) man! Missa Armstrong fi mine how him a leff yu outa him sight – smaddy gwine tek yu weh!"

After my marriage Wilbert had had a hard time trying to call me Mrs Armstrong, and after a while had given up and reverted to the shortened version of my maiden name, thus

"Miss Free" was his name for me.

I perked up at his obviously genuine compliment. I had been feeling a bit down, and had almost decided to go to bed and sulk, forgetting about the party, but I had given myself a mental shake, telling myself that Richard would neither know nor care if I sulked, so I might as well go and have some fun.

The party was in full swing when I arrived. As usual, the cream of Jamaica's society were the patrons – Old Harbour's elite, TV and radio personalities, musicians and sports personalities – even the local Member of Parliament passed through for an hour.

To say that the Barringtons were surprised to see me would be to put it mildly. They had known that the family would be spending New Year's at Walkers Wood, and I had to give them some explanation of my presence. I told them I had had something important to wrap up at work but that I might go down the next day, although I had no such intention.

My cousin Daniel and his wife Darlene, who lived next door to the Barringtons, were even more surprised to see me. My excuse about work did not wash with Daniel, though, and he scrutinised me closely and said, "I bet this has something to do with Delisia's presence, don't it?"

I denied it vehemently, and got angry when Daniel quipped, "Methinks the lady protesteth too much!" I responded angrily, "Methinks the cousin should mind his own damned business!" before stalking off.

I had a wonderful time at the party, and suffered for it later, but I was determined to enjoy myself. I do not know if it was pique at Richard or what, but I drank much more than usual, and even departed from my usual white wine and drank rum punch, far too many of them. I danced like a dervish and altogether had myself a wonderful time.

We rang in 1993 at midnight, and around six a.m. I stumbled to the car, bundled myself in, and started home. I was more than a little tipsy and knew that I should not really be driving, but I convinced myself that it was only a short drive home, and should take no more than ten minutes, and I would be *very* careful.

But oh; how I wished I had gone to Walkers Wood! How I wished I had never gone to the party! How I wished I had never driven Richard's car!

CHAPTER SEVEN

Jungle Telegraph

Six thirty-five a.m. New Year's Day, 1993. The town of Old Harbour was quiet, but a few hardy individuals still occupied the market compound – had probably been there all night – selling a variety of fruit and vegetables. The market never seemed to close; not on Sundays, not at Christmas, not at New Year.

Opposite the market, on the other side of the road, a sugar cane vendor expertly peeled long stalks of ribbon cane with a razor sharp machete, cut them up and placed them into plastic bags for sale. I had already passed him when I decided I wanted a bag of cane, and without checking the mirror, I stepped sharply on the brake, and....

CRASH!

My body jerked with the impact, and the car slid forward a little. Before I could orientate myself an irate face appeared at the driver side window, which was down, and a voice started berating me.

"Yu-a eediat? Or a buy yu buy yu license, or WHA?!"

The Missing Years

Then he saw that I was a woman and continued. "A-hoa! Is a ooman – nuh wanda... Kyaant deal wid oonu ooman driva, y'nuh... dem nuh-fi mek oonu drive pon road – a horse and donkey oonu fi drive!"

By this time a few onlookers had gathered and someone shoved the man out of the way and opened my door. "Yu ahright Miz Armstrong?" I heard a voice ask, and I focused sufficiently to see that it was one of the Village taxi drivers, Uriel.

He continued, "Come out-a di kyar mek A move it out-a di road fi yu," and I meekly complied. I felt extremely foolish. I was dressed in a very low cut, very short, bright red party dress, and four inch red stiletto heels. I gingerly made my way over the uneven surface of the road, around the car, to the even more uneven surface of the so-called sidewalk, wishing I had stayed in the vehicle and just moved over to the passenger seat.

I felt all the eyes on me; some appraising, some leering, some amused. I could hear their conversations; Jamaicans are not bashful, and care not about being overheard – "...di ooman have a good piece-a baddy pan har, man!"

"Shi really look good fi true. A would-a tek piece-a dat..." Someone else said, "A drunk shi drunk, y'nuh... watch deh – him kyan hardly waak..."

Did I say I felt extremely foolish? Massive understatement! I suddenly knew, with defined clarity, what people meant when they said they wished a hole would open up in the ground and swallow them. At this moment, this was my most fervent wish.

The January morning was not very warm – the sun had not woken up properly yet, and I had not brought a wrap, since it was only a short drive from home to the Barringtons'. Now I wished dearly that I had brought one, not so much against the chill, but against the insistent eyes; I felt decidedly exposed.

But other people were coming to my defence. Someone threw a jacket or something over my shoulders, and I smiled gratefully at the donor, who said protectively, "Oonu shet up oonu mout an doan be disrespeckful! Drunk, mi back foot – oonu nuh si seh a di pretty shoes weh shi deh wear mek shi deh stagga suh, oonu eediat oonu?! Dass *Mrs. Armstrong,* oonu dah disrespeck, an Missa Armstrong naa guh like it when mi tell him weh oonu deh seh!"

I did not even know the person who was so stoutly defending me, but I was grateful.

I was beginning to think clearly now. Both vehicles had been moved and were parked along the curb. The other driver was approaching me and demanding to know what I intended to do about the damaged front of his vehicle, which, thankfully, was not extensive. Luckily he had not been driving very fast behind me.

I was tempted to tell him that he should not have been driving so close behind me, but I did not want to prolong the agony, so I took his details, gave him mine, told him to get an estimate for the repairs and I would deal with it. No need to go through the insurance, I said.

He appeared mollified, and having realized that I was *Mrs. Richard Armstrong,* no less, "of *Di Districk Bell* newspapa" he was quite happy. I knew that the estimate would be padded, but I would know how to deal with that. I may be a "Farrinna" but I was on top of the Jamaican 'milk them for all they're worth' mentality.

The Missing Years

Relieved, and anxious to leave the scene, I returned the borrowed jacket and was about to bestow my thanks on the lender and Uriel, and get away from the smirking faces as fast as I could, when who should appear on the scene to increase my already great discomfiture…?

He stopped the marked car and came out, his eyes taking in the small group of people – who had already started to drift away – before moving on to the damaged rear of my vehicle. Some of the people paused as they noticed his presence. He did not look my way, and I thought he had not seen me, but I knew that he knew Richard's car by sight.

The other driver had been about to drive off when Devlin walked up to his car and inspected the front. He said nothing to the man, but came straight over to me, proving that he had seen me all along, and said, "Is you was driving?" I hoped he could not smell rum on my breath from the many rum punches I had imbibed during the night's revelling.

All the while, he was inspecting me from head to toe, hardly trying to disguise the leer on his face. I wished it had been any officer but Devlin; my apparel was making me feel at a disadvantage.

But I was not easily intimidated, and I fixed him with an icy stare and replied, "If you're quite finished with ogling me, yes, I was driving. However, your input is not necessary as the third party and I have already come to a satisfactory agreement."

A few persons snickered, and if he had been white, he would have turned red; he was not able to hide his embarrassment the way I could; but he could, and did, turn it into anger; albeit, a silent, impotent anger, evidenced only by the grim set of his features and the loathing in his eyes.

Claudette Beckford-Brady

He was not a tall man, and my four inch heels and my five-eight height turned me into a six-footer, and I looked down loftily upon him. But he refused to back off, and asked me to produce the vehicle's documents and my driver's license. I walked daintily to the car in my stiletto heels and handed him the documents, removing them from the wallet for him, although I kept no ganja in the wallet, as Uncle Cornell was wont to do in his.

The original documents were kept at home, and all our vehicles carried only photocopies. My drivers were constantly being harassed by police who insisted that they must have the originals in the vehicle, and I was constantly demanding that they show me the statute which so decreed.

Once I had seen that written law, I told the harassing officer, I would comply, but in the meantime I preferred to keep my originals safe from prospective car thieves.

Now, Devlin thrust the photo-copied documents back at me and said, "A waan si di original document dem. Yu suppose to keep yu documents into di veekle."

I sighed. I really wanted to go home. I had partied like a devil all night, my feet were killing me, I had just had a body-jarring impact, the effects of which I was beginning to feel, and I was bone weary. I was beginning to think about Richard's reaction when he heard about this, so I was in no mood for a prolonged argument with Sgt. Devlin.

I spoke forcefully. "Sergeant, I am tired and I would like to go and pick up my baby and go home. If you want to see the original documents, you are going to have to follow me home; alternatively, I can produce them at the station sometime *within the next five days* as is provided for by law.

"Now, since you have inspected my documents, I insist

The Missing Years

that you also inspect those of the third party, who was driving *far too close* behind my vehicle. Had he maintained a proper stopping distance, this would not have occurred."

The man who had berated me and women drivers in general, but who had been all smiles the minute he found out who I was, now scowled darkly at me. But Sgt. Devlin had no choice; there was still a group of onlookers, many of whom disliked him, anyway, because he had a reputation for arrogance. He had to be seen to be fair. He beckoned the man over and he came, document wallet in hand.

The average working class Jamaican, for the most part, appeared to be afraid of, or intimidated by the police. Few would dare to speak to an officer the way I had done, but I was not the average working class Jamaican. I was *Somebody* and I had friends in high places, including the Superintendent at Old Harbour police station, not to mention my brother-in-law Senior Superintendent of Police, Constantine Grant. I was not averse to taking advantage of my connections, if necessary.

I was about to enter my car and leave when Devlin said, "A doan't finish wid yu yet – A might have to give yu a ticket."

I was fast losing patience with him. "A ticket? For what? *He* hit *me.*"

The other driver saw his chance and jumped in with, "Shi stap sudden, bam eena di miggle a di road Affissa. A nevah even get a chance fi brake."

"Which shows that you were *much* too close behind me," I interjected. Devlin regarded me solemnly, his hostility palpable. "Why yu stap suh sudden? A pickney run craas di road or wha?"

I was caught. Obviously I could not tell him that I had

suddenly fancied a piece of sugar cane. I decided to accept the ticket and go home.

"Okay," I said, holding out my hand and lapsing into patois, "write yu ticket mek mi get fi guh home a-mi yaad."

He looked taken aback, but seemed about to go for his ticket book when some anonymous person amongst the onlookers said, "Likkle bad-mind police-bwoy" and others began to voice their agreement. They were brave enough as a group, if not by themselves.

Devlin finally accepted defeat, and said coldly, "Ahright; yu kyan gwaan."

I did not stay to see if the man's documents were in order. I had already agreed to cover the cost of repairs, and I would do so. I smiled my thanks at the woman who had loaned me the jacket and slipped my business card into her hand, telling her to give me a call sometime.

I got into the car and drove, not even bothering to look closely at the damage. I was determined to have it repaired before the family returned in a week's time.

*

Have you ever heard of "jungle telegraph?" Well, there is a superb state of the art one in Jamaica the Beloved Island. It is super efficient, and it never, ever breaks down, come earthquake, come hurricane.

By the time I got back to *Sweet Home* shortly after seven-thirty, with the sun just beginning to get warm, the telegraph system had already sent out bulletins. Wilbert and Lurline were waiting at the gate, a sleeping Estelle in the carrycot. They displayed eminent relief when they saw that I was quite unhurt, and Wilbert said he would take the car to the garage first thing the next morning.

The Missing Years

As I entered the house, the phone was ringing. It was Frank, calling to make sure I was not hurt and asking about the extent of the damage.

I assured him that I was fine and unhurt, and that the damage to both vehicles was minimal. I told him about the exchange with Sgt. Devlin and he told me not to worry about it. I told him I had no intention of doing so, and we laughed a little over the effectiveness of the jungle telegraph. But I was to learn to hate the effectiveness of that 'telegraph' system.

I stripped off, showered and fell naked into bed. I had the house to myself; those who had not gone to Walkers Wood were at Country, making preparations to leave for Ochee. Estelle was never a problem, and I slept deeply for several hours.

I woke up shortly after eleven to hear Estelle mewling in the bassinette beside the bed. I was still tired, and I put her to my breast, half-sitting, half-lying against a mound of pillows, and dozed off again.

I woke up to the sound of a car door being slammed, and by the time I had come fully awake, removed a sleeping Estelle from my breast and replaced her in the bassinette, Richard came striding into the bedroom.

I was stark naked; the clothes I had stepped out of earlier lay on the floor beside the bed, one shoe was lying on its side just inside the doorway where I had kicked it off, and the other was standing in the middle of the carpet. I saw Richard take all this in at a glance, pick up the skimpy little red dress, hold it up, and then drop it back to the floor.

I looked at his body language without meeting his eyes, and felt a little tremor of apprehension run through me. I finally found the courage to look at his face.

Claudette Beckford-Brady

His expression was black; like great thunderheads in a grey sky, ready to erupt and send forth forked tongues of lightning to strike the earth – only I was the earth, and he the thunderheads.

His voice, when he spoke, was the exact opposite of the fiery anger on his face, and sent freezing fingers of ice down my spine.

"Suh, that's why yu didn't want to go to the farm; yu preffa to guh partying wearing next to nothing, cavorting and making a spectacle of yuself all night, and if that wasn't enough, yu had to guh an make a even bigger spectacle in front of half-a Old Harbour Town.

"And to think that it was me who provided yu with the perfect excuse fah not going to the farm – yu mother!"

He paused, as if waiting for me to respond. He had not mentioned the damage to the car and I gave him time to bring it up. I remained silent and only moved to get a robe; I felt at a disadvantage being naked.

If we were going to have a real rip-roaring row, which it seemed we were, because he was pissing me off big time, I wanted to feel dignified, which is very difficult to do when one is buck-naked.

The silence fed on itself and grew. When he realised I was not going to speak he said, "Well? Yu don't have anything to seh?"

I moved to get a clean Pampers for Estelle who had been fed but not changed, and then I went into the bathroom to get a basin of water and her flannel. I was just as angry as Richard was, but I knew that ranting and raving was not going to achieve anything, and quite frankly, I just did not have the energy.

The Missing Years

He *knew* I had been involved in an accident, albeit, a minor one, but he had not asked after my wellbeing as Wilbert and Lurline and Frank had done. That hurt and angered me, but I would hold it down.

He waited until I returned to the room and then said, "At least yu nevah mash up the car too bad, and what a blessing Estelle wasn't with yu. The only sensible thing yu did was to leave har with Lurline."

My hurt grew larger than my anger. Richard was acting completely out of character. In the past, he had never gotten angry, only exasperated, and no matter how exasperated he got, my wellbeing was always paramount with him. Now here he was, far more concerned over a car than he was over me, his wife.

I continued to ignore him as I washed and changed Estelle, who remained sleeping throughout the entire process. I replaced her in the bassinette, then changed my mind, picked her up and took her to her cot in the nursery.

All the while I was aware of Richard's silent scrutiny, and I knew he was only waiting for me to finish with Estelle to pick up the argument. But one person could not argue, and I was not in the mood to accommodate him.

I finished with the baby, turned on the alarm so I could hear her downstairs, and without returning to the bedroom I exited through the passage door and went down the stairs.

A few minutes later, having obviously realised that I had walked out on him, Richard came down and found me making an omelette. I had an extremely healthy appetite, and few things affected it; no matter the situation or the trauma, my appetite remained constant. Now he came into the kitchen and said without preamble, "Get yuself and Estelle ready; A taking oonu back to Walkers Wood with mi."

To tell the truth, I was not against going to Walkers Wood any more. It would be good to be out of Old Harbour for a few days while the dust settled and the gossipmongers had their day. In addition, I had been thinking over the entire situation and realised that I was not actually *against* Delisia's being there; it was more the fact that Richard had invited her without discussing it with me first.

But his words got my back up. I did not appreciate the autocratic way in which he was speaking to me, as if I had no say in the matter.

"Is that an order?" I was tempted to add "Sir" but I didn't.

His eyes found mine and bored into me as he replied. "Yu don't like orders, eh? Well if you weren't so childishly immature I would not have to dispense orders! Yu must learn to hear me when I speak, Michelle, or one of these days yu refusal to hear will result in serious consequences. Look the other night when A sen' yu fah the police – something as important as that..."

He stopped speaking abruptly. I had raised my hands into the air, holding the plate with the omelette on it, and sent it crashing to the floor. Another childish act, but I didn't care. I was not going to try and explain to him that it was fear for his safety which had paralysed and made me incapable of leaving the scene. But his bringing up the subject brought it all back sharply into focus and before I knew what I was saying I had blurted it out.

"Well something happened to you that night to turn you into a monster, and you're still a monster now! You killed that poor boy and now since you can't kill me, you've decided to bully me instead, but in fact you could kill me if you wanted to, couldn't you – I mean, you do *own* a gun, don't you? And I can see you're getting tired of me – staying out half the night every night doing God knows what with God knows who...! Why yu don't just shoot me too?"

What on earth was the matter with me? One of these days my mouth was going to get me into serious trouble. I stopped my tirade and waited for Richard's reaction, barely daring to look at him. He was staring at me, and his features had tightened into the same angry look he had possessed on Christmas night when he had killed the youth.

But he didn't say anything. He picked up a dustpan and brush and started to clean up the broken pieces of plate and omelette from the floor. He put them into the garbage bin, got a mop and bucket, and wiped the area, all the while totally ignoring me.

That was one of the things about Richard – most men would not have even thought of cleaning up the mess, or wouldn't see why they should, but he was very particular about cleanliness, and probably knew that in my present mood I was liable to just leave the mess on the floor.

When he was finished, he went outside, and I could hear him washing out the mop and bucket. All this time I stood uncertainly, waiting for his reaction to my words, but when he came back inside he strode towards the living room, saying only, "I'll be back to pick yu up in two hours. Be ready."

I followed him from the kitchen and watched mutely while he went out the door, got into his father's car which he was driving, and reversed at speed down the driveway and out of the gate.

I felt awful. I wished he had shouted at me; hit me;

anything. Anything but that cold, tight, angry look, and those abrupt words. I wondered where he was going for two hours. Was he going to wherever he had been spending his late nights? *Could* there be another woman, despite his recent over-ardent lovemaking?

I spent the next hour ruminating and at the end of that time I had fully convinced myself that Richard no longer loved me, and that he was having an affair. I made up my mind that from now on I was going to watch for the evidence of his infidelity and when I got the proof, he, and she, whoever she was, would be sorry.

I packed a small case for me and Estelle and was sitting waiting on the veranda when he returned, some four hours later. It was late afternoon and already getting dark. I was fuming, because I had been ready in the two hours he had stipulated, and hated waiting at the best of times. But I said nothing, and neither did he.

He picked up the car-cot and strapped it into the vehicle and I placed Estelle in it and got into the back seat beside her. He locked the grille, got into the driver's seat, started the engine, and drove down the driveway and through the gate. We drove the entire forty mile, ninety-minute journey in complete silence, with not even the radio playing.

I was starving; while he had been gone I had been too busy thinking and been too pent up to remember that I was hungry, but now that we were driving, the hunger came back full force. I wanted to ask him to stop at Faith's Pen so I could buy some roast yam or something, but I was too stubborn, so I suffered in silence.

It was almost seven when we got to Walkers Wood, and full dark. We turned off the main road and drove up the winding private road that led to the house at the top of the rise. As we turned the last corner and the house came into view Richard spoke.

"Fix yu face. There will be guests at the house – no need for everyone to see your sour side."

Inside, I felt like crying. Why was Richard being so horrible to me? I mean, a small car accident was nothing to get all bent out of shape over, and look how he had goaded me into saying those horrible things to him. Now he was freezing me out, speaking only when he felt he had to, and only in terse tones.

Well, I would not cry. Two could be terse, and I could freeze him out just as effectively as he was freezing me out. I would fix my face and be all bright and bubbly to all – except him. See how *he* liked being ignored.

The house and garden were a blaze of lights, music was playing and several people with plates of food in their hands sat out under trees, eating and talking. I suddenly remembered how hungry I was, and decided that food was my first priority. But Richard had other ideas.

I picked up Estelle but before I could head for the house he had taken my hand, which I tried to withdraw without success, and practically drew me over to a group of four persons sitting under an orange tree. His whole demeanour suddenly changed from cold, closed and detached to warm, open and friendly.

"Hey guys, meet my beautiful wife Michelle, and my youngest daughter, Estelle. Honey, say "hi" to the guys…" and he reeled off a slew of names as I pasted on a plastic smile and greeted them all, not really registering which name went with which face.

Claudette Beckford-Brady

All the way in, from the garden to the veranda, and finally to the living room, I was being introduced to a parcel of strangers, and my face was beginning to ache from the forced smiles I was dispensing. But finally, I found people I knew, and my smiles became genuine.

I was hugged and kissed and exclaimed over by my immediate family members who displayed much relief that the accident had not been serious. Estelle was taken from me and I was forced to recount the full details of the incident, while the twins wanted to know which VIPs had been at the Barrington's party. I managed to get through to someone that I was starving, and a plate of curry goat and rice appeared, which I tucked into with gusto, while talking around mouthfuls of food.

When I mentioned that the reason I had stopped suddenly was because I had wanted to buy a piece of sugar cane, Delroy quipped, "First Jacob, and now you; I think they should ban sugar cane."

I knew he was referring to Jacob Miller, one of Jamaica's great reggae artistes, who, rumour had it, had been wrestling with a piece of sugar cane when his car got out of control and he was killed. I have no idea whether or not the story was true, but I replied that the cane should not be blamed for the idiotic behaviour of humans, including myself.

Delisia was having a great time. She was talking to two women, both strangers to me, and they were very animated and laughing a great deal. I asked Mavis if she knew who they were, and she said they were a couple of local lawyers, one of whom Delisia actually knew. I thought what a small world it was.

She saw me, and beckoned me over, and I went, not too

The Missing Years

willingly, but I went. She looked radiant, dressed in a light blue silk dress which was fitted at the top and flared from the waist down. Her ears were bedecked with small diamond earrings and around her neck a teardrop pendant nestled just above the valley of her breasts. She wore silver high heeled sandals, and looked very comfortable in her surroundings. I thought to myself how beautiful she actually was.

She introduced the women to me as Evadne Bacchus and Hortense Samuda. Evadne, she said, had attended some of her classes in college in California back in the Seventies, and she and Hortense had a law firm in Ocho Rios. Me, she introduced simply as "Michelle, Richard's wife."

The two women looked at me, and looked back at Delisia, before exchanging glances with each other. I could almost follow their thought processes. There was no mistaking our remarkable resemblance to each other, and I knew they were curious, but I supposed they were too well bred to actually ask the question. Or perhaps they would wait until I had gone. We greeted each other cordially, and made small talk for a few minutes.

From time to time Richard appeared at my side, introducing me to strangers and endowing me with false smiles of endearment. I responded in kind, being bright and vivacious, until I was ready to vomit at my own duplicity.

But eventually the evening wound down and people began leaving, until finally only the family remained. It was past midnight and all the kids were in bed, while the rest of us sat or lounged around, talking. The conversation returned to my escapade with the car, and again I had to explain what had happened to cause me to brake suddenly.

Richard, who was sitting across the room, seemingly to

be as far from me as possible, said caustically, "Cane! Look how much cane yu have access to between here, yu father place and *Sweet Home*! Yu not helpless; yu could-a cut a stalk of cane not fifty foot from yu back door!"

I did not trust myself to reply, but bit my tongue and held down my anger. I did not want to get into an argument with him in front of the family. I mentally cursed that damn jungle telegraph which was so effective; if not for it, I would have had the car repaired and he might never have known about it, and I would still be in Old Harbour, and he would be here, and we would not be getting on each other's nerves. *Damn that jungle telegraph!*

I turned to Delisia, smiled sweetly, and said, "Isn't it a small world? Fancy you meeting up with a college mate *here*," and she replied, "Isn't it?" and the conversation changed tack.

Eventually everyone went to their various quarters, and Richard and I went up to our room. We were finally alone together, and the atmosphere was stinking with resentment and animosity. I went about getting ready for bed, totally ignoring him, and he seemed to be doing the same. In the bed his leg brushed against me, and I jerked away from him as if I had been burned. He responded by moving further away from me, as if he too hated the thought of any physical contact with me.

He seemed to fall asleep almost instantly, as was evidenced by his breathing, while I lay there for hours, too angry and upset to sleep. Richard obviously no longer loved me – the evidence, if not in front of my eyes, was definitely standing up in my mind. Look how he was treating me, not to mention the fact that he had started staying out till all hours when I knew he was not at the studio.

And up till now he had not even asked me if I had been jerked up by the impact, and the fact that he could go off to sleep so nonchalantly proved that he gave not two figs for what I was feeling – Richard, who was always so in tune with every nuance of my body language.

I couldn't believe that a simple little thing like a minor accident would have him acting this way; I was convinced that it was nothing to do with the car, but that something else was driving him. I knew he was peeved that I had gone to the Barrington's party, but that was also a minor issue and I did not see why that should peeve him so, unless reports of my conduct had been greatly exaggerated.

I mean, I had had what the twins would describe as a "wild time," but I had not been out of order in any way. I simple danced – with men, yes, I admit it – and I supposed I might have flirted harmlessly while I drank and made merry. Perhaps the dress I had worn was a part of the issue... I remembered the look on his face when he had picked it up, looked from it to me, and then dropped it back on the floor.

Of course, there was also the fact that I had initially refused to come to Walkers Wood, which was the precipitator of everything that had since happened...

All in all, I ruminated, it had not been a good start to a new year, and I hoped this was not a portent for the remainder of the year.

CHAPTER EIGHT

I make the News, and Revenge on Devlin

I suppose I must have finally slept, for when I woke it was morning and Estelle wanted her breakfast and a wash. I saw that it was a little before six-thirty and that Richard's side of the bed was empty. I did not take it personally; he was always an early riser, and loved his farm in the early morning; he had probably been gone since five.

I gave Estelle what she needed, and played with her awhile, until she went back to sleep. She was six weeks old now and more aware and staying awake longer. When she had gone back to sleep I gave myself a shower, got dressed in cut off jeans and a tee shirt, tuned the radio to an easy listening station, and lay back down till I was ready to go downstairs. There was no rush; I was on holiday and I was going to take full advantage of it.

It was the second of January, and a Saturday. I was not due back at work till the eleventh; this was my first proper break in a long while – I had not even taken any proper maternity leave. Since I was already here, I was going to have a damn good time, despite Richard.

The Missing Years

A little before eight my stomach said it needed food, so I picked up the carrycot with a sleeping Estelle and went downstairs. As I entered the dining room, Richard, my two dads, and Roy and Tony came in through the kitchen door carrying ravenous appetites to match or surpass my own. Mavis and the other women and kids had apparently had breakfast already and were outside somewhere with Daddy Armstrong and Specky and the others.

I parked the carrycot and Estelle on a chair, greeted everyone cheerfully, not singling Richard out, and sat down around the table. A helper had followed the men in from the kitchen and was asking if she should bring in the breakfast. Richard gave her the affirmative and she left, while they all seated themselves around the table, which was already set.

Richard did not seek to come and sit next to me in his usual chair, but sat at the head of the table where his father usually sat. I made a mental note of it.

Blossom, one of the helpers, brought in a jug of orange juice and a pot of coffee, placed them on the table and went out again, returning a short while later with steamed fish and calalloo, and boiled bananas and fried dumplings.

I did not feel out of place being the only female amongst the men, after all, they were all *my* men in one way or another, and I fed my face while I listened to them talking about the farm and farm matters. The radio was on and the eight o'clock news was about to start.

The conversation lulled while we listened to the news headlines; two men had been killed in a shootout with police in Grants Pen; a gun and a quantity of ammunition had been seized in a police operation in Matthews Lane; there had been several road accidents, including fatalities, over the last forty-eight hours, some of them linked to speed and improper overtaking, some to drunk driving.

And then my heart stopped cold, and I felt the eyes of all my men on me, and I wished I were anywhere but here.

"Mrs. Michelle Freeman-Armstrong, co-owner of SmallRock Publications, publishers of the St. Catherine District Bell and the magazine Jamaican Woman, was involved in a minor motor vehicle collision on East Street, in Old Harbour on New Years Day.

Reports from the Old Harbour police (damn that devil, Sergeant Devlin!) *are that at approximately six-thirty-five a.m. Mrs. Armstrong was heading in an easterly direction toward Spanish Town when she made a sudden stop in the middle of the road, causing the vehicle to be rear-ended by the motorist following behind.*

It is not known what caused Mrs. Armstrong to brake so suddenly, Sgt Devlin of the Old Harbour Traffic Division said, but she appeared slightly unsteady on her feet, and her apparel indicated she was returning from a nightclub or other function.

Sgt. Devlin further stated that he had attempted to breathalyse Mrs Armstrong, but she is a very popular figure in Old Harbour and the crowd which had gathered was being hostile toward him as he tried to conduct his investigations, and he was afraid he would not be able to contain them should he persist in his efforts to interview Mrs Armstrong. He therefore, very reluctantly, had to let her go. As a result, Sgt Devlin was unable to confirm whether or not Mrs Armstrong was inebriated.

In addition to owning SmallRock Publications Mrs Freeman-Armstrong is also a successful novelist, and the wife

The Missing Years

of well known music producer/promoter Richard Armstrong, who recently killed a gunman while defending his family from robbers.

Up to news time Mrs Armstrong could not be reached for comment."

The newsreader went on to report other stories, but I heard none of them. I was fuming with anger over Devlin's malicious innuendos. He was not going to get away with this! I would seek legal advice as soon as I could get Frankie on the phone. He would know what to do. How dare that man make inferences to tarnish my character and reputation!

I did not remember till later that my own mother, Delisia, was a top-notch lawyer, by all accounts. As for Richard, I did not even bother to look at his reaction – there was no need, I could feel his eyes boring into me, and his displeasure was palpable.

I pushed my chair back noisily and got up from the table. I looked at Daddy and the others, totally ignoring Richard, and said, "For all your information, I was most certainly *not inebriated,* and this report is nothing but a malicious attempt by an arrogant little man who does not recognise his own inferiority to tarnish my reputation because I happen not to be intimidated by him!

"If I was unsteady on my feet it was due to my four inch stiletto heels and the fact that I had been in them for eight hours, and he made *no suggestion or attempt* to breathalyse me, and if he had, I would have passed with flying colours, the lying dog! I can get any number of witnesses." I said it with total confidence, believing it. After all I had only been drinking rum *punch*.

Daddy Wilf was consoling. "Nuh worry yuself, Shellie.

Claudette Beckford-Brady

Everybaddy weh know yu know seh yu too sensible to drive drunk; worse yu know seh yu have young baby at home. Mek di bwoy g'weh!"

There was a chorus of concurrence, but I did not notice Richard's voice among them. Then I heard Daddy say, "Come, Richard; doan't look suh dark, man. Yu know seh dat police bwoy deh doan't like needa yu nor Shellie; yu know seh a lie him a tell pan har."

I was gratified at my family's confidence and support, but Richard was not mollified. "Shi should nevah have put herself in that position in the first place; she have a certain standing in the community; this incident will result in some loss of dignity for her."

"My dignity is quite intact, thank you!" I snapped, "and Devlin has not heard the last of this!" and with that I exited the room, leaving them all to discuss, or not, as they wished.

As I stepped through the door the phone started ringing, and for the rest of the day Auntie and the helpers fielded the calls as best they could, including those from my cousin Daniel, Frank and Lynette Barrington, Uncle Bertie, and a few others. I wanted to speak to no-one.

I went outside to find the rest of the family and fill them in. I wanted them to hear my explanation from me before they were made privy to, or before they heard a re-broadcast of the report.

Most of them were sitting out in the garden – I did not see the young adults – Samantha, nor Specky and Rachel's children, and Richards's two sons from his previous marriage. I wished they had all been there because I was only going to explain this once.

The younger kids were romping and paid no attention

The Missing Years

to us adults. I told them about the news report and repeated what I had told the men, elaborating on the exchange I had had with Devlin. Like Daddy and the others, they all professed confidence in me, and gave me their full support. Richard had been the only dissenter.

Specky had been playing with the kids, but had come over when I said I had something to say to everyone. Now he said to me, "Yu want mi to have a word wid him superior officer? Wi could force him to give the media a retraction and give yu a public apology."

Specky waited while I chewed it over. I wondered if he really could get a retraction and apology, and if he did what it would achieve. I knew it would only cause Devlin to hate me more, and probably his colleagues would hate me too, but he was going to hate me more anyway, because one way or the other, he *was* going to pay. I told Specky I would take care of it myself, although I was not sure yet exactly how I was going to do it.

Meantime, Specky was bending over backwards to defend the integrity of the Police Force, contending that officers like Devlin were in the minority. I told him I had not found it so in the six years I had been on the island. I had found the average officer to be of the same ilk as Devlin.

Yes, there were some who were pleasant and polite, and treated people with courtesy; who went about their work with competence, if not dedication. And there were officers such as Specky and Sgt. Newell, who were definitely dedicated to their careers and took pride in efficiency. But it seemed to me that these were in the minority.

Specky said he was sorry I felt that way, but it was a misconception. The vast majority of officers, he said, were

Claudette Beckford-Brady

like himself and Sgt Newell; it was just that I had no opportunity to see the majority at work.

Then Delisia spoke up, her Californian drawl sounding out of place in the St. Ann countryside. "You could possibly have grounds for a lawsuit. He has publicly cast doubt on your sobriety without any evidence to back it up. That is tantamount to maligning your good name. He has impugned both your character and your integrity. I'd say you have a case."

"Maybe in your neck of the woods," I said, "but this isn't the good old US of A." I had spoken more sharply than I intended, and I modified my tone as I continued. "It would be a waste of time and money, and the integrity of the very judges is at times in question. I have as little confidence in our judiciary as I do in the police. Now isn't that a sad state of affairs? What is to become of my Beloved Island?"

Mavis suddenly laughed and said, "Yu rememba di judge at di Rent Board, how yu dress him down and waak out? Bertie seh him doan know how di judge nevah lock yu up fah contempt." I joined her laughter. "That's because him nevah ketch mi," I said, falling into the vernacular.

Delisia had never heard the story, and was curious, and I found myself relating the incident to her. There had been a tenant living in the Big House while Daddy and Mavis were still in the UK. She had kept the place like a pigsty and had been given notice to vacate.

She had been insolent and extremely profane, and tried to get revenge by having me and Uncle Bertie, who was Daddy's agent, brought up in front of the Rent Board Judge, accused of threatening to throw her and her belongings out on the street.

The Missing Years

Of course we had done no such thing, but every time I tried to explain to the judge he cut me off. He accepted everything the woman told him, and accepted nothing that I said. When I complained about his lack of impartiality and her profanity, he had told me that, *"Young Lady, you are in Jamaica now, and yu must expect Jamaicans to curse badwords. It is a national pastime."*

Eventually I had run out of patience, had given him a piece of my mind and walked out of the proceedings, leaving Uncle Bertie to finish dealing with him. He had sent his Clerk after me to bring me back, and I had sent the Clerk back with a message filled with profanity, telling him to tell the judge that since I was in Jamaica he must expect me to curse badwords since it was a national pastime.

Uncle Bertie had said the Clerk had delivered the message to the judge, badwords and all, with a straight face, but he could tell that the Clerk was laughing inside, fit to burst.

Delisia thought the story hilarious and said that was the sort of thing she would probably have done too, and that in fact she herself had had several run-ins with judges in the course of her work, however she didn't have the luxury of being able to dress down a judge and walk out on him, to her regret. She went on to give a few anecdotes about some of the judges and opposing Counsel she had come up against, and we were having a good laugh when Richard and the other men came outside.

They joined in the laughter when they heard what we were laughing about – all except Richard who said caustically, "A guess it's good to be able to laugh when the entire nation has the notion that you are a drunk driver!"

Claudette Beckford-Brady

I smiled daggers at him, and turned to his twin sister and said, "Rachel, can I use your computer?"

"Sure," she said. "Come on, I'll set you up."

Up to that point I had had no idea what I was going to do, but I felt I needed to write, which was always my best form of therapy. Richard was really pissing me off, and I did not want to spoil everyone's holiday by getting into it with him. I asked my mothers (I now had three) to keep an eye on Estelle and call me if she woke up, and then I followed Rachel across to her wing of the house, which had been a later addition made when she got married.

I noticed that she kept glancing at me as if she wanted to say something, and at one point I was sure she started to speak, although no sound came out, but I saw her mouth open, and snap back shut and she gave her head a slight shake. "Rachel," I said, "if there is something you want to say, go ahead and say it."

We had entered her study by way of the veranda door and she removed the dust cover and turned on the computer before turning to me and saying, "Okay. I feel the tension between you and Richard, and I'm puzzled by it. It's not like you two; you've always been so in tune... what's changed?"

Rachel (and Richard) was forty-six, twelve years my senior. She was a paediatrician with a good sized Practice in the town of Ocho Rios, where she invariably had amongst her clientele children of tourists and other visitors.

Rachel was a beautiful woman. As tall as Richard, and still trim, despite having had four children, she moved with a lithe grace and could easily have been a model. She exuded confidence and self-assurance, and she loved all children with a passion, and I had even seen her cry over the ailments of one of her young patients.

Her personality was tranquil – I had never heard her raise her voice – and she had a droll sense of humour. She had never pried into my affairs or my relationship with Richard and I did not think it out of place for her to ask the question, although she obviously doubted that she should.

"I really wish I knew, Rachel," I replied. "He's been acting really out of character; snapping at me for no reason, staying out till all hours... I've come to the conclusion that he's tired of me and is working up to leaving me."

Rachel burst out laughing, and I looked at her in surprised vexation; I didn't see anything funny in what I had just said. She saw my look and controlled her laughter.

"I'm sorry, Shellie, but you are being ridiculous. That's the silliest thing I've ever heard out of your mouth... let me tell you...

"Richard worships the ground you walk on. I have never seen him so happy or contented in my life, and I would know if his feelings toward you had changed. He's my twin and I know him better than he knows himself.

"The first time he mentioned you, I knew he was smitten, even as he was telling me how you dressed him down, and I knew you would get married. I knew he and Dawn were heading for the rocks before he realised it himself, and I am *absolutely certain* that he is as committed to you as ever."

I wanted to be reassured by her words, but I somehow wasn't. "Well how do you explain his sudden personality change, then?" I asked her. "He's treating me as if I have committed a Capital Offence, not to mention the fact that I think he's having an affair..."

Rachel's snort of laughter cut me off. She held me by both shoulders and steered me into an easy chair. "Sit!"

I complied. "Now, listen carefully and don't interrupt. Richard is *not* having an affair, but...."

"How can you be so sure?" I managed to get out before she said, "I *said,* don't interrupt. "Now, as I was saying, he is not having an affair, but he is under a great deal of stress. He is still suffering from guilt over the death of the youth on Christmas night, and he believes everyone is condemning him for it, despite their claims otherwise.

"But what he doesn't realise is that he is condemning himself more than anyone else is condemning him, and until he can forgive himself, he is going to punish himself, and that includes turning you against him as a part of his punishment. It's all a part of the self-flagellation process, but it will run its course. Yu just have to give him time."

She paused, and I risked another interruption. "But I've tried my best to reassure him that he only did what he had to do to protect his family. Any red-blooded man would have done the same."

"Yes, but it's no good till he can come to that conclusion himself. In the meantime, yu just have to be extra loving, and extra patient."

"But he won't let me! I can't do anything right, and how do you explain his new habit of staying out into the small hours when he's not working at the studio, eh? Where is he, what is he doing, and with whom?"

Rachel heard the fear and doubts in my voice and tried again to reassure me. "Michelle, I don't know the answers to those questions, but I do know this – my brother is not having an affair. If he were, he would not be able to hide it from me,

The Missing Years

I guarantee it."

I wanted to feel reassured, but I didn't. Rachel stood up and said, "Anyway, there's the computer, there's stationery; anything else yu want – I'm out in the garden with the others. Think about what I've said."

She exited the room and I sat in front of the computer and stared at the blank screen. In truth, when I had asked to use the computer I had not exactly formulated why I wanted to use it. Sitting there now I stared at the screen and thought about everything that Rachel had said.

Could she be right? Was he hurting me to punish himself? That sounded weird to me, but Rachel had studied psychology as part of her medical training. And she was his twin, after all, and I supposed she knew him as well as, or better than anybody.

I guiltily remembered how I had thrown the youth's death in Richard's face the day before, and realised that I was reinforcing his feelings of guilt. All my previous words and reassurances to him were negated by that utterance – *"You killed that poor youth..."*

My anger toward Richard transferred itself to anger toward my own self. I hated myself. But I would make it up to him, starting tonight. I would convince him that my cruel words had no merit and had only been flung because I was angry at him; and I had only been angry at him because Devlin had caused a minor incident to be blown up out of all proportion and thereby activated the jungle telegraph, which had brought Richard rushing, quite unnecessarily, home.

And then suddenly I knew why I had wanted to use the computer. I started typing and my fingers flew over the keyboard at lightening speed. The words just kept coming and coming, until I was completely written out.

I read over what I had written, and then printed it. Then I picked up the telephone on Rachel's desk and called the two main newspapers, after which I faxed what I had written. I knew the editors of both papers. I arranged to purchase a full page in each of the Sunday papers, after which I would re-publish my article in my own paper's next issue.

My intention of making things up with Richard that night fell flat. When I returned to the garden he was gone, and he did not return home that night. Apparently he had some unspecified business to take care of, according to the family, and he had not even left a personal message for me.

I pretended it didn't matter, but Rachel saw, and knew. She surreptitiously squeezed my hand and whispered, "It'll be okay; give him time," which made me want to cry – me, who was not a crying sort of person...

But I did cry – in the night, quietly and alone.

I went down early the next morning, before six-thirty. The dining room was deserted, but as I entered, Auntie came out of the kitchen with a tray containing a coffee service and two cups, which she said she was taking to Richard and his father, who were sitting on the veranda. She suggested I get myself a cup and come join them, but I declined, saying they might be discussing men's stuff.

I got some coconut water from the fridge and had a long refreshing drink, and then I scooped out some of the succulent white jelly which was in a separate container and ate it. Blossom was cooking liver and pak choy, or pap-chow, as the Jamaicans call it, as a change from the perpetual callaloo, and the smell of fresh Jamaican coffee, which was grown right here on the farm, permeated the kitchen.

The Missing Years

I could hear people in the dining room and when I went back through my three mothers and my two fathers were there. Mavis looked sharply at me, and I thought, *"Oh no; she knows I've been crying..."* but she didn't say anything other than to greet me along with the others.

The table was already set, and Blossom came in with coffee, coconut water, and juice, and said that she would serve breakfast directly. I didn't fancy a cooked breakfast and I picked up Estelle and said I was going to sit out under my favourite tree. I wanted to wait for the boy who would bring the Sunday papers.

I left by the patio door, and as I came out I looked across at the front veranda. Richard and his father appeared to be in deep conversation, and Auntie was just disappearing back through the front door. I called out a communal good morning and Daddy Armstrong looked up and called one back, but Richard did not reply. I turned to walk along the walkway to where I wanted to sit, when his voice arrested me.

"Just a minute, Michelle."

It would not do to be blatantly rude to him in front of his father, but my resolution of yesterday that I would make up with him had dissolved. He had not even bothered to tell me that he would be out all night, and he had never stayed out all night before, apart from when he was here at the farm. Even late sessions at the studio rarely lasted the whole night.

Rachel might be convinced that he was not seeing someone, but I was now more convinced than ever.

I turned and walked over to the veranda. He held out his hands and I assumed he wanted Estelle, so I handed her to him, and he kissed her and held her close. Then he said, without looking at me, "A si yu made the Sunday papers."

I saw a brief smile flicker across my father-in-law's face, and he said, "Your words are sharp, Michelle. I hope you haven't left yourself open to any action or retaliation from the police." He indicated the papers on the veranda table; Richard must have come in this morning and brought them; it was too early for the delivery boy.

I picked one up and opened it, sorting through the various segments. I had purchased a full page spread, but was not sure where it would be featured.

"It's in the main segment –yu certainly don't do things by halves, but then you journalists all support each other, I suppose." Richard's voice was sarcastic and I saw his father send him a sharp glance, which he appeared not to notice, as he nuzzled and murmured to his daughter, who was awake.

Before I could find the page, Daddy Armstrong took the paper from me and guided me to an article. "You should read this first."

It was more or less a word-for-word report of what had been reported on the radio yesterday morning. At the end of the article it said, *see page nine.*

I opened to the specified page. They had found a file photo of me from somewhere and it sat at the top of the page with my by-line.

The article comprised a repudiation of Devlin's insinuations, and a feature article on the shortcomings and inefficiencies of the police force, and the undesirable attitudes of some of its officers.

To the citizens of Jamaica, my family, friends,

colleagues, employees; to every one who knows me, and to those who don't, I wish to say these words.

To all the good and dedicated police officers who go about their duties with integrity, commitment and efficiency; those who Serve, Protect and Reassure, I salute you. The negatives in this article do not apply to you.

Many of you may have listened to, or read reports of a minor collision in which this writer was involved on New Year's Day, in Old Harbour. I wish to give the full sequence of events – which can be corroborated by witnesses – of what transpired, and why it is that a certain officer has sought to malign and impugn my good name, character, reputation, and integrity.

I choose this medium in which to clear my name and air my views, not because I myself am a journalist, but because he himself has used the media as a weapon of spite; making insinuations and telling blatant and bare-faced lies in order to embarrass me and sully my reputation.

His reasons for doing so are based on past disagreements we have had, and my refusal to be impressed by his egotistical self-importance, or to be intimidated by his arrogance or his belligerent attitude.

I am sad to say that I have no confidence in the Police Complaints Authority and their willingness or ability to investigate and bring to book one of their own, and so I have to use whatever means I have at my disposal to have my day in the court of public opinion.

If the officer concerned can disprove any of my charges, let him do so publicly, since he has brought this into the public arena. Otherwise I shall expect a full and complete public retraction and apology.

I went on to give the full sequence of events, taking full responsibility for the collision; even admitting that I had stopped to buy cane. I apologised for my lapse in judgement and good sense and denied being drunk, explaining about my stiletto heels which I had been wearing for eight hours.

I denied that the officer (I deliberately refrained from mentioning him by name) had mentioned anything about a breathalyser test, or that the crowd had been restive or belligerent. In fact, I said, the few onlookers could hardly have been described as a crowd, and the only dissension I had heard against the officer was a lone voice saying what a bad-minded bwoy he was, to which there had been a few murmurs of agreement.

I went so far as to mention the death of my driver, Lizard, (but not by name) and the fact that the investigation had been flawed, resulting in there being no restitution or closure for the family. I was careful not to suggest that money had changed hands.

I repeated his words about not liking "oonu farrinnahs weh come from farrin wid oonu big money" and his remarks about my "dutty Rasta-man." I held nothing back and pulled no punches. I felt safe in the knowledge that everything I wrote was the truth.

I went on to write a scathing attack on the integrity of the Police Force, and individual officers who intimidated, bullied, and brutalised members of the public who did not know their rights, or who had no "backative" or no resources.

I castigated the senior officers for failing to effectively supervise and keep their subordinate officers in line. I berated the Government for failing to instil and enforce in the officers the fact that they are public servants and that their mandate is to "Serve, Protect and Reassure".

Finally, I conceded that perhaps the good officers *did* outnumbered the bad, but said they deserved to be sullied and tainted by the reputations of their corrupt colleagues because they turned a blind eye to the wrongdoings of their brother and sister officers.

I was satisfied with the article. I remembered once telling Devlin that it would behove him well to remember that I owned a publishing company and could generate negative publicity at will. His bid to embarrass me in the public eye had backfired grievously.

I looked up from reading the article, and caught Richard looking at me. The expression on his face was unguarded, and I saw a glimpse of the way he usually looked at me, with affectionate tolerance, but as soon as he caught my glance, his face closed and he bent his head back to Estelle.

I turned to Daddy Armstrong and said, "Well, I don't see any grounds in there for lawsuits. Everything in there is the God's honest truth. My only danger is that some disgruntled cop might shoot me or take out a contract on my life, but a journalist's life is fraught with danger."

The rest of the family were beginning to drift out into the garden in ones and twos, but none of them approached the veranda. My three mothers seemed to have become joined at the hip – I rarely saw one without the others, and they argued good-naturedly about who would hold or change the baby.

I was surprised at the easy camaraderie that existed between them – Delisia and Mavis in particular, but also Mummy Myrtle. They seemed to genuinely get on well, and often I heard them laughing together. It seems that Mavis was filling Delisia in on the antics of my childhood and teenage years.

I recalled Mavis telling me years ago that she had not liked Delisia, and I had understood her sentiments at the time. It seemed those sentiments had changed, and I supposed I was glad.

There also seemed to be no tension between Daddy and Delisia; she had fit right into the family as if she had always been a part of it. My kids had stopped calling her "Other Grandma" and now she was just Grandma Delisia, along with Grandma Mavis, Grandma Myrtle, and Grandma Miriam, who was in fact their great-grandma.

The regular delivery boy brought the papers, and we all spent a lazy day, lounging around the garden, reading, listening to the radio and so on. Everyone (except Richard) applauded my article, and said more people should follow my example and "lick out" against injustice.

If the phone had been busy yesterday after the initial news report had been aired, it became a hotline today. Auntie had had to take it off the hook because of the numbers of calls which had started shortly after eight, and I had turned my pager off, as had Richard. I knew my answering machine would be full by the time we got home.

After lunch the young adults went off on their own pursuits, probably to the river, or maybe into Ocho Rios to the beach, while the younger kids ran up and down and those who could, climbed trees.

Clivey, who was going to be ten in a week or so, wanted to go off with the older group, saying that if fourteen year old Neville could go, he didn't see why he shouldn't – after all he was only four years younger. They told him he should play

The Missing Years

with the younger kids, and he sulked for a while before Specky took him and his six year old brother, Kieran and they went off to the river to fish.

It was a difficult age for Clivey; the person closest to him in age was only six, and for a ten year old boy, that's only a kid. But at the other end of the scale the closest was Neville, at fourteen, who felt *Clivey* was only a kid.

But Specky had the knack of being whatever age he wanted to be, and he became a ten year old boy for Clivey's immediate benefit; good old Specky, the gentle giant. They returned from the river in the late afternoon, boasting several large river mullet and some janga (fresh-water crayfish).

CHAPTER NINE

Reconciliation...at last

On Monday morning I phoned my office, to be told by Debbie that everyone but *everyone* wanted to talk to me, from Superintendent Fergusson at Old Harbour police station, to radio talk show hosts who wanted me on their programmes. The phones had not stopped ringing, she said, and the callers were mainly calling to congratulate me for "licking out." She also said a crowd had gathered outside the police station, demanding that Devlin be fired or transferred.

I admit it; I was shocked and dismayed by the furore the article had provoked. I had set out to embarrass Devlin, and draw attention to the bad attitude and inefficiencies of the police, but I had had no idea how big the thing was going to get. I instructed Debbie to inform all callers that I was on leave and unreachable, which is what she had been doing, anyway.

I spoke with both Cee Jay and Barbara and we discussed the merit of repeating the article in the *District Bell's* next issue and decided it would only prolong the agony. It had already been read by enough people, and those who had not

The Missing Years

read it themselves were given the gist by others.

I took a few numbers to make some return calls, and then told Debbie that I was still on leave and she should only contact me in the direst emergency, and then only if Barbara or Cee Jay were unable to deal with a given situation.

After I finished on the phone I went in search of Delisia. I wanted to discuss what I should do, if anything, and whether, after having read the article, she could see any possible implications or repercussions.

She seemed my best prospect. Richard had been gone since first light, whether he was on the farm or elsewhere I had no idea, and in any case he would probably only say that I had brought this on myself. Rachel had returned to her Practice and Specky had also returned to work in Montego Bay where he was stationed.

I found all three mothers, together with Joy and Auntie sitting out in the back under a gigantic tambrin (tamarind) tree sorting and grading Scotch Bonnet peppers, of which there were thousands. I told them about the uproar the article was causing and asked Delisia if she thought I should let the thing die a natural death, or if I should follow it up.

"Waal," she drawled, "you sure seem to have opened up a can of worms, and one that needed opening, I'd say. But wha' d'you mean by following it up?"

"I mean should I lie low until it all blows over, or should I respond to the requests for interviews…? Should I forget about my demands for a retraction and apology, and let Devlin off the hook, or what?"

Delisia seemed puzzled. "Why'd you wanna do that? It seems to me that this is a wonderful opportunity to mobilise the country into demanding respect and performance from their police force.

"Everyone's in fine fettle right now, and spoiling for a fight with the Establishment, and you are the catalyst for that. All they need is someone to mobilise and lead them. You can't just back away now – you have to follow through – you owe it to the people. You can be a fine instrument for change."

I stared at her in indignant consternation. She had leaned forward and seemed eager in her earnestness; almost excited, as if she herself relished the idea of a fight with the Establishment. But she was setting *me* up as Moses come to lead the people to the Promised Land.

I did not like it. I was no Moses, no Marcus Garvey; no Bustamante. I was simply a small-town newspaper proprietor who wanted a simple life with my family, and to be treated with dignity and respect by the servants of the State. It was not too much to ask.

So how had I suddenly become the people's saviour? And why was Delisia being so *earnest* about it? As if she wanted me to go out and organise demonstrations and marches or some such thing?

"You've politicised this whole thing, Delisia," I said. "You almost seem to be inciting civil unrest. All I want is a quiet life; run my business, enjoy my family and the fruits of my labour. If the people want to agitate for change, let them find another leader. Me? I have said my piece, and the ball is now in their court. I may answer a few interviewers' questions, but I will not be getting involved in any campaigns."

At least talking to her had clarified the issue in my mind. She almost seemed disappointed, I thought, and I wondered if she had gotten involved in student politics during her

The Missing Years

campus days, but I did not ask her.

I still did not know very much about her; somehow we never seemed to be alone together long enough to get into things. And there were definitely things that I wanted to get into with her. We had thirty-two years of catching up to do, but it would obviously take time, and she would be returning to her home in California in a few days.

My other two mothers and Auntie had not taken any part in the discussion, but now Mavis said, "A tink di soona dis matta put to bed, di betta. Don't give nuh intaview – sen' out a general statement sehing what yu juss seh; yu waant a quiet life wid yu fambily, and mek di matta ress."

I decided to take her advice; Mavis was very sensible. I left them to go and deal with matters. I phoned Debbie and dictated a statement to be sent out to the media and also to be included in this week's edition of the *Districk Bell* and then I phoned Superintendent Fergusson.

He and I had always been on pretty good terms, but to say he was not pleased with me would be to understate the obvious.

"Miz Armstrong, why yu nevah taak to mi furse before yu guh dig up ance ness (ant's nest)? If yu did come to mi, A would-a resolve di matta fi yu. Now di whole country stir up, di people dem a crowd di station, an mi affissa dem demoralise an restive. A wanda if yu know what yu really do, eeh?"

I was a little annoyed that he was placing all the blame on me; after all, Devlin had started it with that malicious report of a minor incident.

"Supe," I said, "it was your officer who put it on the national front-burner. He publicly insinuated that I was other

Claudette Beckford-Brady

than sober, and without a shred of evidence to back up his claim. The man is a spiteful, insignificant little idiot, and the Force could do without people like him, but in hindsight, I realise I should have come to you first. I'm sorry."

I realised no such thing, but it was as well to mollify him. He told me that Devlin had been sent on leave and would be transferred out of the Division with immediate effect, but did not say to where. He said disciplinary action was pending for the verbal abuse relating to "farinnahs and dutty Rastas" which Devlin had not denied uttering. He said I had caused discord amongst his officers; some were in Devlin's corner, and some in mine.

"An Am begging yu, Miz Armstrong, don't use yu paper to keep this thing in the public domain." He mentioned nothing about a retraction and apology from Devlin, but I did not bother to pursue the matter, although I would have loved to print it in bold type, large font.

I was relieved to hear that I had some supporters in the ranks. I told him I would try and ensure that the situation died as quick a death as possible, but I suggested he keep a closer eye on the conduct of his officers, and to be more receptive to complaints against them, because I *knew definitely* that there had been complaints previously made against Devlin. It seemed to me that Superintendent Fergusson did not accept my advice gracefully.

But the situation did not die as quickly and as quietly as we would have liked. The paper was inundated with letters of support, so much so, that our mailbox could not contain them and the post office sent them round in a sack.

And another fall-out was that now persons were calling the newsroom with all sorts of stories of police brutality and misconduct and wanting to know how they could take action and get redress. Some of them wanted their stories printed in the paper. When they were referred to the Police Complaints Authority, they said I had no confidence in it, so they didn't either. I instructed Debbie to tell them that the Complaints Authority would do better now that things had been stirred up. I hoped I was right.

None of the media carried my statement about wanting a quiet life and within a day or two people stopped calling for interviews. But the radio talk shows continued to debate the issue of police conduct and accountability and I hoped that something positive would eventually come out of the whole situation.

So far my vacation had not been a stress-free and peaceful one. The five days from New Years to the fifth seemed like a month, and the fact that Richard was still not speaking to me did nothing to help give me a feeling of wellbeing.

He continued to hold me at arm's length, speaking to me only when it was necessary, or to make negative remarks, and I was beginning to despair that we would ever get back to that beautiful loving place where we had previously been. To everyone else, he was the same old Richard, but it had to be blatantly obvious to them that there was much tension between him and me. However, no one, other than his twin sister Rachel, had mentioned it.

I tried to keep in mind what Rachel had said, but he did not make it easy. However, he spent no more nights away from home for the remainder of the holiday, although he might as well have, since the minute he got into bed, he turned his back and fell asleep, leaving me more convinced than ever that he no longer loved me. When I woke in the mornings, he was invariably gone.

But I held it all inside, and now that the furore had quietened, I was determined to enjoy what was left of the vacation. We would all be returning to *Sweet Home* at the weekend and I would be back in the office next Monday, and I did not know when I would get another decent vacation.

The young people had been having the time of their lives. They swam and fished in the river which ran through the property; they made frequent trips into the resort town of Ocho Rios just a few miles away, to go to the beach, shows, and parties. They climbed Dunn's River Falls, and they went rafting on the White River.

They had met up with my Campbell relatives in the town and brought them back to the farm for a tour and an impromptu barbeque. My North American cousins were most impressed with the farm, and the way it was organised and run.

And I noticed that my little sister Samantha, who was eighteen years old, and Richard's nephew Trevor, who was almost twenty, were becoming a twosome. There was no reason why they shouldn't – they were not related by blood.

All of the young people were roughly the same age and got on like a house on fire. Stacy-Ann, at seventeen, was as gregarious as she had been at twelve, with a cheeky and vivacious personality, but if you left the "Ann" off of her name, she would not acknowledge you.

She and Samantha had also become firm friends, and I often found them giggling together, and was sure they were discussing Trevor, or Stacy-Ann's beau if she had one, or just boys in general.

The Missing Years

Richard's two sons, Richie and David were also nineteen and seventeen, like their cousins Trevor and Stacy-Ann. I wondered if it was pure coincidence that a pair of twins had had both their children within months of each other.

I had thought my own sisters Rachel and Rebecca would plan their children together, since they had always done everything else together, but they had not – well, except for the last two, perhaps, who had been born within weeks of each other.

Richie and David, and now Trevor too, attended school in the States, and in fact would be leaving for Miami in another couple of days. Stacy-Ann would also be starting college in Florida next September.

That left Neville, who at fourteen, was often left out of the evening and night-time activities of the older ones, to his chagrin and disgust. At these times Clivey would try to spar with him, but Neville always brushed him off, saying he was only a kid, which was also Clivey's complaint about his own younger siblings and cousins.

But everyone except me had been having a great vacation. My fathers and Delroy spent most of their time on the farm, actually doing manual labour because they wanted to; my mothers and Joy also picked and sorted produce for local or export sales, while the twins and their husbands mostly swam, climbed trees, went to the beach, and partied in the town.

Joy had become the Nanny-in-charge. She, with assistance from the household helpers, or the mothers, looked after and supervised the younger children's hygiene, meals and play. I was sure that the twins' children were not sure who were their natural mothers, and probably thought

Claudette Beckford-Brady

Joy was. Even back home in England she was their regular babysitter while the twenty-six year old twins partied every chance they got.

As for my Donovan and Adele, they seemed to find me redundant while their cousins were around, and they barely stopped to let me hug them, wriggling with impatience to go on their way, but I was gratified to see that they treated their father in the same vein. Richard came and went frequently, but he did not spend any more nights away from home.

We were due to return to Old Harbour on Sunday, and on Saturday afternoon Richard called me into the bedroom and said, "A want yu to come out with mi this evening. Show mi what clothes yu bring."

I was used to him telling me which outfit he liked to see me in when we went out together; that was not the problem. The problem was that there was no friendliness in his tone and it did not sound like an invitation, but more like an order. I told him I did not feel like going out tonight.

He fixed me with his direct gaze and I met it head on. It might have turned into a contest of wills, but I had just about run out of patience with him, and I think my expression and body language said so. I literally saw his thought process as he decided he could catch more flies with honey than with vinegar.

His face relaxed slightly, but he did not smile. "I'm meeting with some international music promoters tonight; their wives would like to meet you." He paused, and seeing that my face remained closed, he continued, "I'd really like it if you would come with me; I'm trying to set up a concert tour for Peace and Love, and one of the wives has read your book and asked to meet you. If yu won't do it fah mi, do it for the guys."

"Peace and Love" was a duo of deejay/singer/songwriters that Richard had recorded and was managing, and who were beginning to make a name for themselves in the business. An international tour would be a great thing for them and for Richard too. I did not want to stymie their chances, although I did not see why my absence should affect their deal. I showed him the two evening dresses I had brought with me and he said neither was good enough. He didn't say it, but I knew he wanted to show me off.

He asked me if I would drive into Ochee with him and purchase one. I gave in gracefully and didn't give him any more opposition, although I was steaming at the fact that he had only asked me because a fan wanted to meet me, and he didn't want to put a business deal at risk. But no problem.

The boutique was a quaint little store which also sold jewellery and a few craft items. The tall slender lady – probably the owner, as was later confirmed – who came to our assistance obviously knew Richard well, because as soon as we entered the store and she saw him, she came over, all smiles.

"Richard! What a pleasant surprise! We never see you these days; how are you?" She kissed both his cheeks. "Come into my office," and she led the way through the store to a small room at the back, Richard and I following behind her, while the two sales assistants looked on in curiosity.

She did not acknowledge my presence immediately; did not even seem to see me, and I stood in the small room, waiting to be introduced. Richard smiled the first genuine smile I had seen from him in days, and said, "I'm a very busy man these days, Cerise."

Claudette Beckford-Brady

I watched the interaction between them and decided that Cerise was far too familiar with my husband. It was time she acknowledged my presence. I smiled sweet poison at her and said, "Yes, he sure is. The kids and I keep him occupied when the farm and studio doesn't."

I was not trying to be subtle. I was defending my territory in no uncertain terms. Richard knew exactly where I was at, and so did she. She finally deigned to see me, and Richard belatedly said, as if I were an afterthought, "Oh; Cerise, this is my wife, Michelle; I need you to outfit her for a special occasion tonight."

He had introduced me to her, but did not introduce *her* to *me*, and I felt as if I were an object and not a person, let alone his wife, and I resented not being allowed the freedom to choose my own outfit. I decided to hate everything she suggested but I said nothing further.

She too seemed to think I was an object, as she looked me over with a professional eye. "Hmm, let me see now. I think... Yes, definitely..." She went to the door and spoke to someone inside the store. "Avril, bring that grey silk... Yes..., I think it will fit..."

"Grey?" I thought. *"Is she trying to make me look drab?"*

But when the dress came, and she fitted it, I found that it was perfect and I decided to forget about hating it. Richard liked it too. It was a strapless dress, which hugged my bosom and contoured to my waist, before flaring away in small neat pleats. It swirled and swished deliciously around my legs when I walked.

Cerise brought out accessories from a closet inside her office; a royal blue choker, a pair of blue high heeled sandals which were the perfect size, a matching silk evening bag, a pair of dainty diamond teardrops with a matching bracelet. The woman knew her stuff, I reluctantly conceded.

When she quoted the price, I nearly had kittens, but Richard didn't bat an eyelid. He simply handed her his credit card and she put through the transaction, and we left, with Cerise telling him not to be a stranger. I was dying to know how long he had known her and whether they had ever been an item. There was a certain possessive quality about the way she interacted with Richard.

Before he and I had become a couple, Lynette Barrington had told me that Richard kept a mistress, but found women in general to be "less than refined and more than mercenary." I wondered if Cerise was included in that assessment, and decided that she fit the bill. But I didn't ask Richard anything about her, and we drove back to Walkers Wood in a silence that was only slightly less hostile than it had been before.

We were meeting the promoters for dinner at the Jamaica Grande Hotel on Main Street in Ocho Rios. As I came down the stairs, all decked out in my new outfit, I noticed with a great deal of surprise that Delisia was all dressed up too, and I was about to remark on it when I got yet another surprise. Daddy Armstrong came from his suite on the ground floor and he too was dressed to kill. He took Delisia's arm and said, "Ready to roll, you two? Richard is outside already."

What was going on here? Why had Richard not seen fit to tell me that Delisia and Daddy Armstrong would be in the party? And hello…? Was something building between my erstwhile mother and my father-in-law?

First Samantha and Trevor, and now Delisia and Daddy Armstrong? If I was right, talk about keep it in the family! I

Claudette Beckford-Brady

would have to pay more attention to what was going on around me.

But I didn't have time to ponder because the family had come to see us off, and were exclaiming over how beautiful I looked. Delisia too got her fair share of compliments, and indeed she looked remarkably beautiful. She seemed to have dropped ten years since the day I had seen her at the airport six months previously.

We finally left, Richard driving his father's BMW. At the hotel gatehouse the security guard said, "Guh straight chew, Missa Armstrong. Missa Clunis just phone chew to si if you come yet. A wi call him room and mek him know seh yu reach."

At the hotel reception we were outfitted with our identity bracelets and given directions to the suite. It turned out that Delisia was here in the capacity of legal adviser. While she and Richard were closeted with Messrs. Clunis and Smith, hammering out their deal, Mrs Clunis, Mrs Smith, myself and Daddy Armstrong drank cocktails and socialised.

Beverley Clunis was a schoolteacher, and, she told me, an avid reader. She had read my book and thoroughly enjoyed it, she said. She had discovered quite by accident, while reading the Sunday paper, that her husband's prospective business partner was married to Michelle Freeman (I still wrote using my maiden name), and had begged to meet me. She even had a copy of my book she wanted me to autograph for her.

She was a white woman; petite, blonde and curvy. From time to time she interjected Jamaican words and phrases into her conversation, and she spoke the best Jamaican I had ever heard from a white person; if one wasn't actually looking at

The Missing Years

her, one would believe her to be a true Jamaican.

Janet Smith was of Barbadian extraction, but had been born in the UK. She worked at Brixton Job Centre and I found that we knew a few people in common. She had not read my book yet, but had purchased a copy from a local bookstore, and also wanted it autographed. Daddy Armstrong was charming, and delighted the ladies with his wit and sense of humour.

After about an hour and a half the men and Delisia wrapped up their business and we had a late dinner, before heading over to the White River Reggae Park where Peace and Love would be performing. I gathered from the men's broad smiles that they had reached agreement, and this was confirmed when I heard them making arrangements for another meeting, this time with the artistes, to sign the contracts.

The White River Reggae Park was packed to capacity with locals and tourists alike. It was to be a star-studded line-up – Dennis Brown, John Holt, The Mighty Diamonds, Gregory Isaacs, Derrick Morgan, Mutabaruka and General Trees, amongst others, and of course, Peace and Love, who gave a sterling performance which left the promoters eager to finalise the deal.

Daddy Armstrong amazed me. For a man of his years – and he was over seventy, although he didn't look it – he partied extremely well. His favourite performer was Derrick Morgan, who was known as the "King of Ska" – ska being the precursor to "Rock Steady" Reggae.

Derrick's performance also "mashed up the place" as he had the crowd gyrating and singing along to his hit tunes; *Ride the Rhythm, Blazing Fire, Miss Lulu* and many others.

Claudette Beckford-Brady

We watched the show from the side of the stage, and when the music "sweet us" we danced energetically. At first Delisia was a little reticent, but Daddy Armstrong's enthusiasm soon had her warmed up and loose, and I watched the two of them in amazement as they rocked to the rhythm of the drum and the bass.

The promoters and their wives too were having a ball, only Richard alone stood to the back of the stage area and did not dance, although he seemed to be enjoying the show, nodding his head and tapping his foot to the beat.

I danced along with the others and decided to enjoy myself fully. I had not been to a stage show in a long while and you could almost say that the entire line-up were my favourite artistes. However, my particular favourites were Derrick Morgan, John Holt, and the Mighty Diamonds.

In fact, Derrick was a personal friend of the Armstrong family; I had met him several times, and after his performance we went backstage to say "hi."

After Peace and Love had performed early on, Richard had given them the outline of the deal, which seemed to please and excite them a great deal. They were both just twenty years old and neither had ever left Jamaica's shores. They were eagerly looking forward to their UK tour, which could lead to Europe, Japan, and the world, if successful.

I was to get a big surprise before we left to go home. The show was still swinging, with the Mighty Diamonds doing their stint, accompanied by the audience; *"I need a roof over my head and bread on my table..."*

Richard seemed to have loosened up a bit and he now stood with the rest of us, who were taking a break from dancing. The Mighty Diamonds finished their performance

The Missing Years

and John Holt came on stage. Daddy Armstrong told us that he was not as young as we were and if Richard would walk him and Delisia out they would get a taxi and go home. Richard did, and came back a few minutes later.

In the event we were not far behind them. John Holt was singing *"Baby I'm-a want you..."* and I was caught completely off guard when Richard pulled me into his arms and started dancing with me. After my initial stiff, surprised reaction I relaxed and enjoyed being in his arms, as Mr Holt sang the loving words which Richard should have been saying to me...

> *"...You're the only one I care enough to hurt about;*
> *Maybe I'm-a crazy, but I just can't live without*
> *your loving and affection, giving me direction,*
> *like a guiding light to help me through my darkest night,*
> *lately I'm-a praying, that you'll always be a-staying,*
> *beside me..."*

It felt so good; it seemed like years since he had held me, and I forgot that we were not speaking as I leaned into him, holding him as if I would never let him go. He tightened his hold on me, and we barely moved to the music, just swayed slightly, and then he kissed my neck.

A wave of desire rushed over me, helped by the lyrics Mr Holt was crooning in his velvet voice, and my knees almost gave way, but I was anchored by Richard's hold. He couldn't fool me; he wanted me too, and he sighed deeply against my neck.

"Let's go home," I whispered, and he didn't seem to need persuading. We said goodbye to the promoters and their wives, and Howie and Wayne who comprised Peace and Love, and left. It took forever to get out of the parking area, because some of the vehicles were parked so badly, but eventually we negotiated our way out and headed for Walkers Wood.

Daddy Armstrong and Delisia had obviously already retired – separately I hoped – as only the hall and stair lights were burning.

Richard and I couldn't get up the stairs fast enough, and started undressing even before we entered our room. Shoes remained where they were kicked off; the very expensive grey silk dress slithered to the floor without a second thought, while the bag was thrown carelessly into a chair. We fell onto the bed and started devoured each other, and at some point Richard removed the choker from around my throat and in the morning I found it clear across the room where he had thrown it.

CHAPTER TEN

Malicious Gossip

In the morning we made love again; slow, sensuous love, with Richard being his old gentle self. There was no rush to leave the bed; I had expressed milk for Estelle and she was with Joy.

Afterwards I lay in his arms, sated, but not quite contented. The air had not been cleared; passion had overtaken us, but there were still un-discussed issues between us. Neither of us said anything for a long while, both of us probably afraid of breaking the spell.

But we had slept late – it was past nine o'clock; something unheard of for Richard, and late even for me – and we would all be leaving for Old Harbour after lunch, so like it or not, we eventually had to move. He finally let out a deep sigh and said, with a hint of his old humour, "Well, A can't run the world from this bed; guess I gotta go."

We showered separately, him first, while I picked up our clothes and tidied the room. When he was dressed and heading out the door, he pecked my cheek. "Si yu downstairs."

Claudette Beckford-Brady

I stripped the bed and left the sheets in a pile on the floor for the helper. Then I packed all our things before bathing and getting dressed. Everyone was downstairs when I got there and all had already had breakfast. I was starving and was gratified when Blossom brought me some roast breadfruit and ackee and saltfish, and orange juice. She said Richard had eaten and gone down on the farm to talk to Derrick, his cousin and farm manager.

Delisia was very upbeat and lively, and declared that she couldn't remember the last time she had had so much fun. Daddy Armstrong too, said it had been years since he had been out so late, but it had made him feel ten years younger.

I watched him and Delisia carefully to see if there was chemistry between them; it had seemed so to me last night, but that might just have been the excitement of the time. I don't know if it was my imagination, but it seemed to me that his smile, when bestowed upon her, was extra warm, which warmth seemed reciprocated.

Chuh! I was probably imagining it.

Richie, David, and Trevor had all left for Miami the previous Thursday, leaving Samantha dejected and Stacy-Ann consoling. Auntie said that the place was going to seem like a morgue when we had all gone, she didn't know how she was going to fill her time. Daddy Armstrong spoke the first patois words I had ever heard out of his mouth.

"Gwaan! Yu always find something to do, all when yu don't need to, yu ole workaholic, yu!" He chucked his sister under the chin and she slapped his hand away, saying mock-severely, "You gwaan yu ways, Sarr!"

I studied my father-in-law carefully. He was acting out

of character. Never, in the six years I had known him, had he spoken a word of patois in my hearing, or acted so jocular. He was laughing a lot, too, and had said he felt ten years younger, and did indeed *look* ten years younger. I turned my attention back to Delisia and caught what I swear was a secret smile pass between the two.

My God! I *was* right! There *was* something going on there!

I saw it again when we were leaving. Everyone was kissing and embracing and remembering last minute things to tell each other, Samantha and Stacy-Ann in particular. Clivey couldn't find his favourite cap and had to go searching for it, delaying our departure. Delisia and Daddy Armstrong stood a little off to one side, seemingly in earnest conversation.

When we were finally ready to leave, he kissed her cheek and said, "Call," and she answered, "A shore will."

Well! If that didn't beat all! I wondered if Richard was aware of what was happening between our two parents, for something surely was. And Daddy Armstrong must be at *least* twenty years her senior.

We made good going and got back to Island Farm in a little under ninety minutes. Delisia was leaving the island tomorrow and was going to Country to pick up her suitcases and say her goodbyes. Richard parked the bus, picked up his car, which Wilbert, as good as his word, had had repaired, kissed my cheek and said, "Don't wait up," kissed the kids, and he and Delisia drove off.

He did not come home that night.

In the morning he turned up early with Delisia in tow, before I left for work. She had come to say farewell, and it seemed that Richard, instead of Daniel, was taking her to the airport. I held down my angry and insecure feelings, and said a pleasant bon voyage to Delisia, who remarked that the time had flown so fast, and so much had happened that she and I had had no opportunity to catch up.

I left for work as soon as I could decently get away, leaving Delisia and my parents in conversation, and Richard playing tag with the kids, since her flight was not till around noon.

It was good to be back at work. My return sort of caused a small flare up of last week's excitement but I squashed it as quickly as I could, saying that it was over and done. I tried to avoid being in public, and skulked like a thief from the car into the SmallRock building and back again, not venturing onto the streets of Old Harbour. Give them time to forget the whole damn thing.

My partners and I had been thinking for some time about expanding our local readership base, and we were in the planning stages of changing the *St. Catherine District Bell* from a single parish paper to cover the whole of the south coast. The new product would be called the *South Coast Weekly* and would incorporate the *Districk Bell*.

We were in a meeting discussing our plans, when Denise, the receptionist buzzed through to say there was a woman in Reception to see me. She said her name was Lydia Campbell and that she was my cousin.

I groaned inwardly. No doubt *Courts* was coming to repossess her furniture, or her light (electricity) was about to be disconnected, or perhaps it was one of the kids needing to go to the doctors, or needing school shoes. There was always someone needing something, and I tried to accommodate them all as best I could, knowing that times were difficult, and that not everyone was fortunate enough to be as solvent as I was.

But there were an awful lot of them, and sometimes it seemed that the multitude of wants and needs would overwhelm me. I had asked them not to bring their problems to the office, but to see me at home, or otherwise, phone. I supposed if Lydia was actually here, it must be more urgent than usual.

I didn't think it was anything to do with Grandma, because Lydia had moved down from Country and was living at Freetown with a new baby-father. I told Denise to tell her to wait in the reception area and I wrapped up my meeting in another twenty minutes and called her into my office.

Lydia was Uncle Kingsley's oldest daughter, and she was a few years older than I was. Lydia did not like me very much; she resented the fact that I had been the recipient of so much generosity from my Grandma and North American relatives, who had not only assisted me financially in the setting up of my business, but had also contributed to the building of the house on the hilltop.

Lydia coveted both the hilltop and the house; I had overheard her and another cousin discussing me, and their resentment had been palpable. However, she had no idea that I knew how she felt, for I had kept it completely to myself, not even mentioning it to Grandma.

I greeted her with a pleasant smile. "Hi Cousin Lydia; how yu do? Here, sit down. Yu want some juice, or some water?" I held a chair for her and she placed her now ample bottom in it. When I had first met her back in 1978 she had been a slim twenty-year old; now she was a very fat thirty-four year old and looked more like forty-five.

Claudette Beckford-Brady

She sat down and said, "Yu doan't 'ave nuh Pepsi?" I wanted to tell her that she should lay off the sodas and try to lose some weight, but I refrained. She would probably take it the wrong way. I went to the fridge and opened it; there was no Pepsi, but there was a bottle of *Ting* which I handed to her. Then I said, "So, it must be important for you to come to the office; if you remember, I did ask oonu not to check mi here-suh. What's the problem?"

"A get a chance fi guh Cayman fi work, but A haff to let the woman know by dis evelin. The trouble is a doan't have di money fi mi fare. A was wandering if yu could len' mi some?"

Now, generally when they asked to 'borrow' money, it was not usually repaid, but we maintained the fallacy that it would be. I did not want lack of funds to stand in the way of her trying to make a better life for herself, and asked her how much she needed. She told me, and I wrote a cash cheque which she could take to the bank and change straight away.

She did not seem in any particular hurry to leave, and I humoured her. She chatted about various things, told me that she was leaving her new baby-father because he beat her, and then floored me with the statement; "Yu need to watch Delisia, yu-nuh. Memba seh she's a man-stealer; she did try fi t'ief yu faada from Mavis, and now it look like shi deh try a ting wid yu husban'."

She was being ridiculous of course, and in any case I was sure there was something brewing between Delisia and Daddy Armstrong. I was slightly annoyed at what I considered to be Lydia's spitefulness, and I had no idea why she should want to cause contention between Delisia, who was her aunt, and me. I hid my annoyance and laughed.

"Don't be daft, Lydia. My husband does not stray, and if

he did, it would not be with my mother. They happen to be very close; Richard was very kind to her when she first came back, even when *I* myself wasn't."

I realised belatedly that I had actually referred to Delisia as my mother, but did not have time to dwell on it. Lydia responded, "Well, why him spen' suh-much time a Country wid har, an which part dem guh naily every evelin, den, an nuh come back till before-day, eeh? An sometime him sleep eena di house a Country an doan leave till maaning. Mi may nuh live a Country aggen, but mi know everyting weh gwaan up deh."

I had not been back to Country since Christmas night when the robbery had taken place, and I did not often see any of the Country cousins, unless they wanted something. I was quite shocked to hear that Richard had been spending time up there, and with Delisia in particular.

But I was sure there was a good explanation, although why he should see fit to keep it secret from me, I had no idea. And I knew Grandma would not countenance anything out of order, and Lydia must know it too.

But it did explain where he had been on the nights he had not come home. Did that account for *all* of the late and missing nights? I wanted to know a great deal more, but I was not going to give Lydia the satisfaction. I had my own way of gleaning information; I *was* a journalist, after all. I needed her out of there.

"Well, Lydia, I have a whole heap of work to catch up on; yu know I just came back from a week in St. Ann. I hope things work out for you in the Cayman Islands." I had opened my office door and stood waiting, while she heaved her bulk out of the chair and put the *Ting* bottle on my desk. She was being dismissed. On the way out she said, "Mi like how yu hangle di police bwoy, Cousin Shellie. Big up."

When she had left I sat down at my desk and stared into space. *Why* had Richard been spending time at Country, and where did he and Delisia go off to, not returning till late? And why hadn't he told me about it, and explained their reasons?

Did any member of my family know about it, and know the reasons? Did Daddy and Mavis? Grandma? Daniel? It would humiliate me to ask any of them – well, perhaps not Grandma – but then I shouldn't have to. I deserved an explanation from Richard himself. And, now that Delisia was gone, would the late and all night business stop? Well; we would see.

But try as I might, I could not get the conversation with Lydia out of my mind. Could Delisia *really* be making moves on Richard? I shook myself mentally. Ridiculous, of course. And Richard was bigger than that. He would not humiliate me that way.

But *could* she? She could be devious; had entered into a relationship with Daddy when she *knew* he was living with Mavis and that they had a son. And I suddenly recalled that she was only five years my husband's senior – they were closer in age than I was to him, since he was twelve years older than me.

But what about the interaction I had noticed between her and Daddy Armstrong? Was it a blind to cover up her and Richard's relationship? The thoughts tumbled around in my head and I could give myself no satisfactory answer.

In the evening Richard himself came to pick me up. He had been at the studio next door and came to see if I was ready, and it so happened I was. He was gradually returning

The Missing Years

to his old self, and he kissed me and asked if I had had a good day. I said I had, although after Lydia's visit the day had rapidly gone downhill.

My temper had been short, and a reporter and Prento, the clerical assistant and trainee printer had felt the sharp edge of my tongue, for which I later apologised. It was not fair to take out my feelings on them.

Richard chatted about inconsequential things on the way home, and I asked him if Delisia had gotten off okay. He said she had and changed the subject, asking me what I was doing about Adele's birthday, which was the next day.

I told him that a joint party was planned for the weekend, because Clivey would also be having his tenth birthday on the fifteenth, just three days after Adele's fifth. I wanted to add that if he spent a little more time with his family he would have been aware of the plans, but I didn't. Neither of us mentioned the fact that he had not come home last night.

Over the next few days he was almost his old self. On Saturday we had a joint birthday party for Adele and Clivey, and on Saturday evening Richard went away and again did not come home till almost five a.m. Sunday morning.

So, Delisia was gone, but he was still staying out with no explanation. I was going to have to have it out with him, but I decided to wait until after Wednesday when everyone would be on their way back to the UK.

Many of the overseas visitors had already returned to their respective homes, and the rest would all be gone before the end of the month. My immediate family were leaving on Wednesday, and it would once again be just me and Daddy and Mavis.

Claudette Beckford-Brady

Richard disappeared again Sunday afternoon, but returned home just before midnight. I said nothing, but bided my time till Wednesday.

I said my goodbyes at home and did not accompany them to the airport with Mavis and Daddy, who drove the bus. Their departure left *Sweet Home* feeling deserted and I quite understood Auntie's saying the place would be like a morgue.

On Wednesday evening I decided that there was no time like the present. Everyone was gone, and Richard and I were totally alone in the house for the first time since before Christmas. Estelle was sleeping contentedly, Donovan and Adele were in their beds and Richard and I were downstairs having a late supper.

"Richard," I said without preamble, "are you having an affair?"

His hand stopped halfway to his mouth, and he replaced the forkful of fish onto the plate. "WHAT?!"

"You heard me."

He regarded me in silence for a very long few seconds, and then he said, "Whatever gives you that idea?"

"Well," I said, "you've been staying out till all hours; sometimes all night, and I know you're not at the studio. And someone suggested that you and Delisia had gotten mighty close, going off someplace together on a regular basis and not returning till late in the night, and I mean, she *is* closer to you in age than I am…"

His expression became even more incredulous and I wondered if he were playacting. "Yu think I'm having an affair *with yu mother?*"

"Well… I don't know… *You* tell *me*."

The Missing Years

"Yu know how ridiculous yu sound?"

"Yu know how lonely and insecure yu been making me feel?"

We stared at each other. Finally, after a long silence, he said, "I am not having an affair with your mother. Satisfied?"

I was not. "Then can you explain where you and she have been going, why it keeps you away from home at night, and why it has been kept a secret from me?" I hurried on. "Can you tell me why I had to hear about it from a malicious bad-minded person, and be made to feel so small because it's an open secret and I was the last to find out?"

He pushed back his chair from the table and stood up, leaving half his food on the plate. I stood up too; I do not know where he was going, but he was not going until he had answered my questions fully.

He sat on a sofa and patted the empty place beside him. I ignored it and sat in a different chair. He shrugged his shoulders and began to speak.

"First of all," he said, staring into my face, "I *can't believe* you'd think I was having an affair, let alone with *your own mother*! What kind of person yu take mi for, eeh? Where is your trust? I'm mortified, Michelle.

"Secondly, I can't believe that you, a journalist and writer who is supposed to be super-observant, has not seen the sparks and interaction between our two parents."

So he *had* noticed, and I had not been mistaken. Okay, fine; but what business did he and Delisia have which involved them being out late at night? I said nothing, and he continued to speak.

"A didn't broadcast what A was about because A didn't think it was anyone's business. I intended to tell yu at some point, but A decided to wait until I'd done what A set out to do. A didn't intend to mek yu feel lonely and insecure, and as a matter of fact, A don't see any reason why yu should have. Yu were surrounded by your entire family, and I had no reason to believe you would ever doubt my love or respect fah yu."

He stopped speaking and bored into me with his dark piercing eyes. Was he waiting for me to make some response? But he still hadn't told me what he and Delisia had been doing.

And why *wouldn't* he think I'd feel lonely and insecure, when he had been totally ignoring me for the most part, except to chastise or criticise me, and when he had not even respected me enough to let me know when he was not coming home, or trusted me enough to tell me what he and Delisia were up to. I said, "You still haven't told me what you and Delisia..."

He held up a hand, and I stopped speaking. "A would have asked you to help me, as my wife, but you'd just had a baby. So A did the next best thing and asked yu mother, who was more than willing, and – no disrespect to you – was probably the more appropriate person."

I was beginning not to resent so much Delisia being referred to as my mother. I had accepted the fact that I now had three mothers. But what did he mean by "more appropriate person?" I said nothing, and he continued.

"I felt a burden of guilt and responsibility to the two families of the dead and injured youths. A decided to visit with them and do what A could to assist them. I had initially intended only to pay medical and funeral expenses, but when I saw how they lived, I felt I needed to do more.

The Missing Years

"The grandmother of the dead youth, for instance, lived in a tumble-down old shack which leaked. She slept on a thin piece of sponge on the floor, and depended on the charity of her neighbours for sustenance. The boy had been her only family, and means of support, even if it was mostly from ill-gotten gains; his father, her son, was doing life in a New York prison for murder.

"I wanted to move her into a good Golden Age home that I know of, but she has not left her Country for fifty years and wanted to stay there. So I had the shack torn down, and built her a new house, and employed the injured boy's mother to look after her. They too, the boy and his mother, will live in the house and when the old lady dies, it will become theirs outright; Delisia has drawn up all the paperwork.

"As for the reason we were out late so often, it was usually evening before I could get the chance to go and check on things; and Miss Esme is an old woman with no-one – I had to make all the funeral arrangements and organise the set-up. Sometimes I was so tired that it was just easier to stay at Country rather than drive all the way from Connors to come home."

I privately wondered if he was a little afraid of the country road at night, bearing in mind what had happened there on Christmas night. But he was still speaking.

"But it's finally over now; the set-up was Saturday night; the funeral Sunday. They will get their money in the bank every month. The money will stop when the old lady dies and no longer needs looking after – I am not going to support the other boy and his mother for life; he will make a full recovery, and they have a house that he can return to when he has served his sentence. No need to reward him for his wrongdoing. I will have paid my dues.

"So, as I said, it's over. I'll have no more reason to go there. That's all."

He stopped speaking, and I stared at him in amazement. He had been doing all of that, and didn't think he should have said something to me about it? Did he think I would have objected, or what? I was about to ask him when he spoke again. "I'd rather you kept this to yourself. It's nobody's business."

"Does Grandma know?" I asked. He nodded. "Yes, but she and Delisia are the only ones, apart from the people in Connors District. Sooner or later it will become common knowledge, I suppose, but for now we have tried to keep it low key."

"Well!" I said, for want of something better to say. I didn't know *what* to say. I began to feel extremely foolish. Imagine, I had accused my husband of having an affair with my mother! God! He must think I'm deranged!

But I was glad he had done what he had. It would help him as well as the beneficiaries; perhaps now his guilt would be assuaged and he would return to his former self. I told him that I was glad for what he had done, and that it was the sort of thing which made him stand out from other men, and which made me love and respect him all the more. My words sounded trite and inadequate but were sincerely spoken.

I only hoped, I thought privately, that he would never, ever have to use that gun again.

Thinking of the gun sent a chill down my spine and I suddenly realised that we had not discussed it. I wondered where it was now; was it here, in our house? I wanted to know, and since we were clearing the air, we might as well dispose of all outstanding issues. I didn't want to upset him over again, but I felt I had a right to know if a weapon of death was in my home.

"Aahm, Richard?"

"What?"

"What about the gun?"

"What about it?"

"Well," I said, "the fact that you have one at all. Don't you think you should have told me?"

"Why?"

I was getting exasperated. "Well, I don't know – because I'm your wife, maybe...?"

"There was no reason for you to know. It's not something one broadcasts and the fewer people who know about it, the better."

I sighed. "Richard, I am not *people*; I am your wife. Where is the gun now? Do you carry it on your person at all times, just sometimes, or what? Where did you take it from on the night – one minute your hand was empty, the next it had a gun in it? Do you leave it in the house sometimes? Could my children inadvertently get a-hold of it...?"

Here he interrupted me. "I didn't realise you took me for a fool, Michelle. Like I would be stupid enough or irresponsible enough to leave a gun where a child could get at it... Thanks!"

I started to speak to tell him I was sorry, but he cut me off. "I own a gun, not because I want to hurt or kill people, but because we live in a society and climate where it is expedient for some persons to have added protection. My business interests and our position in society make us a target of criminals; that is the only reason I possess a gun.

"Now, you can rest assured that I will *always* protect my family at any or all costs, and *that* is *all* you need to know. You need know *nothing* about the gun; just trust me. Can you do that Michelle? Can yu trust me? Now, let's put ourselves and the matter to bed, shall we?"

It was not a request. His voice told me he had had enough of the discussion. I cleared up our half-eaten suppers and tidied the kitchen so Lurline would not come in to dirty plates in the morning. When I returned to the living room he had already gone upstairs.

I felt a little better in myself. I had not gotten all the answers I had been seeking, but my main concerns had been addressed. I hoped things would get back to normal now; that Richard and I could get back to that beautiful place in our relationship where we had been since our marriage. I did not want ever to leave that place again; it was lonely and distressing to be without the mainstay of one's life, and I was extremely thankful for having Richard. I never ever wanted to be without him.

I looked in on the children, had my bath and joined him in the bed. I felt lighter and more relaxed than I had in a very long time, and when I turned to him and initiated our lovemaking, he responded with fervour, and we rode the waves of passion until we fell exhaustedly asleep.

CHAPTER ELEVEN

A Pleasant Interlude with Delisia

Nineteen ninety-three had not gotten off to a very good start, but now that things were rosy again between Richard and me, everything else seemed to improve too. SmallRock Publications opened a small office in Mandeville with two staff members to co-ordinate the news from the parishes of Manchester and St. Elizabeth, and things were in full gear for the launch of the new publication.

I had been extremely busy, but more and more I found my mind being invaded and my work interrupted by thoughts of Delisia. Richard had been singing her praises, telling me what an intelligent woman she was, and how I would benefit from having a closer relationship with her. He said I had let a good opportunity to bond with her slip by while we were all at Walkers Wood, and that I should communicate more with her by phone, and he even suggested that I take a trip to California to visit her.

I still could not help feeling a little peeved at his continued championing of Delisia, and I was jealous of their easy friendship. I kept remembering the fact that Delisia was only five years Richard's senior and I wondered had Richard met her first, would he have fallen in love with *her*?

Richard, always very intuitive about my feelings, told me point blank that I had no reason to be jealous of Delisia; he loved *me*, and only wanted to see me and my mother develop a close loving relationship. I denied being jealous.

"Don't be ridiculous, Richard Armstrong. Of course I'm not jealous of my own mother."

"You *are* too. You practically accused me of having an affair with her."

"I never *accused* you; I only asked you *if* you were. Anyway we were all under a lot of pressure at the time, and I guess I *was* a little irrational. But I realise now that I was being foolish, and anyway, as you yourself pointed out, there seems to be something brewing between her and your father."

Richard was rubbing my feet while I lay back against a mound of pillows. I loved having my feet rubbed; it was so relaxing. He responded to my last statement. "Now ain't *that* something? Your mother and my father. I like it."

"You *would*," I said. "And don't forget your nephew Trevor and my sister Samantha. This family is becoming far too intertwined."

Richard left off one foot and started on the other. "There's nothing wrong with that. It's not as if any of them are directly related by blood."

I was intrigued by the intricacies of such tangled relations. If my mother and Daddy Armstrong got together, my mother would become my husband's stepmother as well as being his mother-in-law, and my father-in-law would also become my stepfather. Samantha, who was Richard's sister-in-law, would become his niece-by-marriage if she and Trevor wed. Rachel, my sister-in-law, would become my sister's mother-in-law...

I decided to stop trying to work it all out. I felt relaxed and drowsy, and Richard had left off my foot and was lightly trailing his fingers up my leg, and along the sensitive parts of my inner thighs and my attention turned to more urgent matters.

We made slow sensuous love which left me utterly sated and happy, with no doubts in my mind that my husband loved me.

The following day I had decided to call Delisia. California time was some four hours behind ours, and so I waited till I knew she would be about arriving at her office, and called her there.

She seemed delighted at my call. I told her I was sorry that I had not spent more time with her at the family reunion and at Walkers Wood, and that next time she was on the island I would be sure to make time for her. She replied that with all the drama that had taken place over the holidays – the armed robbery and Richard's shooting of the two youths, and my drama with Sergeant Devlin – she quite understood. She said I could always take a trip to California to see her, if I wanted to. She would pay my expenses.

I told her that as soon as I could find time from work I would take her up on her offer, and I actually started to forward plan to see when I would be able to take a trip.

Despite myself, I was beginning to like Delisia. She had blossomed at Walkers Wood, and I noticed that she and my other two mothers had become great friends, and had often been heard giggling together like young girls. I still felt that

Claudette Beckford-Brady

she and I had some unresolved issues, but those could be addressed at some future time, and without antagonism and drama.

As it turned out, before I could take up her offer to visit, Delisia herself returned to Jamaica at Easter. She had called a week before to say that she would be staying at the *Jamaica Grande* in Ocho Rios and that she would be glad to book a room for Richard and I to come down for a couple of days, if we wanted to, just the two of us.

She said this was a spur of the moment trip, and we could use the opportunity to start getting to know each other better. She belatedly added that David, Richard's father, would also be her guest, and that the two men could keep each other company while she and I rapped.

So, I thought, things are progressing on that front. I wondered seriously if my father-in-law was slated for becoming my stepfather. Well, stranger things have happened, I suppose.

I agreed to go. Since that initial phone call we had been in constant touch, and I too thought it was high time we started getting to know each other better. And then of course I was nosey enough to want to know about her relationships over the years, if she had had any. I rather got the impression that she had been an ice maiden where the opposite sex was concerned, and I was rather surprised at the sparks between her and Daddy Armstrong.

We took the children with us as far as Walkers Wood and left Adele and Donovan with Auntie; it was the Easter holidays and their two half-brothers whom they adored, and who adored them in return, were on vacation from Miami. On the way home Richard and I would pick them up and the

The Missing Years

two young men would spend the rest of the holidays at *Sweet Home.*

Daddy and Mavis had opted not to go to Walkers Wood this time. They had been home now for some eight months and had settled into island life, happy and comfortable with their farm and their home.

Daddy woke "before-day" every morning and was down on his farm, sometimes while it was still dark. He said he loved to feel the early morning air and see the dew on the plants. I asked him if he had drunk dew water from coco leaves as he had told me he used to do before he had gone to England. He said he had planted a few roots of coco specifically for that purpose.

He had bought a pregnant cow that he named Doris. Doris had just dropped a calf and Adele had named her Star because she had a little white star in the centre of her forehead. Every morning we had fresh milk, together with the fresh eggs from Mavis' layer hens, of which she had two dozen, and from which she supplemented their income by the sale of eggs to the locals.

Daddy's farm supplied the local higglers (market women or informal traders) with red peas (kidney beans), callaloo, peppers, pumpkins, cucumbers, tomatoes, okra, pak choy, and when in season, sorrel and gungu peas. He also had mixed orchards of citrus; oranges – various varieties – limes, tangerines and grapefruit; he had many varieties of mango too, and bananas and plantains, breadfruit, ackee, and coconuts. Daddy had taken Richard's advice and was running the farm as a business concern and keeping books, which I had shown Mavis how to do.

She and Daddy had never been happier or more

Claudette Beckford-Brady

contented. I remember back in England Mavis had always had trouble getting up in the mornings, and had been perpetually late for work; now she delighted in getting up early, because she "wanted to" she said, and not because she "had to." It made all the difference, she said.

She and her household helper, Miss Pearl, had become fast friends, and worked together side by side, be it cleaning, cooking, in the garden, or whatever; and whatever they were doing it was always accompanied by lots of gossip and laughter.

Neither of my parents had reached pension age and both were still young enough to really enjoy being home on their beloved island. Before going to England Daddy had traveled the island a bit, but the farthest Mavis had been from her home in the country district of Ginger Ridge, and later from Joe Grung where she had been living with Daddy, had been to Spanish Town and May Pen.

Since coming home she had been to Walkers Wood and Ocho Rios, eaten roast yam and saltfish at Faith's Pen, and fish and festival at Helshire Beach. She had plans to explore the entire island at her leisure and I wanted to be her tour guide, whenever I could fit it in with running my business.

Richard and I, and even Adele, were experts on the island and its culture; we had been almost everywhere – to the known places, and the unknown; all the little nooks and crannies and places off the beaten track that tourists know nothing about, and which is the real Jamaica, our beloved island.

But until I had the time to show her, she could take herself and Daddy to the main tourist areas of Montego Bay, Negril, and Ocho Rios; she could visit all the other parishes

The Missing Years

and the various attractions; Green Grotto Caves in St. Ann, Lover's Leap in St. Elizabeth, Reach Falls in Portland; she could visit the mineral baths at Milk River in Clarendon, Rockfort in Kingston, or Bath Fountain in St. Thomas. This beloved island was full of places to go, and to see.

But for now, she and Daddy were quite happy just running their home and farm, and on Good Friday morning when the rest of us left for Walkers Wood and Ochee, they waved us off with smiles and instructions for us all to have a wonderful time, and Mavis said she hoped Delisia and I would bond.

As usual we drove by way of the Bog Walk Gorge and that horrible structure known as the Flat Bridge, which I hated. It seemed far too narrow, and had no guard rails, and I did not like it one bit. Adele and Donovan did not seem fazed by it, and looked out of the windows at the waters which were churning and foaming after some recent rains. However, we got across quite safely and I breathed a silent sigh of relief.

At least, I had thought it was silent, but Richard glanced at me sideways and said, "You'll never get used to this bridge, will you? Every time we cross it, you heave a sigh of relief and unclench your fists. A can't understand why yu suh fraid-a it...?"

I couldn't understand why, either. I was not afraid of many things, and logic told me that the bridge was quite safe – I mean, look how many thousands of vehicles travelled over it every day with no problems. I just could not understand my irrational aversion to the thing.

As usual fruit vendors tried unsuccessfully to tempt us with their offerings but we already had a large box of fruit

Claudette Beckford-Brady

which we had picked for Delisia.

We left the Flat Bridge and the Bog Walk Gorge behind and by-passed the market town of Linstead, famous for its market and its ackee song; *Kyaa mi ackee guh-a Linstid Maaket – nat a quattie wut sell* (carried my ackees to Linstead market, not a penny-ha'penny's worth was sold).

We passed through Ewerton and started up Mount Rosser, which was another place I did not like, because the road was narrow and winding, with barely space for two vehicles to pass, and many blind corners, yet the road users did not seem to value their lives or those of others as they rushed to overtake slower moving vehicles.

But again we negotiated it safely, finally coming down off the mountain at Faith's Pen, where more roadside vendors sold authentic Jamaican cuisine. A short distance up the road we passed Moneague, where a Jamaica Defence Force training camp was located, and then on to Walkers Wood.

The small farming community of Walkers Wood boasted its very own internationally famous brand-name food company, named for the district, which produced a range of spices, seasonings, preserves, jerk sauces, and so forth. All the ingredients for these products were produced by local farmers, who also part-owned the company. I had toured the facility with Richard and was most impressed with the order and industry of the place.

And then we reached the turn-off which took us up the hill to the private road leading to the Armstrong farm and residence. Richard and I did not linger. After depositing Adele and Donovan, who ran off excitedly without saying goodbye, we drove on into Ocho Rios and to the hotel, passing through

The Missing Years

the world famous *Fern Gully* on our way.

Fern Gully was an old river course around three miles long, and had hundreds of varieties of ferns, many of which were found nowhere else on earth. It had been badly damaged during Hurricane Gilbert in 1988, and many of the ferns had been damaged or destroyed, but it was beginning to recover, some five years on.

We checked into the hotel and went to our room before knocking on Delisia's door, which was right next door to ours. She was there; she had been waiting for our arrival, and Daddy Armstrong was there too, having checked in the night before. I couldn't wait to find out if he had a room of his own, or whether they were sharing.

We exchanged greetings and Delisia and I embraced briefly and she remarked on how much Estelle had grown since Christmas.

For the next couple of days we did absolutely nothing but eat, drink, swim, and just generally relax. Delisia and I spent quite a lot of time alone together – it seemed to me that Richard contrived to make it so – but I wasn't averse to it. In fact I really realized for the first time that Delisia could actually be *fun*.

She seemed to have burst right out of the shell that she had been hiding in when she had first returned to the island, and we giggled like two naughty children as we watched and good-naturedly ridiculed the other guests and holiday-makers staying at the hotel.

I was in fact quite surprised at the easy way she and I had slipped into being buddies, and I was beginning to realise that we were very much alike in more than just physical appearance. We could almost have pass for twins; she was slightly taller than me, but with the same build and similar facial features and, I soon realised, the same dry wit and sense of humour.

And something else struck me about Delisia. She showed me that she was eminently maternal. She had practically commandeered Estelle away from me; she changed her bottom, bathed and dressed her and constantly played with her. I would have been redundant had I not still been breastfeeding her.

This in itself should not have been strange – after all, she was the child's grandmother and could be allowed some doting, but I happened to overhear her crooning to the baby and I heard her say, quite distinctly, "I love you Michelle Delise."

Had she gone back in time to when I was a baby?

She had not had the chance to be a mother to me, and it seemed that she was now playing out a fantasy and substituting Estelle for me. I only heard her call Estelle by my name the one time, and she acted quite normally otherwise, so I did not think she had 'gone off'. I proceeded to watch her very carefully, nevertheless, until I was sure.

She and Daddy Armstrong had separate rooms, I had discovered, but I noted that her room was situated in the middle between ours and his. I couldn't stop myself from speculating about what might be taking place during nocturnal hours; David was still a virile man despite his advancing years.

When they were together during the daytime they held hands frequently and laughed a lot together. When Richard and I had spent our two days and left, Daddy Armstrong remained with Delisia for the rest of the week.

The Missing Years

But during the two days Delisia and I had made progress in our relationship. We had talked a little about her life in California and I had taken the plunge and asked her about boyfriends. She had replied that during college she had not had time, and since, had not had the inclination.

However, she admitted that she had accepted a few dates, mainly with older men, she said, as they were more likely to be more interested in conversation and less interested in sex; some of them, anyway, she had added dryly. She did not indicate whether or not she had had any sexual relationships, and I was not quite brave enough to ask outright, but I was sure there were sexual feelings between her and David.

I was dying to know more about her relationship with him. "You and Daddy Armstrong have really hit it off, though, haven't you? Is my father-in-law about to become my stepfather?"

She had laughed. "We're just having fun. I feel as if I've just discovered life, and it's something to be explored. Why complicate it by attaching expectations and ties to it? Am gonna just go with the flow." I supposed she was right.

We had also talked about Richard. Delisia liked him just as much as he liked her, and she told me how lucky I was in having him. "You two compliment each other perfectly," she said. I'm real happy for you, Shell."

She asked if he had fully recovered from the ordeal of the shooting, and I told her that he seemed to be fine, on the outside at least, and I had seen no indications that he was brooding on the inside. He had returned to his normal confident and self-assured self. She said the fact that he had been able to assist the families had helped him a lot, and then she had floored me with her next statement.

"It was a good thing that Richard had been able to flush his system by having a good cry," she had said. "Men generally find it hard to cry, but more of them should; crying has great therapeutic value."

Richard crying? I could not envisage it. When and where had he put on this display of emotion and how come this was the first I had heard of it? Had he cried on Delisia's shoulders? In her arms? A pang of...what...irritation...jealousy...? struck me. Why had he not released his emotions to *me*? *I* was his wife, after all. *I* was the one he should have turned to.

And why hadn't he told me about it? Was he embarrassed? I hid my internal feelings; I would take it up with Richard later. I wanted to know the full details, but did not want Delisia to know that I knew nothing about it, so I resorted to subterfuge to make her think I already knew all about it, in order to get the information I required.

"You are so right," I said. "I can't imagine why it is that men feel that it is less than manly to be able to cry. I'm glad Richard is big enough to realise that crying does not make a man any less a man." I went on artfully, "I'm really glad you were there for him during that time, Delisia. He said he had not wanted to burden me because I had just had a baby, but he said you were the next best thing."

I was not lying. He *had* said that. I put the next phase of my interrogation into action. I lowered my voice and said softly, "I don't think I would have been able to bear seeing him cry, but I'm glad he had you. Did he cry an awful lot?" I was throwing out a wild card. Maybe he had only told her that he had cried; maybe she had not actually witnessed it; maybe he had not used her shoulder.

The Missing Years

"It was heartrending. I had never been in a situation like that before, and hadn't quite known what to do, but I suppose instinct guided me, and I just held him and let him cry it all out. When he was through, he was able to talk, and that helped him too. But I think the fact that he was able to give physical assistance was the healing factor."

She said the episode had taken place in the car one evening when they were returning from Connors, and Richard had had to stop driving and park the car while he cried. I was glad no-one else had witnessed it, it was night and the car had tinted windows. I realised belatedly that I really was glad that she had been there for him, and no longer felt irritation or resentment about it.

I left Ocho Rios feeling a lot closer to her than I had previously done. I still wanted to know her life story, but I supposed it would come in little pieces as we got more comfortable with each other.

On the way home we had picked up the kids and Richard's two sons from Walkers Wood. Rachel's four children, Trevor, Stacy-Ann, Neville and Grace, all wanted to come to *Sweet Home* too, and so Trevor, who had passed his driving test and had been driving for a year or so, borrowed his mother's car and followed behind us. They spent a week and then returned to Walkers Wood.

I did not tackle Richard about his crying. I had thought it over and decided that he was entitled to keep some things private. I was still slightly peeved that he had not confided in me, but I supposed he might feel a little embarrassed, although I did not see why he should. But then, I had always hated for anyone to see me cry. I had shed many secret tears over the years, as well as public ones – too many for someone who was not a crying sort of person – and so I sort of understood why he had not said anything to me.

Mavis was pleased when I told her that Delisia and I had gotten on well. Sometimes it struck me anew just how much I loved and respected Mavis. When I looked back on the brief period of hatred I had felt for her during my teens I felt ashamed. Throughout my entire life she had been there for me. I had not appreciated this during my school days, but I absolutely appreciated it now.

Mavis had been instrumental in giving me the first link with my birth family. She had made contact with my grandma and opened up the lines of communication which had led to my finding my large extended family, and at no time had she shown the slightest hint of jealousy or resentment at my relationship with my other family. Indeed, she had done everything she could to facilitate it, including constantly encouraging me to forge a bond with Delisia.

Mavis and I were now as close as any mother and daughter could be, but I had discovered that there was room in my heart for Delisia too. Of course I was still hurt that she had not made any attempt to have a relationship with me, but I supposed I could see a little more clearly where she had been coming from. Anyway after those couple of days together in Ocho Rios we kind of drew closer together and spoke on the phone at least once a week, which pleased Mavis very much.

Grandma Miriam, too, had been a little worried about my earlier dislike of Delisia; I was now happy to be able to tell her that we were beginning to bond.

I had not visited my Country for several weeks, so one afternoon I decided to leave work early and go up there to

The Missing Years

spend an hour or two with Grandma Miriam. I had made arrangements for Wilbert to pick me up, which he did at the appointed time, and we left.

The clock in the centre of the town was where all the country taxis parked; the ones going to Bannister, Red Ground, Bartons, and beyond, also the ones going to Bois Content and Bellas Gate in my Country. The Bellas Gate stand was devoid of cars, and there were four people waiting, two of them my cousins. I told Wilbert to stop the car so I could offer them a lift. The four of them got into the car and we continued our journey.

We had just passed Colbeck when the argument started. My cousin Blossom was a large woman with very ample hips, and took up considerable space in the back of the car. Jamaicans were generally expert at "smalling up themselves" in order to squeeze into overcrowded vehicles, but it seemed she had not "smalled up herself" enough to suit the other passengers, who were almost sitting on top of each other.

One of the other women said to Blossom, "Small up yuself nuh; yu one kyaan' tek up summuch space."

The other woman voiced her agreement, and even Poonchie, my other cousin, who was Blossom's niece, agreed. Blossom haughtily replied that she could take as much space as she liked, since this was her cousin's car, and if the women didn't like it, they could always get out.

I decided to pacify the argument by letting Blossom sit in the front seat, and I, who was somewhat slimmer although much taller, would sit in the back. I indicated this and told Wilbert to stop the car so the exchange could be made. I had thought that this would suit Blossom much better, but she

Claudette Beckford-Brady

took extreme umbrage at the idea.

"Cousin Michelle," she said, "mek di dutty people-dem come out-a yu kyaar. Yu is a high-class somebody – dem kyaan't expeck yu fi ride eena back seat eena yu own-a veekle, an'-a rub-up rub-up 'gainst dem frowzy self."

The car had stopped for the exchange to take place, but instead of getting out of the car Blossom opened the door and said to the two women, "Oonu come out-a mi cousin bl..d cl..t kyaar!"

I was beginning to get annoyed with Blossom, and I did not like profanity at the best of times, but I remained calm. The two women had gotten out of the car and were standing around uncertainly. I suspected that they were more intimidated by the fact that I was, in their eyes, a "somebody", than by Blossom's aggressiveness, and I also suspected that if I had not been present they would have taken Blossom on. But for now, they were not sure exactly what to do.

I knew I could not leave them at the roadside; every vehicle coming from Old Harbour to Bellas Gate would be full, because no driver would leave the taxi-stand without a full load, which meant two or three in the front passenger seat, and at least five in the back, if not more.

And indeed, I did not want to leave them. I had already made a commitment to them, and I was not going to allow my cousin to dictate who could travel in my vehicle.

I told the two women to get into the front seat, since Blossom obviously was not going to, and I got into the back seat beside her, and we resumed our journey. She was not pleased, to say the least, and continued to grumble as we went.

The Missing Years

Finally I ran out of patience and said to her, far more mildly than I was feeling, "Yu know, Blossom, it is *my* car, and I don't have any objections to helping out a couple of neighbours so I don't see why you should be so upset about it."

Blossom saw several reasons why she should. First of all, she said, they were no neighbours of ours, because they were not from Gravel Hill, Bois Content, or even Joe Grung, but all the way from Bellas Gate. Secondly, I should not be relegated (although she did not use that word, and probably didn't even know it) to sitting in the back seat of my own car just to pacify "nayga people". Nayga is the vernacular for Negro or nigger and is commonly used in a derogatory way by Jamaicans against each other.

I told her mildly that I did it to pacify *her* and that I did not think it right that she should style people in such a derogatory fashion, and she decided to take me on.

"Di trouble wid yu, Cousin Michelle, is dat yu waant everybaddy fi like yu."

"And is there something wrong with that, Blossom? Don't *you* want people to like you?"

"Afta mi nuh kya (care) ef dem like mi aar nat. Mi naa beg nuhbaddy nutten, an yu, Cousin Michelle, should-a hole yuself far above di likes a dem; shoulden even chat to dem – afta raal, yu is "Somebaddy" an dem a nuh nuhbaddy."

I thought to myself that if they were "nobody" then she was too, since she was in the same social situation as they were, but of course I did not voice my thoughts. In any case she would probably dispute it; she was "somebody" by virtue of her connection to me, no doubt.

I had not paid much attention to my other cousin,

Claudette Beckford-Brady

Poonchie, who up to now had not said much, except to agree that Blossom was taking up too much space. Poonchie was in fact Blossom's niece, being her brother's child, and that made her my second cousin. My mother, Delisia, was Blossom's aunt, and Poonchie's great-aunt, or as they say on the island, "gran'-aunt."

Poonchie was about nineteen; a tall, slim girl, with a model's figure and a beauty queen's face. She had long straight hair, and was of very 'brown' complexion, courtesy of her mother who was a St. Elizabeth "white" Jamaican who had migrated to St. Catherine.

This meant that Poonchie was light-skinned – more so than the average Campbell cousin, who were generally darker and showed more features of the Indian heritage in our blood. Unfortunately, this made her think that she was a cut above the average person, including her Campbell relatives, especially those of darker complexion.

This perceived superiority caused her to be "speaky-spokey" which is a derogatory Jamaican term for someone who puts on airs and graces and tries to speak in a superior manner. In addition, Poonchie was a student at CAST (College of Arts, Science and Technology) in Kingston, where she was furthering her education in the field of computer studies and business administration. This too, I suspected, made her feel superior to her country relatives, and closer to me in status.

Now she decided to put in her tuppence-ha'penny's worth. "Hanty Blassum his roight, Cousen Michelle – famillarity breathe cantemp, y'know. Yu needs to mantain di prapper distant betwix' yu an di lower straatas."

I wanted to laugh out loud. She obviously did not consider herself a member of the "lower straatas". I wondered what she would say if I suggested giving her speech lessons, but the question was moot since I didn't have the time or the inclination.

I answered her. "Well, you know, Poonchie, I don't feel that I'm any better than the next person. I may be more privileged, yes, but that doesn't make me better or more superior."

"Haf cose hit do." Poonchie was indignant. "Yu lays down wid daags, yu ketch dere fleas!"

I caught Wilbert's eye in the mirror and made a grimace. He grinned back at me. I couldn't be bothered to argue with my cousins, and I also didn't want any more insults levelled at the two women in the front of the car, so I didn't bother to answer Poonchie. I turned my head and looked out of the window.

I idly wondered whether Blossom and Poonchie considered themselves inferior to people like Frank and Lynette Barrington and other professionals. And what were the criteria for superiority, anyway? Affluence and material possessions? Professional status? Skin colour?

I knew that many Jamaicans considered that the lighter one's skin colour was the more superior they were, but I'd had no idea there could be such snobbery amongst people of the same social situation.

We made the remainder of the trip in silence with only the car radio playing. We deposited Blossom at Free Marlie Crossroads to walk the remaining short distance to her home, and Poonchie alighted at the bottom of Gravel Hill where her own family lived.

Wilbert left me at Grandma's and then went on to Bellas Gate with the other two women, who had relaxed somewhat and had become talkative once my cousins were out of the car. They did not say anything against my cousins while I was in the car, but Wilbert told me afterwards that the minute I was out of the vehicle they had vilified Blossom and Poonchie in the most virulent manner. Me, they had developed a great liking and respect for.

Grandma Miriam was keeping well. She would be eighty seven this year, and no longer moved as easily as she used to, however, all her faculties were still intact, and there was nothing wrong with her sight and hearing, but she no longer went to the sunrise hilltop in the mornings. As usual she was glad to see me, and I told her about spending two days with Delisia at Easter.

She said Delisia had written and told her about her visit and had apologised for not coming to Country, but had said that it had been a spur of the moment trip and she had only spent a week. She promised to visit again soon, but Grandma kept harping on about her age, saying that Delisia had best make it sooner rather than later, since time was running out for her.

I wished Grandma would not keep on anticipating her death, but she had been doing it for as long as I had known her, and I knew I was not going to get her to stop, so I said nothing, but went on to tell her about my visit with Delisia. I told her that we were beginning to draw closer, and that made her so happy that I was glad I had changed my attitude toward Delisia.

In June Delisia wrote and invited us to come and spend some time with her during August when the kids would be on holiday. She invited Grandma too, but she declined, saying she was not up to the travelling at her age. I told her about an eighty six year old woman, who had just made her first parachute jump from an aeroplane, and Grandma said good for her, but she was still too old to travel. Delisia would have to come to her.

So we made our plans to go to California in August; Richard and the kids and I. Mavis and Daddy had been included in the invitation but they too had declined, saying they would take up the offer some other time. I knew Mavis wanted to give Delisia the chance to further bond with me and her grandchildren, and I thought again what a remarkable and unselfish woman Mavis really was. She had shown no signs of jealousy or possessiveness; had accepted Delisia into the family rather more readily than I had, and did everything she could to facilitate our fledgling relationship. I loved her dearly.

CHAPTER TWELVE

A History Lesson, and
A Californian Vacation

It was the middle of July and the sweltering heat outdoors was somewhat relieved by the prevailing Trade Winds which blew in from the sea by day, and out from the land by night, but indoors one had to have the use of fans or air-conditioning.

Outside, the lawns were burnt brown, except where sprinklers were at work, and the National Water Commission was now imploring people to turn off their sprinklers in order to conserve the precious commodity. In the city of Kingston water lock-offs were the order of the day and people only had water in their taps for a few hours each day, usually from midnight to four in the morning. People were advised to utilise used dishwater to flush their toilets and find other means of water conservation.

The country was beginning to settle after the General Elections in March which had returned the Peoples National Party (PNP) to power, allowing the incumbent Percival James Patterson, who had inherited the mantle from the ailing

The Missing Years

Michael Manley, his own mandate.

The elections had been marred by political thuggery and violence which seemed a hallmark of island politics, but nevertheless the opposition Jamaica Labour Party (JLP), led by Edward Seaga had conceded that the landslide victory of the PNP could not be challenged. However, the JLP had boycotted the new parliament for several months, and were only just now taking up their seats in the House.

It had been an extremely busy few months at the paper, primarily due to the plethora of political and related stories; our political correspondent had been kept on his toes, and other reporters had been temporarily removed from their beats to assist with the election coverage. I too had taken on the role of reporter myself, for a few weeks, and had conducted several interviews, including one with the newly returned Prime Minister and one with our local Member of Parliament.

I had thoroughly enjoyed myself, not having realised how much I had actually missed being out in the field, but now things were back to normal and comparatively quiet again and I resumed my normal duties of administering and overseeing the running of the paper.

School was out, and usually the children would have been at Walkers Wood for the summer, but this year we would be spending a week in California with Delisia, and before that we wanted to take Daddy and Mavis to the eastern parish of St. Thomas, which they had never visited, and in particular to the hot spring mineral spa at Bath.

We hired a mini-bus and took Miss Pearl, and Lurline and her two children with us. We set out very early one Friday morning, taking our time, and sightseeing on the way.

Claudette Beckford-Brady

The Old Harbour Road was empty at five in the morning, and we had a clear run to Spanish Town and all the way to Kingston and beyond.

We drove into the face of the newly risen sun. It was a truly beautiful Jamaican morning and we drove with the windows open to catch the cool morning breeze. We passed through Kingston, passed the Rockfort mineral bath, but didn't stop, since we were headed for the one at Bath in St. Thomas; passed the cement factory and the Jamaica Flour Mills and on to Harbour View, then took the roundabout exit which led to the eastern parish of St. Thomas.

The road was not good – nothing unusual in the island, unfortunately – and it was narrow and winding. We passed a lot of traffic heading into Kingston, including some great big lorries whose drivers thought they were driving racing cars at Dover raceway or Brands Hatch.

Richard was maintaining a steady pace, but not driving that fast, since we were sightseeing, and sometimes impatient drivers behind us tailgated and honked their horns, because overtaking was difficult along these narrow roads. Some drivers, though, took chances that made me cringe, and overtook around corners and on roads with precipitous drops. However, Richard did not allow this to cause an increase in his speed, and wherever he could he pulled to the left to let faster moving vehicles pass.

I had been giving everyone an educational tour along the way, and we had made our first stop at Eleven Miles, Bull Bay, to view the monument which commemorated one Jack Mansong, alias Three-fingered Jack, a Coromantee runaway slave of the late 1700s who had harried the British plantation owners and the soldiers who were sent to apprehend him.

The Missing Years

"There are countless legends surrounding Mansong," I told my audience. "And he's pretty famous. Believe it or not, he was the subject of a play at the Little Theatre in the Haymarket in London, no less, from as far back as 1800."

Richard had not known that, and showed great interest. "Really?" he asked. "Well how about that? Tell me more."

"Well," I said, "it was a pantomime and it opened on the 2nd of July 1800. A few Englishmen had already written about him, including a William Earle, Jr. and a Dr Benjamin Moseley, and the play was based on their versions of the story. The play was actually written by a comedic actor named John Fawcett, with music by Samuel Arnold."

Mavis was impressed. "God, Shell, how yu manage fi rememba suh much tings – all dem name and date deh – yu good!"

"Well, that's because I love my island and want to know everything about its history, Mum. I can never read enough and I am on a constant voyage of discovery."

"Me too," piped up Adele. "Mummy is taking me with her on the voyage of discovry, aren't you, Mummy?"

"I sure am, Putus," I replied.

Adele's thirst for knowledge equalled my own. She was already an avid reader, devouring books for an age group two or three years above her own, and she asked endless questions. Donovan, on the other hand, did not seem particularly interested in accompanying us on our voyage, although he was fascinated by insects and lizards; in fact all wildlife fascinated him and he loved to watch nature and wildlife programmes on TV.

Lurline's two children, who were aged nine and seven, were not particularly interested in a history lesson and were anxious to resume the journey as they were excited and impatient to get to the fun part of the trip, meaning the beach, I suppose.

Miss Pearl, Mavis' helper, wanted to know the full story of Three-fingered Jack, so as we drove along I recounted what I had learned about him. "He is said to have lost two of his fingers in a fight with a Maroon fighter named Quashie, and that's how he got his nickname. He had escaped from his master's plantation around 1780 after leading a failed uprising, and he continued to terrorise the planters from his hideouts in the hills.

"The planters, assisted by government troops, tried their level best to capture him, but couldn't, so eventually they placed a bounty of three hundred pounds Sterling on his head and let it be known amongst his followers that whoever among them brought in his head and the hand with the missing fingers, that person would be pardoned.

"According to legend he was a sort of Robin Hood – stealing from the rich British plantation owners and sharing the spoils. And apparently, despite his willingness to kill soldiers and planters, it is said that he would never kill a woman. In the end it was his old arch-enemy, Quashie, along with two other Maroons, who captured and killed him. They preserved his head and the hand with the missing fingers in rum, and took it to the authorities and collected their reward."

"Imagine dat!" Miss Pearl exclaimed. "An yu seh dem mek play about him clear a Inglan'?"

"Absolutely; our beloved island and our people are world famous, Miss Pearl."

After leaving Bull Bay we continued along the winding

The Missing Years

mountain road, revelling in the scenic beauty of the terrain. Here the vegetation was still green, testifying to the fact that this section of the island had had recent rains, unlike the parched dryness of our own parish. Fortunately, however, the rains had not been heavy or prolonged, which would have rendered the Yallas River crossing un-fordable.

During dry times the Yallas River could be a mere trickle, but during prolonged rains it became a torrent, causing traffic to be diverted, and often washing away people and property. We crossed without mishap.

At a place called Mt. Sinai we stopped to read a plaque which told the story of Judgment Cliff. In 1692 there had been a great earthquake in Jamaica – the same one that had broken off a part of the city of Port Royal and sent it crashing beneath the sea. Here at Mt. Sinai it is said that a part of the mountain broke off, and fell into the river, burying an entire plantation and its owner. It was seen as Devine Retribution, as the plantation owner was reputed to have been a very wicked man.

Driving along the coast road, we arrived at the village of Yallahs, the home of yet another Jamaican legend. The Yallas Ponds are two fairly large bodies of salt water a short distance inland from the sea, separated by narrow spits of land. Legend has it that the land was once productive agricultural land, but that it had been bequeathed to two brothers who fought so bitterly over it that the land had sunk to below sea level and become two briny ponds.

To give credence to the legend, the ponds sometimes had a red colour which is caused by drought-loving bacteria; the local folks insist, however, that this hue is caused by the blood of the two still warring brothers.

Claudette Beckford-Brady

We left Yallahs, still enjoying the verdant countryside and the view of the beautiful Caribbean Sea as we followed the coast. We passed a small waterfall right at the roadside, which was surrounded by lush green vegetation, and on to Morant Bay where we stopped for another history lesson, much to the disgust of Lurline's nine year old son, Kemar, who kept wanting to know when we would get to the beach.

It was still pretty early in the day – not yet eight o'clock – we had left home early and made good time, although we were not hurrying. Now we parked the mini-bus in the Morant Bay square where the subject of the lesson was situated, and we had a bathroom break and gave the kids a breakfast snack.

After everyone was satisfied I directed their attention to the statue of Paul Bogle which was in the courtyard of the old court house, right there in the Morant Bay Square. This was where Bogle, one of Jamaica's National Heroes, along with others who had been tried with him, had been convicted and subsequently hanged in 1865 after an uprising dubbed the "Morant Bay Rebellion."

It had been some twenty seven years since the abolition of slavery in the island, and the recently emancipated Negroes were having a hard time of it. Despite their new-found freedom they were scarcely better off than they had been under the slave masters; indeed it could be argued that some were worse off – at least as slaves their basic needs had been met – but now many were finding that freedom was not all it had been cracked up to be.

Finally the pressure became too much, and a natural leader emerged in the person of a man named Paul Bogle, from the district of Stony Gut. Bogle was a small farmer and a

The Missing Years

Baptist deacon, and he had attempted to make representation to the Governor of the island, Edward John Eyre, but after he and two of his followers had marched the forty six miles from Morant Bay to the Seat of Government in Spanish Town, the then capital, the Governor refused to see him.

The pressure became too much and on the 11th October 1865 the valve burst and rioting erupted. Martial law was declared, and the warships *Onyx* and *Wolverine* were dispatched to Morant Bay, and troops sent from Kingston and the military base at Newcastle in the St. Andrew hills. Eventually, on the twenty-third of October Bogle was captured by a group of Maroons who were assisting the British; he was tried and convicted, and hanged the following day from the arch of the courthouse, which had been burnt during the rioting.

Meanwhile, back in Spanish Town Governor Eyre had declared that the rioting had been incited by George William Gordon, a Baptist minister who had ordained Paul Bogle as a deacon in the church.

Gordon had been born of a union between a slave woman and her white master around the year 1820, some eighteen or so years before the abolition of slavery. He was not officially acknowledged by his father or his white half-siblings, and had received no help from them, but he learned to read and write and keep accounts, and eventually set himself up in business. He met and married one Lucy Shannon, the white daughter of an Irish editor.

George William Gordon was very concerned about the plight of the former slaves, and agitated for better conditions for them. This did not endear him to the ruling class, nor to the emerging coloured middle class of half-whites of which he was a member.

Gordon was brought to trial on the twenty-first of October, and hanged on the twenty-third along with eighteen others. He too is honoured as one of Jamaica's National Heroes.

I loved being able to relate the nation's history to my parents and my children, although the kids would of course not understand everything, but they were learning bits and pieces and over time they would become well steeped in the knowledge of their history and culture.

After we left Morant Bay we headed for the mineral springs at Bath. We passed several public beaches along the way and the kids were beginning to get impatient, but we assured them that they would like Bath Fountain, although it was not a beach, and that they would get the opportunity to go to a proper beach later. At Port Morant there was a road that would take us inland through the district of Airy Castle and direct to Bath, but it was not a very good road, and we decided to continue along the coast and then inland to Golden Grove, doubling back west to approach Bath from the east.

We drove through miles and miles of coconut and banana plantations; the bananas wearing their protective blue plastic bags; and we passed the ruins of Stokes Hall Great House, which is one of the oldest structures on the island, but did not stop because the kids were becoming fretful, even Adele. Donovan had slept and awoken, and was now demanding lunch, although it was only just past ten. I gave him a packet of banana chippies and then had to give the other three kids some too. Estelle, as usual, was being an

The Missing Years

extremely good baby. She was now nine months old and I had started to wean her, although I still allowed her the breast at night.

Eventually we arrived in the town of Bath where the Bath Fountain hot water mineral springs is located, the waters of which are reputed to cure all manner of ailments. The curative ability of the waters was supposedly discovered by a runaway slave whose leg ulcers were miraculously healed after he had bathed in the river, and he had, again supposedly, braved his master's wrath to tell about the miracle waters.

We intended to spend a couple of hours; have hot towel massages, eat lunch and then head on into Portland, arriving around two o'clock, where the kids could get to spend a couple of hours on a "proper beach" before we headed home by way of Friendship Gap and St. Andrew. It would be a very long day for the two younger children, but they took "puss-naps" as we drove.

It was now approaching eleven and we wanted to leave by at least one o'clock to give us time to drive leisurely to Portland and allow the kids a couple of hours on the beach, so we wasted no time, but set off up the hill to the hot spring for our massages.

The massages were informally offered by a group of local men, mostly dreadlocked Rastafarians; not in the hotel which had hot and cold water piped in from two different springs, but up at the stream itself, where the water came out of the rocks so hot that it was unbearable.

The informal masseurs saturated the towels in the hot water and then placed them, as hot as one could bear, on the body. When they had thoroughly opened up your pores and supposedly drawn out the impurities, they would use natural oils extracted from local plants to give you a good body massage right there on the flat rocks.

I was mortified at the palpable disappointment of the kids when they saw the place, and I realised belatedly that they were rather young to appreciate the therapeutic value, or the rustic natural beauty of the place. However, they cheered up after they had donned their swimwear and started splashing in the cooler river waters that were not hot, and Richard and Daddy took them upstream and out of sight. Richard took Estelle with them while Mavis, Miss Pearl, Lurline and I had our hot massages.

Apart from its mineral bath attraction the town of Bath is itself an historical place. The once spectacular Bath Botanical Gardens is located near the spa and is the second oldest botanical gardens in the western hemisphere, and the first on the island of Jamaica. It was the incubator for all the plants brought in from abroad during the early years of European occupation, including flowering species such as the croton, jacaranda and bougainvillea, and fruit trees such as the Otaheite apple, the ackee and the breadfruit, some of which were brought by Captain William Bligh of *Mutiny on the Bounty* fame.

Sadly, it was discovered that the site of the gardens was under constant threat from the nearby river, and also lacked the soil nutrients which were required for it to thrive, and after several incidences of flood damage it fell into disuse. Finally, in 1862 the plants were removed to Castleton Gardens in St. Mary.

After our massages and lunch we left Bath and headed for Portland where we found a beautiful secluded beach at

The Missing Years

Boston Bay that was not overcrowded, and Daddy, Richard and the kids had a wonderful time in the water, while the other women and I relaxed under beach umbrellas and gossiped.

All too soon it was time to pack up and head for home. It was past five in the afternoon, and we had been on the road for a round twelve hours. As soon as we started the homeward journey Donovan and Adele fell asleep, and it was not long after that Lurline's two children followed suit.

We eventually arrived home, tired but happy just before eight in the evening and we put the kids straight to bed and Richard and I spent a relaxing evening with a bottle of wine and some soft music, before having an early night ourselves.

*

August came, and we departed Jamaica to spend a week with Delisia at her home in Santa Monica, California.

Her home was impressive. Built on a half-acre sloping lot, it was a single storey building, consisting of two bedrooms, each with its own en-suite bathroom and private veranda, and a split-level living room, all opening onto the patio and swimming pool. A separate two-bed guest house was also on the property; Delisia said she often had guests in residence, but that she liked her own solitude for the most part, which is why she had had the second house built.

The house was in a beautiful neighbourhood, alongside other resplendent homes, boasting manicured lawns, landscaped gardens, and swimming pools. To the north, south and east, the city of Los Angeles almost surrounded Santa Monica, but this was redeemed by the backdrop of the Santa Monica Mountains to the north of the city and the warm blue waters of the Pacific to the west.

Claudette Beckford-Brady

On the evening after our arrival Delisia held a small dinner party to introduce us to her business partner and a few of her close friends. I was curious to know what she had told people about us; she had told me that it had been easier to just put me out of her mind and get on with her life, and for thirty years she had done just that. I could not imagine that she had told many people, if any, about the daughter who had been stolen from her.

For thirty years she had, to all intents and purposes been childless, and now suddenly she was producing, not only a daughter, but a son-in-law and three grandchildren to boot. Her friends and associates must be inordinately curious, and I was eager to hear how we would be introduced.

I mean, to anyone seeing the two of us together, there would be no mistaking the fact that we were closely related. We could actually pass for sisters; Delisia had only been seventeen when I was born, but my children now called her "Grandma Delisia" which would let the cat out of the bag. But perhaps she no longer wanted to keep the feline hidden.

I could see that she was in two minds about being called "Grandma." On the one hand she was proud, but on the other hand I could almost see her cringe and grimace every time they used the title. I was mildly amused by this, and teased her about it; we had reached that comfortable place in our relationship which allowed me to do so. She had laughed and admitted that I was absolutely right, but she would not exchange being a grandma for anything.

But the children would not be at the dinner party tonight to call her "Grandma" so she could keep the relationship hidden a while longer, if she wanted to.

There were ten people present, including Delisia,

The Missing Years

Richard and myself. The first to arrive was a retired doctor who lived a few houses away from Delisia, and had walked over. He was a native of Trinidad, of East Indian descent, and had been in the United States since his early teens, and sounded very American.

He was a widower, and it was obvious to me that he really liked Delisia. I noted the way his eyes followed her as she moved around, and he contrived to be near her as much as possible. He seemed about the same age as Daddy Armstrong, and I recalled that Delisia had said she favoured older men. I realised that Grandpa Carlton had been around that age when he died, and Delisia had said she felt partially responsible for his death. I wondered if she was looking for a father-figure in a relationship.

But on close observation of Delisia, she seemed oblivious to the fact that Rashid Ranjeet liked her above the norm, and did not favour him with any special attention. The other guests comprised her business partner, Geraldine Chambers, also a Jamaican, with her white American husband Clement, who sold real estate. The couple were in their fifties.

Next, a young couple, about my age; he was a supporting actor on some soap opera or the other that I had never heard of, let alone seen, to his sore disappointment; she was a news anchorwoman on a local news channel, and seemed pretty likeable. He, I knew I was not going to like – he fancied himself far too much and thought everyone else fancied him too – but she turned out to be someone worth knowing, and I knew that Delisia had invited her specially to meet me.

They were a couple, but not married. Their names were

Claudette Beckford-Brady

Omar Silk, and Elaine Wynters; he was an African American, and she black British who had been in the States for just over two years, and had lived near my locality in London, although we had never met.

Finally there was an elderly couple in their early seventies named Ralston and Evelyn McCallum, again Jamaicans, who I subsequently learned had been surrogate parents of sorts to Delisia. Evelyn was a retired gynaecologist, and Ralston an orthopaedic surgeon, also retired. Delisia had boarded with them whilst attending college and law school. They were childless, and had welcomed the apparently parentless and solitary young woman.

Delisia introduced us as "Michelle and Richard Armstrong, my daughter and son-in-law," and no-one batted an eyelid or otherwise showed surprise. Either they were all extremely well-bred, or she had already apprised them of our relationship.

Dinner was catered. Delisia said that Conchita, her housekeeper, was a superb cook, but seemed unable to cook in larger quantities – she could not get the proportions right – which was strange for a Mexican woman, so whenever Delisia had guests for dinner she either cooked herself, which she was quite good at, she said, or else she had food brought in. I wondered why she had opted for a formal dinner when it could just as easily have been a barbeque or buffet supper.

The conversation at the table covered a diverse range of subjects. Omar Silk tried to keep the conversation centred on himself and his career; specifically his intention of being the next Denzel Washington – it was only a matter of time, he said.

He was a good looking man, but he had a weak chin and

The Missing Years

his eyes, although beautiful and dreamy, rarely made contact with yours, and when they did, they slid away within a second or two. I definitely did not like him or his curly perm.

I discovered that Elaine was an aspiring writer. She had read my book, which Delisia had introduced her to, had thoroughly enjoyed it, and wanted to pick my brain about my style, and how to get published. She said her first attempt at a novel was three quarters complete. I promised to have a look at it for her before I left.

Mr Ranjeet and the McCallums had also read my book, so had Geraldine Chambers; only her husband Clement, and Omar Silk had not. They all professed to have greatly enjoyed it and congratulated me heartily.

We discussed a little world politics and the role of the United States; we talked a little about the economic situation in Jamaica and the crime problem. I told them about my newspaper and magazine and Richard told them about his farm and his recording studio.

Omar Silk suddenly remembered that he was also a great singer and wondered about the possibility of recording an album. He had never been to Jamaica, he said, and would love to come and visit. Richard skilfully avoided giving an answer and started talking about my next book, which held absolutely no interest for Mr Silk. He poured himself more wine and retreated into his own little world, probably weaving fantasies of his imminent stardom.

After dinner we sat out on the patio in two little groups, the men in one, and the women in the other. Mr Silk had wanted to insinuate himself into our group but Elaine repelled him, telling him that we were having "girl talk." He wandered off and sat by himself at the poolside without joining the other men. Suit yourself, I thought.

I liked Elaine. She reminded me of my friend and business partner Cee Jay. She was perhaps not quite as gregarious, but she had a bubbly personality and laughed easily. Her South London accent made me feel really comfortable with her, as if I had known her before.

She had lived in South Croydon before moving to Streatham, just a few miles from my own home in Brixton, and we knew all the same places, if not the same people. She had also done her journalism course at London University, as I had, but three years behind me. She had worked briefly at Channel Four Television before migrating to the United States along with her Jamaican parents.

Elaine said her job was okay, but not exactly fulfilling. She said she wanted something where she could make more of a contribution and an impact, and thought the print media might suit her better than broadcast journalism. She said if I wanted another journalist on my paper or magazine she was not averse to coming to Jamaica.

As she said this she looked across at Omar sitting alone by the poolside, and I caught a flicker of – I don't know – how could it be dislike... *they were a couple...*? Anyway, I got the distinct impression that she would not mind getting away from him. I realised that they had not spoken a word to each other at dinner, and decided to watch their interaction more closely if I got the chance.

Throughout the entire evening no one had mentioned my relationship to Delisia. Now the Chambers had left, and so had Elaine and Omar, leaving us alone with Mr Ranjeet and the McCallums.

Delisia obviously felt very much at ease with these

three, because she kicked off her shoes and curled up in a chair, her legs tucked under. In fact everyone seemed a lot more relaxed now, and the conversation became more personal. Mr Ranjeet said how nice it was for Delisia to have her family to visit; his own two sons still lived in New York where he had retired from, and he rarely saw them or his grandchildren. Mrs McCallum said, "You be grateful, old boy; at least you *have* grandchildren to 'rarely see'."

She spoke frankly of her regret at not having children. She had been pregnant once, she said, but had developed complications and had finally miscarried. She had never been able to conceive again, to her eternal regret.

I wondered why she had not tried any of the various options that were available to her, and then I remembered that she was of an earlier generation. The first birth by In Vitro Fertilization had been in 1978; probably much too late for her. Still, she could have adopted.

Since she was speaking so frankly I ventured to ask if she had ever considered adopting. She said she and her husband had thought about it, but then they had decided against it, and she had thrown herself into her career and building a successful Practice.

She had met Delisia through her niece; they attended some of the same classes, and had become friends. Delisia had been struggling; trying to attend her classes and work two jobs at the same time. She had been sharing digs with three other students, but still found things financially difficult.

Mrs McCallum had taken a liking to the reserved young woman, sensed a kindred soul, and adopted her, so to speak, taking her into their home, where Delisia had lived until she had graduated law school and started her first job in the

D.A.'s office.

I reflected on how lucky both Delisia and I had been with the people who had nurtured us. I had had Mavis and Mummy Myrtle. She had been alone in a strange country, but she had somehow found a familiar mother figure, a Jamaican, one of her own, and had been nurtured. I was glad for her, and I could see that the McCallums regarded her as a daughter, and she them as parents.

Oh, my God! Not another set of great-grandparents for my kids?! Did ever a family consist of so many parents and grandparents?

Just before they left, Mrs McCallum, who told us to call her Evelyn, turned to me and said, away from the others, "It's been a pleasure to meet you, my dear. I am so glad that Delisia finally found her lost child; she carried the burden for many years – cried fountains of tears.

"I always sensed that there was deep heartache, but I had put it down to a broken romance; it took your mother many years before she confided in me about you. I'm so happy you've found each other."

Her words astounded me. When Delisia had told me that it had been easier to just put me out of her mind and get on with her life, I had assumed she meant she had totally forgotten about me. It had never occurred to me that she would have shed tears over me. But I had no time to ponder Evelyn's words because they were taking their leave, and I had to watch my manners.

Evelyn and Ralston invited Richard and me to visit them whenever we wished, and to bring the children. They kissed Delisia and me, and shook hands with Richard, and left. Mr Ranjeet was also leaving, but I noticed that he lingered, and I

The Missing Years

bade him goodnight and diplomatically steered Richard away. I don't know if Delisia appreciated my effort, or deplored it, but I would guess the latter from the reproachful look she threw me.

I looked in on the kids and when I returned to the living area Mr Ranjeet had gone and Richard and Delisia were laughing over something, which I discovered to be Omar Silk's ego and conceit, and I joined in the laughter. Delisia said that Elaine had been trying to drop him for some time but he was clinging, and she was not assertive enough to send him packing. So instead she wants to run away to Jamaica, I thought.

It was almost midnight, but the three of us sat chatting for a while longer. I thought how comfortable and natural it felt, sitting here chatting with my birth mother, and I remembered ruefully how I had stated emphatically that I never wanted to have anything to do with her. Thankfully, I had gotten over that sulk.

I was beginning to see her in a newer, softer light, I realised, as we chatted and laughed together. I had been gradually progressing toward this, but I think the new discovery that she had really mourned my loss for many years, as Evelyn had said, endeared her more to me.

When we went to bed I told Richard about what Evelyn had said, and he said he had had no doubt of it. He had never envisaged Delisia as the cold unfeeling and vindictive woman I had, and truth be told I did not see that same woman now, twelve months on.

During the past months we had exchanged several letters and many phone calls, and the couple of days we had spent together at Easter had helped to bring us closer together. The fact that it had taken nearly a year for us to reach that stage was more my fault than Delisia's; she had probably been waiting for my cue. I had been rather hostile toward her initially, and had attacked her verbally – I supposed she had not wanted to risk such a confrontation again.

Well, that was all water under the bridge now, and we were working our way toward a closer relationship. Mavis was a very intuitive woman, and I'm sure she had only declined Delisia's invitation in order to maximise our opportunity of bonding further.

We were only spending a week, and the next few days were full. We visited Delisia's offices and met her staff. The Practice was almost ten years old and not a large one, having only the two partners, but it was flourishing and she said the workload was ever increasing and they might either seek additional partners or take on more Associates.

There were many large law firms with multiple functions and many attorneys in the area, but small firms could also cream off some of the lucrative business. The area supported, apart from the movie and television industries, many light manufacturing companies producing aircraft and aerospace equipment and electronic components.

Delisia's client list was impressive, as she told me about some of the companies and individuals who retained her services, and indeed, as we were leaving her office a well-known actress from one of the daytime "soaps" came in. I did not watch soap operas, but I had read her profile in my own *Jamaican Woman* magazine – the "soap" was very popular on the island and we had to give our readers what they wanted – and so I was familiar with her name and face.

The Missing Years

We were briefly introduced, and for the first time I really noticed the proud way in which Delisia introduced us. "My daughter and son-in-law, Michelle and Richard Armstrong, and my grandchildren. Richard is a music producer/promoter and export farmer, and my daughter publishes a newspaper and magazine in Jamaica, and is also a novelist – perhaps you've seen her book, *My Idyllic Days*?"

I was sure the actress had not, but to my surprise she smiled directly into my eyes and said, "You wrote that marvellous piece of literature? I bought it last year while I was vacationing in Montego Bay. I thoroughly enjoyed it; in fact I identify totally with Sylvia, and I knew a bastard just like Ricardo. Good work; I'm sorry I don't have my copy on-hand for your autograph."

I was impressed; she really *had* read it. Many people profess to read books, but can tell you nothing about the plot or characters. She seemed rather more impressed by the fact that I had written a book than I was at the fact that she was a soap opera star. I assured her that I would arrange to give Delisia an autographed copy for her. As she was leaving I heard her express surprise to Delisia that she even had a daughter; Delisia had never mentioned that before...

Santa Monica is a resort city. It is situated on Santa Monica Bay down the coast from Malibu, and has a vibrant tourist industry, alongside the entertainment and light manufacturing industries. There were so many places to go to, and so many things to see that we had to sit down and decide which we would see and which would have to stay for some other time.

We went to Disneyland at Anaheim and visited San Diego Zoo and Sea World. That excited and wore out Adele and Donovan and we were able to leave them and Estelle, who was now ten months old and weaned, with Ralston and Evelyn McCallum, who were eager to baby-sit, while Richard, Delisia and I went off on our own adventures.

We visited Beverly Hills; Rodeo Drive, went into Saks Fifth Avenue and all the other exclusive stores. We visited the movie studios, taking the children with us, this time, and all in all, we had the most marvellous week of our lives.

CHAPTER THIRTEEN

Delisia's Story; The Finale

Delisia and I were alone. Adele and Donovan had been pleading to be taken back to Disneyland and Richard had obliged them, accompanied by the McCallums who were more than glad to go.

They had left early, since Anaheim was some distance away, and Delisia and I were in the pool with Estelle, who loved to splash. She was already familiar with swimming pools; she had been inducted into the Barrington's pool very early on, and was quite happy in the water. Both Adele and Donovan were already fairly competent swimmers, and I expected Estelle to follow suit.

It was another glorious Californian day. The sun blazed down out of the sky with an intensity that seemed hotter than our own Jamaican sun, and it was unrelieved by even a breath of breeze. Delisia's pool was most welcome, and we swam and lounged around in the shady area of the poolside.

We had been in California for five days, and we would be leaving in another two days. We had done so much during that time that it felt as if I had been there for a much longer period of time. I felt extremely comfortable and at home; there had been no awkward moments with Delisia, and in fact we had fallen quite easily into being a family unit.

We bathed and dressed the kids together, prepared meals together, laughed and joked just like any normal mother and daughter, but we didn't discuss the past, although as far as I was concerned it was still unfinished business.

A year ago Delisia had actually requested that we leave the past in the past and start fresh, and I suppose I had tacitly agreed, but I did not feel as if I had gotten any closure. Now I saw our being alone together for the entire day as a good opportunity to approach her on some of my main issues.

I did not want to spoil our new-found camaraderie, but until I had resolved the outstanding issues I could not be totally, one hundred per cent at peace with Delisia. My earlier antagonism toward her was no more, and my feelings that she did not deserve to have a ready-made family dropped into her lap – they had gone too.

But I was still hurt by the fact that she could have found me so easily if she had only tried. A simple letter to her mother, or my father's parents and we could have been reunited many years ago, or at the very least, we could have kept in touch by written correspondence, phone calls and photographs. Her failure to have done so, in my mind, meant that she had simply not wanted to and that meant she had not wanted *me*, or anything to do with me.

Outstanding also, was the fact that when we had met at the airport, she had not greeted me with the hugs, and the tears of joy, nor the exclamations of delight I had envisaged and looked forward to over the years, instead she had been rather hostile, to my way of thinking.

Of course she had been in shock; to be suddenly, and without warning, confronted by the daughter who had been stolen from her thirty one years before, but had the boot been on the other foot, I would have grabbed her and hugged her for dear life.

Of course Richard would say, and in fact *had* said, that I could just as easily have hugged her myself, instead of laying into her verbally and putting her on the defensive. He was willing to bet that had I done that, she would have hugged me back, the tears and emotions I had wanted would have flowed, and all the unpleasantness would have been avoided.

I suppose I could concede that point, and wipe that part of the slate clean. But there still remained the fact that she had made absolutely *no effort* to even get me back. Again, if the boot had been on *my* foot, I would have kicked down Hell's gate to get my child back, and I think I still resented her a little for not having done that.

We had a cheese salad for lunch and while Estelle was taking a nap Delisia and I sat chatting about generalities and inconsequential things, when she suddenly said, "Y'know, Shell, I know I told you that I didn't believe in regrets and 'if onlies' but *if only* I had not been so stubborn and selfish, I would not have missed out on so many years of pleasure with you and the children. I regret to have to say it, but I *do* have regrets."

I could not decide if it was a selfish regret: did she only regret because *she* had missed out on the pleasure...? What about the years of worry and distress she had caused to the family at large, especially to Grandma Miriam – did she regret those too?

I did not respond straight away and she continued. "I really wish I could go back and change things, but of course I can't. But I wish I had made the effort to get you back. I'm sure George and Mavis would have been reasonable about it."

Aha! She had opened the gate. I could enter. "Why *didn't* you – *really*?"

She stood up and said, "Fancy some wine?" I would rather get an answer to the question, I thought, but I nodded. I did not think she was trying to avoid answering – rather it seemed as if she wanted to fortify herself before we got into it. I thought wine was a good idea. It might free up her speech.

She returned with a bottle in an ice bucket, and two glasses. She poured, sat back down, and said, "Now then – *why* didn't I – really…?"

We talked for ages, or at least Delisia did, with only occasional input from me. Estelle woke up and I fed her and put her in the playpen which Delisia had bought for her, along with the many toys she had also bought. If I were not strict she would spoil the children. But Estelle amused herself happily while Grandma Delisia and I continued our talk.

She had not answered the question immediately, but said that if I had the patience, she would start at the beginning and tell me her story. I had the patience. She had begun.

"The entire thing was of my own doing. I alone am responsible for everything, and no one else is to be blamed for any of the subsequent events or consequences; not my father, nor any of my family members.

"I had no right to have held them responsible, or to have

The Missing Years

ostracized them for something I alone was responsible for. I myself started the entire chain of events, and I had no right to have caused so many people so much pain over so many years."

She paused, and I was about to say something, when she raised a hand and said, "Don't break my stride." She went on, "I'm going to tell you the whole story from the beginning; I am not going to try and excuse my actions – I was wrong – I accept and acknowledge that.

"I was sixteen when I realised that I was in love with George Freeman. I had known him all my life; our two families had been neighbours for generations, and sometimes George or other members of his family, along with other men in the district would come and give 'day's work' to my father and brothers when it was digging, planting or reaping time.

"George had known me since I was a baby, and was extremely difficult to seduce – and I admit with no degree of pride, that I had set out to seduce him. Apart from my age, the fact that I was still in school, and the additional fact that he already had a baby-mother, there was also my father and three of my eight brothers who were still at home to contend with. George wanted no part of me.

"But I had been spoiled; had always been given everything I wanted, and was not to be denied. George was no match for me, and one night, at my grand-uncle's ninenight I finally got my way. George had been partaking freely of the rum which was in plentiful supply and when I managed to lure him away to a dark, un-inhabited corner of the yard, and showed him my favours, he was lost. After all, he was only a normal, hot-blooded young Jamaican male."

I tried to envisage Daddy as a young man in his early

twenties trying to run away from a determined Delisia. I was willing to bet he had not tried very hard to run, but as Delisia said, he was a hot-blooded young male. I was convinced she was trying to make him look not so bad in my eyes, and I respected her for it. But her next words convinced me that he really had tried.

"Of course when he had sobered up and remembered what had happened he was aghast, and extremely angry. He tried his best to avoid me, but I pursued him relentlessly. He managed to elude me for nearly three weeks, but eventually I cornered him and told him I had missed my period and thought I might be pregnant.

"I didn't really think I was, but desperate times called for desperate measures and it got me what I wanted; at least temporarily. George was terrified and I persuaded him that we needed to meet to discuss what we would do about my 'pregnancy.' Once I got him alone I intended to convince him that since I was already pregnant there was no danger in indulging in some more sex.

"It had been an extremely hard sell. I had never met anyone more stubborn, apart from myself and my father. (No wonder I was so stubborn; I got it from both parents *and* my grandfather). *George was intent on going to my father with a full confession, and to suffer the consequences, be they what they may. It took all my powers of persuasion to sway him from that course. I told him that he was courting death, or at the very least, severe injury. I did not see how my brothers could restrain themselves from giving him a beating, even if my father could.*

"I had everything planned, I told him. I would hide the 'pregnancy' until it became impossible to do so any longer.

Between now and then I would think of what to tell my father and brothers. In the meantime, since I was already 'pregnant' there was no danger in our having sex.

"George wanted none of it, but he had no choice. If he crossed me, I would go to my father and brothers, but if he complied with my wishes I would protect him from them by keeping his name secret. After all, they couldn't beat it out of me."

As Delisia spoke my mind flashed back sixteen or so years to the time I had been relentlessly pursuing my first boyfriend, Clive, for sex, and his refusal to rush into it. I had been determined, and had even got Mavis to take me to the doctor and have me put on the contraceptive pill at only age sixteen. Instead of being glad, Clive had been very angry and had refused to make love to me, causing me to run off in humiliation and tears.

I could imagine Delisia's determination, if it had been anything like mine. But she was still speaking, and I brought my attention back to what she was saying.

"We settled into a secret sexual relationship," she continued. *"My plan was that after a couple of months, I would take to my bed for a few days with "belly-ache" and emerge to tell George that I had miscarried. I was afraid to 'miscarry' too soon for fear that the relationship would end with it. I was not sure if George would be sufficiently 'addicted' to me to keep up the relationship afterwards.*

"But I was too clever for my own good. I had planned to 'miscarry' with my third period, some three months into the 'pregnancy.' But I waited in vain for the first period. It never came.

"I did not know what to do. I had already told George

that I was pregnant and dealing with it, so there was no help there. I had no sisters, and the only brother I would have been able to talk freely about it with was Keith, and he was in England. I dared not tell Cornell, who I was in fact closest to, because I knew he would go looking for George with his cutlass.

"I wrote to Keith and told him how excited I was to be having a baby, but that I was afraid of the consequences when Pappa found out. I asked him if he couldn't come home to give me some support. He said he could not leave England at that time.

"Later when Pappa did find out, I wrote to Keith again, asking him to intercede with Pappa so he would allow me to keep my baby. He wrote back telling me that it would do no good, because once Pappa had made up his mind about something, there was no changing it. I wrote to my other brothers in North America, too, and some told me I had made my bed and must lie in it, while others said what Keith had said about Pappa's stubbornness."

I made a mental note to tell her that Uncle Keith had in fact tried to intercede with their father on her behalf.

"There was help from no quarter; Mamma said she would take you and raise you herself – even Bev and Eula offered – so that I could return to school, but Pappa would have none of it, and his word was law. He said if I gave you up he would still be willing to send me to university, despite the fact that I had let him down grievously. I was willing to forfeit university to keep you, but I was not given the choice."

Her voice became softer as she stared off into space and continued. "It was January, 1961. You were four weeks old, and the most beautiful baby I had ever seen. I played with *you, and sang to you, and then I fed you and bathed you as I did every evening, and then we went to bed. When I woke around midnight to feed you again, you were gone. Pappa had removed you whilst I was sleeping, and given you to George and Mavis.*

"I was hurting, and livid enough to kill. I wished on Pappa agonising pain such as I was feeling; I even wished him dead to his face. I stopped speaking to all the members of my family, even those who had tried to help me to keep my baby.

"I continued to live at home, but it was not comfortable. I spoke to no one unless it was compulsory. After a few months Pappa gave me an ultimatum – stop sulking and return to normal, or leave his yard. By this time I had secured a job teaching at Ludford Mount Elementary School, although I was untrained, and I was able to rent a cheap room at Breeze Mill, so I obliged him and move away from Gravel Hill. Mamma came up to the school to see me on several occasions, but I refused to see her or to have anything to do with the family. As far as I was concerned, they were all dead, and so was my baby.

"By that time George and Mavis had moved down to Old Harbour, and I later heard that they had gone to England and taken you with them. I continued to teach at the school until 1965 when I got my first lucky break.

"Luck, in fact, seems to have played a big role in my progress and achievements. One of the teachers at the school, Miss Elsa, had a sister living in Trench Town in Kingston, and she said I had too much potential to stay buried in the country, so she arranged for me to go and stay with her sister, Maude, while I tried to further my education.

"Two months after I left Country and went to Trench

Claudette Beckford-Brady

Town, I got news that my father had fallen from an ackee tree and broken his neck."

Here, she paused for a while, but I did not say anything. I could see that she had travelled back in time to 1965. It did not seem to be a pleasant journey, and why would it, I thought as I watched the emotions play over her features. She resumed the story, speaking in a voice which was so low I had to strain to hear what she was saying.

"It was all my fault, of course... I had wished him dead..."

Her voice trailed off, and I broke in with, "Of course it wasn't your fault – you know Grandpa Carlton was a law unto himself – he had sons and grandsons capable of climbing trees; he had no right being up a tree."

She shook her head. "Thanks for saying that, Shell, but I'm convinced that had it not been for my actions, he never would have climbed the tree."

"What are you saying?" I asked. "Surely you're not suggesting that he committed...?" I was afraid to say the word. "...that he did it *deliberately*?"

There had been rumours, I had been told, that Grandpa Carlton had had his heart broken by Delisia's betrayal – she had been his unashamed favourite – the youngest child and the only daughter amongst eight sons. She had also been extremely bright, and he had been looking forward to sending her to the University College of the West Indies to study law.

He had been so proud of her. She would have been the first from the district to attend the university – some of her brothers had university degrees, but they had been obtained abroad – and the fact that she was a female made him even prouder still. He must have been devastated when he saw his hopes for her come crashing down, and that devastation had turned into searing anger.

But *suicide?* Ridiculous! I had not known Grandpa Carlton, but from the things I had heard about him, I could not envisage him as a man who would commit suicide.

Delisia responded to my question with a long drawn out sigh. "I don't know. Elsa told me that there were rumours to the effect…"

I cut her off. "Ridiculous. You knew Grandpa Carlton and I didn't, but from what I've heard about him, I can't conceive of him doing anything like that. The man simply slipped and fell out of the tree. We will never know why he was in the tree in the first place, but I'm sure if he had wanted to kill himself he would have chosen a more foolproof method.

"I mean, he had been a *doctor*, for heavens sake; the tree he fell out of was not that tall, I gather, and if he had not fallen awkwardly he might not have died. He could have been severely injured and permanently disabled and he must have known that. If he had wanted to kill himself he would have chosen a taller tree or used another method."

I spoke emphatically because I really believed what I was saying; I wasn't just saying it to make her feel better. She shrugged her shoulders and said, "Well, anyway, where was I…? Oh yes…

"On the death of my father my friend Elsa felt obliged, although I had asked her not to, to let my family know where I was, and my brothers Kingsley and Cornell came to Trench Town to inform me of my father's death. I told them that as far as I was concerned my father had died the day he took my baby away, and I refused to go back with them to Country.

"I had wanted desperately to go – wanted to make up with my family, but I remembered that I had wished my father

Claudette Beckford-Brady

dead, and knew they would all be blaming me, so I internalised – hid the problem inside and threw myself into work and study.

"I could not afford to attend UCWI, but Miss Maude was active in party politics and I was introduced to a number of politicians, political aspirants, and university students who frequented her yard and shop, some of whom are now prominent in business and government, others are faculty members at the university. I listened to their discourse, and learned from them, occasionally making a tentative contribution myself.

"Miss Maude also arranged for me to get a job at the Trench Town Elementary School, where I taught for only four months before she found me a sponsor, her own niece, to accept me into the United States. I successfully applied for a US Visa and left Jamaica in 1966. I subsequently discovered that Miss Maude had paid her niece to accept me. That woman was a real treasure, God rest her soul."

She paused and poured herself more wine, before handing me the bottle. I topped up my glass and said, "To Miss Maude," and Delisia held up her own glass and said "Amen, to that."

I was impatient for her to continue the story, and I did not want her to lose her thread, so I said, "Your story is fascinating; go on." She complied.

"I arrived in Los Angeles in July of 1966. By this time I was twenty-two and was anxious to start college, but my sponsorship did not extend that far; I was being accommodated, but the rest was up to me. I was lucky enough to find a job as a Nanny pretty quickly, and I worked and saved as much as I could. At times I was working three

The Missing Years

jobs at a time; I took whatever I could get. My ultimate intention was to get into college as quickly as possible.

"By the fall of 1968 I was able to enrol at UCLA. I continued to work, doing whatever jobs were available. I was a waitress, a babysitter, a maid. At one point I even worked as a car valet. It was hard; a constant struggle, but tired as I was, my school work always took precedence.

"I continued living with Miss Maude's niece for two and a half years, and then, out of the blue, the husband started 'putting question' to me. At first, I thought he was just teasing, or perhaps testing me to see if I was game. I even wondered if his wife had put him up to it to see if I would violate her trust, but then I thought it unlikely. Either way, I was taking no chances, and so I moved out and began to share digs with three school-mates, all much younger than myself.

"Life became harder then. I had been living as a part of a family, and had made only minimal financial contribution, but I had had a full meal every day, and had a private room to myself. Now I often went to bed hungry; I had to contribute to the rent and utilities, as well as buy food, **and** *I had to share a room with someone. And I still had to save for books and future years' tuition.*

"I became very despondent. I cursed the fates that had caused a previously pleasant gentleman to suddenly turn into a lecher. I knew I had done nothing to encourage him, but took it as divine retribution for my sins. I had not been punished yet, and so far life had been far too easy.

"Eventually, though, the pressure of work and study, hungry belly and un-air-conditioned room took its toll on me, and I gave up. I returned to Jamaica in 1971 without

completing my studies. Miss Maude was once again a tower of strength. She used her connections to get me a job at Excelsior Girls' school, and she fed and nourished me for a year, and then sent me back to the States.

"*I had told her the truth about her niece's husband, and she arranged for me to stay temporarily with a different family until I could find alternative accommodation. I returned to my studies in the fall of 1972 and although it was still hard, this time I was determined to succeed, more for Miss Maude's sake than my own, at first.*

"*I had thwarted the Devine retribution. Shortly after returning to school I struck up a friendship with another mature student and she invited me to a family barbeque where I met her aunt, Evelyn McCallum and her husband, Ralston. They were both doctors, and childless. They soon adopted me and invited me to come live with them.*

"*I insisted on paying board, and remained with them right up to my graduation from law school, when I discovered that they had been saving the 'board' money I paid them, and had invested it for me.*

"*I worked in the D.A.'s office for six months, hated it, clerked for a Judge for a year, and then found a great job with a large firm of lawyers, where I stayed for seven years and gained experience in all aspects of the law, from criminal justice to corporate law. With this wealth of experience I decided it was time to strike out on my own, and in 1983 I did just that. I approached Geraldine and we set up our own partnership, which I'm glad to say has proved successful and lucrative.*"

She stopped speaking and looked at me. I had been listening spellbound to her story, and although she had not

The Missing Years

addressed the issue of why she had not tried to get me back, I was very interested in the path her life had taken. She nodded in the direction of Estelle in the playpen and I saw to my surprise that she had lain down on the rug and was fast asleep.

I had totally forgotten about her, and I picked her up and carried her into Delisia's room and laid her on the bed. It was late afternoon, and I guessed that Richard and the kids would be back shortly. When I came back out, Delisia was making batter as a prelude to frying chicken wings and I began making a salad and blending fruit to make fruit-punch. We worked comfortably alongside each other and I picked up the conversation.

"So, you've brought me up to date on the sequence of events that brought you to where you are, but you haven't really touched on your deeper feelings, and my main question; why you didn't try to get me back, or at least keep track of my progress till I was old enough for you to write to."

Delisia looked sheepish. "I had made up my mind to go away and make a big success of my life, and show them all. When I was rich and a big successful lawyer, I would begin legal action to get my daughter back. And then when Pappa died, I sacrificed you on the altar of my guilt. I had caused his death; therefore I had to make atonement by giving up my rights to you.

"And as the years passed and I realised that you were getting older and older I started imagining the stories they would be telling you about me, if they mentioned me at all, and I was sure you would grow to hate me, as I was sure all my family, as well as George and Mavis, hated me."

She emptied out the fryer and put more wings in before

adding, "Of course I realise now that I wanted them to hate me, because I hated myself, but I didn't realise this until I finally confided to Evelyn about why I was always so sad, and she made me talk it all out."

I told her what Evelyn had said to me about her crying a fountain of tears, and she looked embarrassed, but continued. "I had not cried at all from the night they had taken you until the time I told Evelyn about you. I had not cried at my father's death. I had kept all the tears that I wanted to cry tightly bottled up inside, but when I was talking to Evelyn they started to flow and continued for months. I just couldn't stop them, although I was able to control them sufficiently, and confine them to the night-time, for them not to affect my work.

"Evelyn tried to encourage me to write to my family; she said they would welcome me with open arms, but I was too much of a coward to make the attempt, despite my wanting to. She even offered to write for me, but I refused to be specific about the address, only saying I came from St. Catherine."

I thought it strange that *nobody* Delisia knew had seen any of our advertisements and photos of her over the years. We had advertised in most, if not all, of the Caribbean press in North America and the UK, and yet we had not had a single response. Didn't any of these people read their own native country's newspapers?

I posed the question to Delisia. She shrugged. "I always just skim the papers to keep abreast of current events in the news; I have no time to read it from cover to cover, and I have never even glanced at the personal columns."

Estelle chose that moment to wake up, and made a little

experimental sound to see if anyone was around. We had about finished in the kitchen and I went to get her. The conversation stalled while I spoon-fed her creamy mashed potatoes and carrots, and Delisia prepared water for her bath. When she was all fed and washed we took plates of mashed potatoes, wings and salad out to the patio and had our own evening meal.

Richard and the kids had still not returned, and I guessed that they, Adele in particular, would not want to leave until forced to do so. I was all too familiar with her "Just another few minutes, *pleeease* Daddy," and she would bat her eyelids at Richard and he would be lost.

We finished eating and washed up the few utensils, and then I said I wanted to shower and change. Elaine Wynters was coming by later for drinks, and the advice I had promised her. I hoped to God she was not bringing Omar Silk with her tonight.

I had read a good portion of her almost completed manuscript, and written some notes for her. I was really no critic, but I could render my own opinions which I thought were fairly credible.

She was writing a *Mills & Boon* type romance such as my friend Lynette Barrington loved, and I wondered why an obviously intelligent and well educated woman like Elaine did not attempt something more substantial. The plot was full of clichéd situations and jaded phrases, and I did not want to hurt her feelings or dampen her ardour, but I wanted to be honest with her.

She arrived while Delisia was changing; alone, by herself without Mr Silk, and a few minutes later Richard, the kids, and the McCallums came in. Delisia and I would have to finish our conversation tomorrow, because we were leaving the following day.

The kids were tired but happy. They brought pizza which they appeared too tired to eat and we dunked them in the bath, gave them a quick once over, and put them to bed. They were both asleep as soon as we tucked them in.

The McCallums were almost as excited as the kids had been. They couldn't remember the last time they had had so much fun, and lamented the fact that we would be gone so soon. They had told the kids to call them "Gran and Gramps" and the kids had taken it in their stride. I suppose they were used to getting new members of their family.

Elaine and I sat off to one side and discussed her manuscript. I tried to be gentle in my criticisms, and she took them well, although I could sense her disappointment. But there was no point in my lying to her, and I encouraged her to keep trying. I told her that I knew she had a good command of words and could come up with creative situations and phrases of her own instead of using the same old same old.

After we had discussed the book she brought up the subject of Omar Silk. She said she had been captivated by his good looks and dreamy eyes, and also perhaps by the fact that he was a TV actor who was intent on going places, but she had soon found out that he was an egotistical "wannabe" with mediocre talent and an even more mediocre role in his "soap." She also said that he was immature, insecure and jealous, and she had tried several times to ditch him, but he was clinging for dear life.

I told her that if she really wanted to get shut of him she would have to be more assertive and send him packing in no uncertain terms. If he persisted in being a nuisance she should consider a restraining order or something. "Why don't you talk to Delisia about it?" I asked.

Then she said that if she could get a job elsewhere it would solve her problems and I told her no, she would only be running away from them. Nevertheless I promised that if we needed another journalist on the paper I would ask my partners to consider her, although it would mean a substantial drop in remuneration for her.

We rejoined the others and chatted for a while before they all said goodnight. Evelyn and Ralston invited us to a farewell barbeque the following afternoon and we accepted. It was by now pretty late and we all turned in for the night.

We left the children sleeping in Delisia's guest room under her care, and Richard and I walked across to the cottage. I couldn't wait to fill him in on everything Delisia had told me about her life, and I started relating her story on the walk over. He was very interested, and we sat up in bed, sipping wine and talking. He said that both Delisia and I had been born under lucky stars; we had both been extremely fortunate in our family and friends.

I told him what Delisia had said in response to my question of why she had not tried to get me back or even to have some sort of long distance relationship; how she had sacrificed me on the altar of her guilt over her father's death. He asked if all my outstanding issues with her had been resolved and I thought it over for a while before I answered.

"Well," I said, "I suppose so. I feel quite comfortable and at ease with her now; no lingering feelings of animosity, although I suppose I am still a little hurt by the fact that my fantasies of the happy first meeting and reunion had not played out."

Claudette Beckford-Brady

Richard laughed. "You had your entire life all planned out, but you had to realise that *even you* couldn't control every single drama and how it played out. Anyway, I think you should put that away completely and concentrate on moving forward.

"You have to admit that you are one of the luckiest young women in the world. You have three mothers, two fathers and possibly a new stepfather in the offing; you have a large loving extended family, plus your own nuclear family of three gorgeous kids and your devastatingly handsome and charming husband. What more could a girl want, eeh?"

I thumped him playfully. "I'll tell you what more – she could want to be made love to *right now* by that devastatingly handsome and charming husband of hers." Richard leered at me and said, "Christ, woman, you're insatiable," but he needed no persuasion and we made love and fell asleep in each other's arms.

A few days later we arrived back at *Sweet Home*, having spent a wonderful week in California. The air between Delisia and me had been well and truly cleared, and I was well and truly happy. I thought back to the day nearly nineteen years ago when Mavis had delivered the devastating news that she was not my biological mother – news that had changed the entire course of my life.

Had I not made the discovery, I would never have found my extended biological family, including my beloved Grandma Miriam; I would never have met Richard, would not have had Adele, Donovan and Estelle. The entire course of my life would have been charted differently; I might have remained in England and never discovered my beloved island; might have ended up as one of a bunch of anonymous

The Missing Years

newspaper reporters, and not be running my own publications.

And I would not be living happy and contented in my *Sweet Home* on my Beloved Island; Jamaica.

ABOUT THE AUTHOR

Claudette Beckford-Brady was born in Old Harbour, Jamaica. In 1964 she joined her parents in Gloucester, England, where she attended school. After leaving school in 1973 she held various clerical and administrative positions in the civil service and local government, finally ending up as Personnel and Training Officer at London Borough of Lambeth. In 1990 she returned to Jamaica where she now permanently resides.

This is Beckford-Brady's second novel and is the sequel to her first, Sweet Home, Jamaica which was published in two volumes in May 2007 and subsequently republished in a single volume in June 2012. She is also an accomplished short story writer and has won many awards in that category.

OTHER BOOKS BY CLAUDETTE BECKFORD-BRADY

Return to Fidelity is Beckford-Brady's third novel.

Enid Maynard-Livingstone is disenchanted with her fifteen-year marriage to Basil, who has a predilection toward girls young enough to be his daughters. However, Edith is not about to leave him and give up the comfortable lifestyle she has become accustomed to after having grown up dirt-poor in a rural Jamaican parish. However, when she runs into an old friend the temptation to give Basil a taste of his own medicine and have a fling is overwhelming.

Leroy Duncan has a happy marriage but lately a difference of opinion is threatening the relationship. Having lived in England for years, Leroy now wishes to return to Jamaica, but Evadne his wife has no such desire. She considers the island to be a backwater, lacking in modern amenities, full of criminal elements, and prone to natural disasters such as hurricanes and earthquakes. She fails to see why she should give up her comfortable existence in the UK for a life of uncertainty.

Set in the UK and the Jamaican parishes of St. Catherine and Trelawny this story gives an insightful and sometimes humorous look at the marital conflicts which can arise when couples find they no longer have the same objectives.

Sweet Home, Jamaica, Volume One is the first part of the two volume edition. Michelle Freeman, affectionately known as Shellie, was born in Jamaica but migrated to the UK with her parents when she was three years old. At age thirteen she accidentally discovers that her father's wife is not her biological mother. This shocking discovery leads her to begin a search for her birth mother and this search eventually takes her to Jamaica where she finds a large extended maternal family and develops a deep and abiding love for the island of her birth.

After leaving school and university in London, where she studied journalism, Shellie decides to leave the UK and practise her profession in Jamaica. However, all is not plain sailing, as she encounters culture shock, prejudice and jealousy and comes to the realisation that her beloved island is not the idyllic paradise she had supposed it to be.

Set in South London and on the beautiful island of Jamaica the story spans seventeen years, following the fiery and feisty young woman through her teenage years, young love and tragedy and into adulthood with more conflicts and clashes.

Sweet Home, Jamaica, Volume Two completes the saga of Michelle Freeman and her extended family as the story moves into the 1980s where Michelle has become a young woman with ambitions of becoming a famous writer and to live in Jamaica, her homeland. It follows the story of her progress and the path her life takes to the fulfilment of her dreams. Join her in her travels to hot sunny climes as she integrates with her birth family and the local community as a resident rather than as a visitor to the island. Her extraordinary family causes tears and laughter, but through it all Michelle learns to build a life for herself in the land of her birth and becomes accepted into the local community. It is not an easy ride as she discovers that her beloved island is not the idyllic paradise she had envisioned it to be. A bittersweet story of the intricacies of human relations over time and distance.